RAVEN TALKS BACK

RAVEN TALKS BACK

A RAVEN MORRESSEY MYSTERY

Beth Anderson

www.krillpress.com

Raven Talks Back

© 2011 by Beth Anderson

All rights reserved. No part of this book may be used or reproduced by any means, graphic, electronic, or mechanical, including photocopying, recording, taping or by any information storage retrieval system without the written permission of the publisher except in the case of brief quotations embodied in critical articles and reviews.

Raven Talks Back is a work of fiction. The characters, incidents, and dialogues are products of the author's imagination and are not to be construed as real. Any resemblance to actual events or persons, living or dead, is entirely coincidental.

Published by Krill Press LLC. All rights reserved.

ISBN 978-0-9821443-9-8

Printed in the United States of America

To all of the guys in my life:

Bob, Chris, Cody, David, E.J., Eric, Isaac, Jarrett, Jeff, Rick, Riley, Rob, T.J. and Tony

I love you all

*"Every murder turns on a bright hot light,
and a lot of people have to walk out of the shadows."*

—Mark Hellinger, American journalist

The Fog

The spirits of my ancestors live in the towering Chugach Mountains that surround my world in Valdez. I know they are there. I can see them most mornings, great cottony masses of gray fog rolling down the mountains, sinister characters in a black and white movie, shivering and mourning their inevitable disintegration above the marina before they disappear over Prince William Sound.

They call to me through that fog, whispering my name. I hear them, soft, desolate sounds you can only hear if you're really a part of this beautiful land.

My people will always tell my story to future generations of Athabascans, and tourists from the lower forty-eight who come to walk through our villages and see for themselves how little is left of what we were. We have no written ancient history. Everything known about our past has evolved only because of stories told in the dark of night before our children go to sleep, when wind screams over the mountaintops and roars down through the passes, bringing the icy chill of our glaciers spiraling into our homes in spite of insulation invented by modern man. The wind is still bitter and we know it.

Even so, we lead a lovely, slow-paced life in this part of Alaska, where all the flowers burst with fragrant beauty everywhere in the summertime, and deep undercurrents of love and laughter seem to hover beneath the surface of our daily lives.

At least to me it had always been that way, until the Saturday morning in early June, when my world of gentle laughter disappeared and violent death entered the soft space I had occupied all my adult life.

ONE

The thought had never entered my mind that I might find myself standing in my back yard shuddering with nausea and disbelief, staring down at a nude female body with no head or hands, and equally horrifying, a painted rock close to where her head would have been. The only other thing missing was blood.

Mark Taylor's men had graded and leveled our yard the previous week, ready to set the foundation for the attached greenhouse my husband, Red, had been promising for years. Alaska winter days are so short and dark that nothing grows without a heated greenhouse and ultraviolet light. Of all the things I longed for in the wintertime, I missed fresh flowers most.

As was often the case in Valdez, things got done whenever they got done no matter which day it was. I hadn't known they were coming on Saturday. Mark and his men had simply pulled into the driveway and started working.

My eight-year-old son Timmy stood under the tall pine in the northeast corner of the yard with his thumb in his mouth. I froze when I turned and saw him because he hadn't done that for three years, ever since he'd started school. I hurried over to him, pulling him close. He shivered when my fingers brushed over his arm and his skin felt cold, although it was quite warm that morning and the fog was already beginning to dissipate over the Sound.

"Timmy, are you hurt?" I forced my voice to stay calm because his black eyes were ringed with white and his lips were a bluish tint.

He pointed toward Jack O'Banion, our chief of police, without making a sound.

I frowned, puzzled by his silence. Timmy had never had a problem speaking; he'd been talking nonstop since he was eleven months old. Now he just shook his head and looked back down at the ground.

Alice, my daughter, was still at the door, where we'd brushed past her in our rush to get outside after she'd awakened us from a sound sleep a few minutes before. I beckoned for her to come.

A surrealistic film seemed to float over the yard as she headed my way. Although she was only twelve, she was constantly swiping her long black hair away from her eyes the way girls did on TV, and lately she had taken to walking in slow motion, her hips moving in a deliberate way that made me nervous. Her voice, shrill with fear before, was now flat and emotionless. "I don't think he can talk. He saw it first."

I glanced down at Timmy again. One of the straps on his overalls had come unbuttoned. His black hair hung down over his eyebrows, reminding me as it always did of my father and his father before him when they returned, sweaty and exhausted, from their caribou hunting trips.

His feet were bare, as usual. They were never cold until after termination dust, first snow, appeared on the surrounding mountains early in September, when the temperature would dip below twenty degrees at night. Other than that he went barefoot everywhere, but today his feet were blue and mottled. I tried to pick him up to carry him into the house where I could warm him, but he seemed to have gained twenty pounds overnight. I could not lift him and he could not move.

"Red," I called, "I need help here. Come carry Timmy into the house for me, will you?"

Red turned to face me. "Why can't he walk?"

"I think he's in shock, Red. He's ice-cold."

At that, Jack strode over to us and knelt, lifting Timmy's chin with his finger.

"You okay, son?"

I'd never before heard such a compassionate tone of voice coming from Jack. I'd always thought him distant and unreadable, but this time even the look in his eyes had softened somewhat, a real departure from his usual all-business behavior, and for the first time I found myself drawn to him, whereas before there had been nothing to like or not like.

Timmy turned away from him, still silent.

Jack felt Timmy's forehead then glanced up at me. "He feels clammy. You're probably right, I'm pretty sure he's in shock. Mark told me he was watching while they were loosening up the dirt a little more and he saw it first."

My heart almost stopped. "What did he do?"

"They told me he ran over to the tree where you found him and hid his eyes with his hands. He hasn't made a sound. Let's get him inside so you can call Doc Martin. Tell him I said to get on over here, he can check Timmy first and then I'll need him out here."

Timmy shuddered. Jack picked him up without effort and slung him over his shoulder. What a picture they made, Jack in his silver-tipped snakeskin boots and cowboy hat, long legs striding across the lawn toward the house, worn leather holster moving as he walked, and my sad, silent little boy lying limp on Jack's shoulder with his eyes closed.

I followed them into the house but found myself glancing up into the nearby mountains as if someone were crouched, hidden from sight with binoculars trained on us, watching our every move.

Someone had to be watching. I could feel the certainty of it snaking along under my skin. Otherwise, why had the body been left in our yard?

TWO

At eight-thirty that morning Jack had been on his way to the Eagle, Valdez's only grocery store except for the warehouse-type store on Egan Drive. This morning he was still half asleep and everything was peaceful. For those who left the lower forty-eight and came here to live, the slow pace was welcome, but for those who became chief of police it was usually boring as hell, a far cry from Dallas. Just the way he liked it.

He wanted to stop and pick up a box of donuts for his men before he checked in at the station, which was really just a couple of rooms in the main building that also housed the city hall and fire house. He had to admit the donuts weren't really for his men, but probably more for his own insatiable sweet tooth. It hadn't affected his weight though. He glanced ruefully down at his waistline while he drove. *Well, not much.*

At first, when he spotted Mark Taylor waving him down and saw the big mound in the Morressey's back yard as he pulled in, he thought somebody had shot a bear. The Alaska media would play that up big time, because bears were news no matter what they were doing. They'd mosey on down the mountains from time to time and the cops would always try not to shoot them unless they had to.

In fact, it was like a big holiday when anybody spotted a bear in town. They'd call him and he'd come racing over with a handful of firecrackers. Everybody would run outside to watch him light a few and toss them in the general vicinity of the bear, which would think it was being shot at and haul ass back up into the mountains where it belonged. Then everybody would go inside and have coffee and cake.

Not this day, though.

The corpse in the Morressey back yard was not a bear, it was a woman who had been so brutally murdered it made his eyes swim for a minute while his mind tried to deny what he was seeing. This was the last thing he ever expected to see in the Morressey's back yard, or in anybody's back yard up here, and the thought of a murder like this in Valdez sickened him.

He stood over the body to examine it as much as possible without touching it, wondering who it was and what she could have done to deserve anything this violent and senseless, but he couldn't spend time right now wondering about the unknowns. He could see the knowns without any problem. He pulled out his recorder and began to dictate as he moved around the body.

"At approximately eight-thirty this morning, an unidentified nude female body was discovered buried in the back yard of 4355 Moose Haven Avenue, located where a foundation is being dug for construction of a greenhouse on the property of Red and Raven Morressey, residents at the same address.

"We have no identification as yet. The victim's head and both hands have been severed from the body. A white rock approximately twelve inches in diameter had evidently been placed where her head would have been, although it's crooked and adjacent to the body now, probably from being moved by the scoop loader used by the builders this morning. The rock appears to be a replica of an Alaska Native ceremonial mask, with two black dots for the eyes and a red circular mark indicating a mouth. There are faint blue signs of blood inside the skin toward the bottom of the torso. Rigor has come and gone."

He clicked the recorder off for a minute. Spiders were crawling around over the body fighting over the maggots and flies were everywhere, mainly the top of what was left of the victim's neck and between the legs. He didn't see much sense in adding that to his report, the rest would get them close enough to time of death, and the bugs were common enough here.

He sighed, clicking the recorder back on. "Blisters two or three inches across have formed on various parts of the body, indicating the victim has been dead at least three days."

There'd be no way anybody could pick this one up without skin coming loose. It reminded him of floaters found out in the Sound every once in a while among the driftwood and seaweed, bloated, nasty as hell, completely unrecognizable.

"The victim's torso appears to be completely covered with tattoos."

He knelt, trying to see whether they were real without touching the body.

"Correction, the apparent tattoos are raised cuts which have healed to form what looks like tattoos but is actually scarification, which is a method used by some tattoo artists to ensure permanence.

"There are no visible blood spatters anywhere in the area. It appears the killer let her bleed out at the murder scene and washed her before he brought her to this location, dumped her, and covered her with some of the loosened dirt."

He clicked off his recorder and glanced up at Mark, owner of the construction company. "This is not your everyday cutter. Somebody pretty good had to have done this over a long period of time."

"I never saw anything like it," Mark said. "Do you have any idea who it is?"

Jack shook his head and looked around at the other men. "Has anybody touched anything?"

They all said no.

"Is it real?" asked Red, squinting because the sun was directly in his eyes.

"It's real."

"Who is it?"

Jack looked up again, his eyes narrowed. "We'll find out sooner or later. I've never seen cuts like that on anybody before, at least not in the flesh. I've seen photos on the Internet, that's it."

"I've never seen it at all," said Red. "I wonder how she got out here?"

Jack peered at him from under the brim of his Stetson. "You tell me. It's your yard."

Red's face, normally ruddy all year round, turned a couple shades whiter and he looked as if he might throw up.

Jack felt nauseous too, but he didn't want to let anybody see it. He never showed that side of himself to anyone. Not since his last murder case, anyhow.

"I didn't know it was out here," said Red. "If I did, I'd never have had the yard dug up, that's for damn sure. I never saw whoever this is before, that I know of anyhow." He hunched over and peered down at the body. "Who around here would do something like that?"

Jack looked up at him again. "I don't know, but you can be damn sure I'm going to find out." He turned toward Mark and his men. "All of you, walk single file out of the yard, don't step on anything that looks like it could be a footprint. Go sit in the truck and I'll call for somebody to cordon off the area."

The minute he said, "cordon off the area," he knew his easy days in Alaska had come to an end. He'd never cordoned off an area in Valdez for a murder like this. There hadn't been any murders here like this until today.

He was so sick of grisly crime scenes. That last one back in Dallas...well, best not think about that right now, although there were similarities. Then again, most all murder victims had similarities, except in the scale of brutality. This killer was brutal all right, and definitely had good control with a knife. All the cuts were clean. Whoever it was had done each cut in one swift, vicious slice.

He got on his cell and told two of his officers to pack up a body bag and get on over here.

Red was still looking down at the corpse, his forehead wrinkled like Jack's old Setter's whenever he spotted a bird on hunting trips in Texas.

"But how the hell did it get here, Jack? This yard was just dug up last Saturday, before that it was rock-solid. Somebody who saw the yard being dug up had to have done this." He glanced over at Mark and his men. "I wonder if one of them could have anything to do with this. Both of Mark's men are Alaska Natives, and that rock definitely is a replica of those masks they use in their ceremonies."

Jack was already thinking about questions to ask them. He was also, for the moment, wishing he'd stayed in Dallas, where a squad of detectives would have taken care of things like this, and maybe it wouldn't be his squad for a change. Here, he was the squad, and in Valdez kills were almost always bar fights, or if it was a marital thing it usually happened in the winter. The locals liked to call them Alaskan

Divorces.

Jack's men showed up and got busy taping off the area, snapping digitals, drawing pictures, setting up a grid, searching the surrounding yards. He had to help Doc with the body because by that time his men, both rookies, were gagging behind their vehicle after they tried to pick it up and it slipped away from them, leaving skin residue on their gloves and shoes.

He spotted a green thread on the victim's arm as they rolled her onto the body bag. It could have come from the yard, but he pulled it from the body with some tape and dropped it into a plastic bag, then wrapped the rock in a tarp from the back of his vehicle and marked that too.

The whole time he was taking care of business, he could hear the soft voice of his grandmother, who had raised him after his mother left and his father died, and whose voice had been stilled several years ago.

"You know what you need to do to make this right, son. Go do it."

THREE

I had expected Doc to take care of Timmy first but he took a quick look, told me to keep him covered and give him something warm to drink, then disappeared out back for over an hour while I lay cuddling Timmy, trying to keep him warm.

He shivered, as he had the previous winter when he was sick with a virus, then fell asleep, making strange, guttural noises deep in his throat that reminded me of an ancient Athabascan chant my father used to sing when I was a kid. I could have sworn it was the same chant, but my father died years before Timmy was born and Timmy had never heard it.

Still, it sounded like my father's voice and I found myself wondering how it was Timmy could have done that. Then again, when children are in the throes of a nightmare, who knows what sounds might come out of them? Nightmares are deep and powerful events and voices in them are often surreal.

I put it out of my mind when Doc came into the bedroom. Timmy was half asleep and didn't respond, even when Doc tapped his knee with a rubber hammer.

Doc, a heavy-set man with a pale complexion and thick flying sandy hair that as usual hadn't been cut in a while, glanced my way. "He walked into the house, didn't he?"

"No. Jack carried him in."

Doc frowned. "Was he standing when you were outside? He didn't pass out and hit his head on anything, did he?"

"He was standing when I went to him. I just can't get him to say anything."

Doc touched Timmy's forehead and he opened his eyes.

"Son, did you get hurt out there?"

Timmy shook his head and closed his eyes again.

Doc looked up at me. "He saw it, right? Out back?"

I nodded.

"Did you?"

"I did." Flashes of the scene in my yard were coming back to me now, a slide show running a little too fast.

I lowered my voice. "What I can't figure out is why anyone would bury a body in my yard. It's beyond frightening. I feel very threatened. I don't like this feeling at all."

Doc patted Timmy's arm. "Let's go into another room and talk, Raven. He'll be okay here."

We went into the kitchen and I poured him a cup of coffee, black like he always took it. Doc had delivered all three of my children so he wasn't just our doctor, he was family, as he was to so many people in town. He was also the town's unofficial medical examiner. Valdez was so far from the Alaska State Troopers' main location that quite a while back they had licensed him to perform autopsies rather than try to transport the body to them.

I made myself a cup of Earl Grey tea, which I'd been drinking all day, every day, since I discovered it in college, while he settled into one of the kitchen chairs and took a sip. "Timmy's probably going to have a hard time for a while," he said. "Keep him warm but try to get him back into the normal family routine as soon as you can. Don't make him sleep without a night light if he wants one. I know a good child psychologist in Anchorage who treats Post Traumatic Shock Disorder. Timmy's got all the signs of it."

I was dismayed. It was such a long trip to Anchorage, especially to drive there. We'd have to fly every time. "I have to take him all the way up to Anchorage? Can't you treat him here?"

He shook his head. "I don't know that much about this kind of thing with kids. We need to get him to somebody who does. Call me Monday morning and I'll set something up for you, but if you have any problems over the weekend, no matter what time it is, call me right away."

He took a last sip of coffee and stood. "Looks like I've got a busy day coming up. You don't happen to know any female who's covered with cuts that look like tattoos, do you?"

"No," I said, "I have no idea who it could be, but then I don't see people running around town naked." I realized what he'd just said and looked up at him, frowning. "What do you mean, cuts that look like tattoos?"

Doc pulled at his ear. "Well, some people have cuts made on their bodies and the design is formed by raised scars as they heal. They rub indelible colored ink on them while the wounds are still fresh and the color forms what amounts to a three-dimensional tattoo, or in her case, a couple hundred or so."

My jaw dropped. I'd never heard of anything like that, although I had toyed with the idea of a tattoo while I was in college. "What kind of person would do a thing like that?"

His mouth formed a wry grin. "Somebody who likes pain, I guess."

"I wonder who it could be."

"I don't know, but there can't be many like that around here. I know none of my patients have ever been decorated like this body is."

I shuddered. "I can't imagine doing anything that must hurt so much."

"Well, our dead friend must have liked it a lot," he muttered, heading out the door.

A few minutes later, while I was still sitting at the table, Alice came into the kitchen.

"They took it away. I watched the whole thing. It was gross." She opened the breadbox. "I guess we're not having breakfast, huh?" She took a quick glance at my face.

"I don't see how you can eat anything after seeing that." I sipped my tea and watched her carefully measured movements. "Are you sure you're okay? That's got to have been an awful shock."

"I'm okay now." She started to drop her bread in the toaster, then changed her mind. "Besides, I see stuff almost that bad on HBO all the time."

"But this was real and it was in our back yard, Alice. I can't figure out how anyone could have buried someone out there without being seen."

"Easy. They did it at night." She spread peanut butter all the way to the edge just as she always had.

"It's not that dark at night now, Alice. Someone had to have seen it."

She gave me a sideways smile and bit into the bread, shrugging. "Maybe a ghost did it. You're always talking about the spirits of our ancestors hanging around, so hey, maybe one of them..." She rolled her eyes. "Mom, I was just kidding. Maybe Charlie saw something. He's always up at night."

"Speaking of Charlie, go get him."

She returned about five minutes later with Charlie, still in his underwear, stumbling down the stairs behind her, his eyes heavy with sleep.

"Did Alice tell you what happened this morning?"

He rubbed his eyes. "She babbled something about somebody getting killed someplace. So? Is it anybody we know?"

Alice grinned. "Not unless you know somebody with full body tattoos, numb-nuts, and I do mean full body. She even had them on her—" She stopped abruptly at the look on my face and giggled, turning away to pour a glass of milk.

"What the hell is she jabbering about? Isn't there anything to eat around here?" Charlie lowered his head almost to the tabletop. His thick red hair, which he usually spiked with some kind of gel every day, hung down over his forehead, obscuring his eyes.

Charlie was a typical sixteen-year-old male, bored all the time. The town had built a teen center on West Hanigeta but there was nothing else for kids to do in the evenings. No movie house, no bowling alley. The center was pretty much it.

Red had started a senior scout troop for the boys several years back. The older kids mainly messed around on their computers at night and ran in and out of each others' houses at all hours, but at least Charlie and his friends still belonged to the scout troop.

To me, they seemed like normal kids, playing CD's at night and talking while they goofed around on their computers. We let it pass, since he slept on the opposite side of the house and we rarely heard the noise. It was comforting just to know where he and his friends were most of the time.

"Charlie!" I said sharply because he was beginning to doze again. His head shot up. "I need to know if you've seen anything strange in the back yard in the past week."

"Not if you mean somebody burying a body out there."

"I mean anyone walking through the yard."

Charlie scratched his armpit, glaring at his sister, then shrugged. "The guys walk through there at night all the time, Mom. How am I supposed to know who's been back there? My room's in front." He gave Alice a wicked grin. "Maybe you ought to ask her. Right, Alice?"

"What are you talking about?" I turned to her. "What did he mean?"

She flushed a deep pink. "Oh, Mom, once in a while some of the girls sneak out in the middle of the night and come over here, too. We don't do anything wrong, just sit around and talk about boys and stuff." She gave her brother a malevolent glare.

"We'll have a little talk about that later," I said. "Meantime, have you noticed anyone or anything out back at night?"

"Mom, animals walk through the yards around here all the time. I hear stuff, sure, but nothing like you're talking about."

Our house was on the edge of town in a cul-de-sac bordered by the highway on one side, halfway hidden by tall bushes and trees on the outer edge. One new two-story house had just been built on the other side, and several houses sat in a row across the street from ours.

The fourth side, at the back of the house, was pretty much hidden from a side street which ran into the highway. About a mile or so across from the highway stood a mountain range, cold and forbidding in the wintertime, but in the summer, filled with fireweed and tall green pine trees.

Alice was right. Anyone could walk into our back yard at night and we'd probably think it was deer or a bear and never give it a second thought.

FOUR

Jack headed back inside after Doc left. He wanted in the worst way to find out what was really going on in the Morressey household. He'd always felt something was not the way it seemed in that family, although he could never put his finger on it.

The coupling of those two puzzled him because they were so different. She came from an Alaska Native family. Her natural black hair and high cheekbones, as well as those haunting deep-set dark eyes, testified to that. He thought she was one of the most beautiful women he'd ever seen, not only on the outside but inside, too. Listening to her talk was like listening to Joan Baez sing an old Seventies folk song, soft and somewhat sad, but always worth honing in on.

On the other hand, some town people seemed leery of Red, although Jack wasn't sure why, he'd never seen Red do anything out of the way. Now his gut was telling him to go slow, be careful, because why would anyone pick this yard to bury a body, when they could easily have hidden it up in the mountains where it might not have been found for months or years? Maybe never, if the animals found it first. There had to be a reason.

It wasn't going to be easy finding it. Everybody in town knew Raven was finally having her greenhouse built and the yard was being dug up. There'd been a lot of talk about it all week in town so at least he was clear on one thing. Whoever murdered this woman knew about the digging and wanted the body found in this yard.

He settled himself into a chair in the kitchen where they were all four sitting, staring at each other.

"Alice? Charlie? Have either of you seen or heard anything out back this past week?" He knew he was just yanking his own strings. None of the teenagers he'd been around ever seemed to notice anything except what was going on in their own lives. He was that way himself when he was growing up. Girls, cars, sports, that was about it.

Naturally, both kids said no.

He turned back to Red. "For the record, can you account for your time during the last few days?"

Red's eyes narrowed. "Sure, I guess so."

"Would you mind writing it all down for me, including anyone who saw you?"

Raven got up and got two sheets of paper and two pens. Red started to write his movements over the past week and Raven began writing her own without being asked.

After they were done, Jack pointed toward the new house that had recently gone up next door. "Do y'all know anything about those people? All I know is, it's a couple and somebody's mother."

The house was visible out of Raven's window and he thought, as he had before, how strange it was that there were no windows anywhere on the first floor except for one small window high up. It had to almost reach the ceiling because right above that, four large windows spread across the back of the house.

Even though snow often reached twenty-three feet or more in Valdez in the winter, whenever there were good days it was nice to let a little natural light in. He couldn't figure a house with only one window that high up on the first floor, but there it was. There were no windows on the other three sides either. These people had brought their own contractors in, complete with their own city builders' license. As long as they didn't do anything wrong, they were on their own.

"I've never seen anyone there except for the builders," said Raven. "Red, have you?"

Red shook his head.

Raven glanced at Alice and Charlie, her eyes questioning.

"I've never seen anybody," said Alice.

"How about you?" Jack asked Charlie.

"Nope," said Charlie, "they don't have any kids my age or I'd have seen them. We haven't had anybody new all year at school except for the freshmen and I know all of them."

Jack pushed back his chair and headed for the door.

"I'm going to go find out if anybody's there now," he said.

"That's as good a place as any to start."

Just as he reached the dividing line to the next yard, his cell phone rang. He answered it, glancing at his watch.

It had to be Vera, he could smell the pheromones. She had enough of them to fill the countryside and then some.

"Hi, baby," she purred. "I can be at your place in fifteen minutes."

"Uh...Vera, I'll have to call you back. Something's happened here and I have to talk to some people."

"Can't you talk later?" she half-whispered. "I'm horny as hell and I need my Jack fix right now, know what I mean?"

He cleared his throat, trying to shake the voice that had been revving his world for the past few months. "Not right now, honey, I'm working. There's been a murder here."

"A murder? Who?"

"That's what I'm trying to find out. Right now we don't know who she is but believe me, she's dead. I'll have to call you later."

"Want me to come pick up your key and go on over to your place and get ready?"

His eyebrows rose when he heard the low seduction in her voice. A little thing like murder didn't mean a whole hell of a lot to her, that was clear, but he didn't let anybody have the key to his house, even Vera. He'd been dodging this issue for a while, so he tried to sound regretful. "I don't have time right now. I'll have to call you. I'm right in the middle of things here."

That was true enough, he was standing halfway between the Morressey house and the new one. "Later, okay?"

There was silence, then a click. He shook his head. Vera had a fierce temper when she was crossed. He knew he'd be in for it that night if he saw her, but probably not what he was hoping he'd be in for.

He went to the front of the house and knocked on the door. A female voice shouted, "Hold your horses, I'll be there in a minute!"

He waited a couple of minutes, then knocked again.

The same voice, a little closer now. "Just hold your damn horses, for cryin' out loud! I'm comin', I'm comin'!"

When the door opened and he looked in he saw the entire first floor was what amounted to one fully furnished great room, separated only by a huge stone fireplace in the middle, with a see-through opening into the kitchen right behind the front door. They had everything anybody could need and more, all of it first-class.

Nobody in the Morressey house had seen anything being moved in? He found that hard to believe, considering what all was there.

The furniture wasn't his only surprise. Attached to the back wall, which faced the Morressey house, was a motorized chair with a track leading up only to the small window he'd seen from outside.

"Well, come on in," barked the same voice from behind the door. "What the hell're you waitin' for, after poundin' like that?"

A head peeked out. "Takes this old body a long time to get to the damn door, young man. You gonna stand there all day scratchin' your balls, or are you comin' in?"

He edged into the open foyer eyeing the woman, who kicked the door shut with her foot, then wheeled herself across the room like she was coming in second at the Tour de France.

She motioned toward the sofa. "Sit," she ordered.

He sat, still trying to eye the track without letting her know he was staring at it.

"I had that built in," she said. "They didn't want windows on the first floor on account of the high snow. I wanted one and it's my money so I had it installed when they weren't here. I knew it'd drive 'em crazy and it does." She grinned, obviously proud of herself.

He nodded, still surprised by a chair that could only go up to nowhere and then back down. They eyed each other while she set her wheelchair brakes.

"You're the chief of police, ain't you?" She smiled with satisfaction at her own cunning.

"I am," he agreed while he gave her a quick once-over. She couldn't have been more than four-foot-ten, ninety-five pounds. Probably close to seventy-five years old. Long white hair flew wild around her face, half-shielding wide open blue eyes, but there was something about those eyes.... He took another look and realized one was glass.

A purple housedress with two top buttons open hung from her

shoulders, and knee-hi stockings that barely covered a slew of varicose veins were rolled almost down to her red and white Reebok running shoes.

"Nice shoes," he commented.

"Ought to be. Cost me a pretty penny, but it's my pennies and I'll spend 'em any damn way I want." She raised her chin, daring him to contradict her. He waited.

"If you're wanting to talk to my son and his…" she hesitated, then spat out the word "wife, they ain't here. They drove up to Anchorage yesterday, should be back a little later on today."

"Shopping trip?"

She nodded. "Bitch wants new drapes. The ones my decorator picked out ain't good enough for her. I'm payin' for them, too, like everything else." She drew herself up into a tight knot. "My husband left me a skunk-load of money, plus what I had anyways. She's spendin' it as fast as she can."

He smiled inside. "What did your husband do?"

"Oil. He was a CEO, flew in and out of here a lot. We were going to build a house here, then he croaked on me so I built it anyways. And besides that, don'tcha know, I used to be a famous movie star!"

He tried not to look surprised, although when he looked closer he could see flashes of fading beauty underneath her wrinkles. "What's your name?"

She grinned, toying with him. "My movie star name or my real name?"

He shifted in his chair to get a closer look. "How about your real name first."

She laughed out loud, a cackling, hacking sound, and slapped her thigh. "I'm Kimberley Clarke. Used to be Kim Stiletto back in my movie days."

Stiletto? He thought back because he didn't want to offend her. "I'm sorry," he had to admit, "I never went to movies much. What movies did you make?"

She laughed again and unbuttoned a third button, then leaned toward him. "Take a look." She grabbed both sides of the top like she was going to rip it open.

He held up his hand to stop her. "Ma'am...Mrs. Clarke, I'm here on official business. I need to ask you a few questions and I'll be on my way."

"You don't want to hear about my movies?" she wheedled.

"Okay, tell me about your movies." Anything to keep her from showing him whatever was under that dress.

She grinned at him. "Pornos, sonny. I did pornos. Made a hell of a lot of money at it too." She chuckled, eyeing him while she re-did the top button, leaving the two middle ones open.

"So," she said after she got her dress arranged to her satisfaction, "I saw 'em take that body away while ago. That's why you're here, ain't it?"

"Yes, ma'am. What can you tell me about it?"

She shrugged and he noticed one side of her mouth smiled more than the other. He leaned closer, all business now. "Did you see who buried that body in the Morressey's yard, Mrs. Clarke?"

She glanced up at the window. "I don't spend all my time looking out that window. I ain't that bored with life, not yet anyways."

"I don't know how much time you spend there, Mrs. Clarke. I just want to know if you saw anything unusual over there."

She leaned toward him, tapping him on the knee. "Did you know I used to be a famous movie star?"

"Yes, I did, Mrs. Clarke. That's very nice. Now, about the Morressey's back yard. Have you seen or heard anything different over there in the past week or so?"

"I made porno movies. My son's wife hates it." She chuckled under her breath. "She's a school teacher, didja know that?"

He shook his head, trying to suppress a smile.

"Well she is, she teaches English. She's applied for a job here. I got a way to get even with her for stealin' my son and my money. Guess what it is. Go ahead, guess."

His hopes were sinking fast. "I don't have a clue."

"I fracture every damn word I can think of. Drives her crazy, so I do it all day and all night. I know better, but I do it anyways." She laughed again. "Can you think of a better way to drive an English teacher nuts?"

"No, I guess I can't." He stood and held out his hand. "It's been a pleasure talking to you, Mrs. Clarke. I'll stop by later and speak with your son and his wife."

"Wait, don'tcha want to see how my chair works?" She hopped out of the wheelchair, took two firm steps, then realized what she'd done and spun back around to face him, perfectly steady on her feet. "Don't you dare ever tell them I can walk."

Her voice had completely changed. It was deeper, stronger, more definite, and her diction was clear. "Don't you dare ever. I absolutely mean that."

"No, ma'am," he agreed. "I won't say a word."

Her left eyebrow rose. "Just keep that in mind when you cash your paycheck, young man. I pay the taxes here."

She strode over to the chair, settled herself into it, pushed a button and the chair carried her up the wall. She looked down at him, then out the window.

Her voice rose and her fractured grammar returned. "Yes siree, I can see real damn good from up here. I can see nearly everything." The chair slid back down the track.

"But you haven't seen anything unusual this past week, is that right?"

She gazed at him for a long minute while she settled back into her wheelchair. "I did over five hundred of them movies." Her voice had noticeably softened now, drifting, her speech slurred again. "Over five hundred."

This wasn't getting him anywhere. God only knew what she'd seen or if she remembered anything about it.

"Thank you, Mrs. Clarke. I'll check back with your family later." He was about to let himself out when he heard a noise in the yard. He opened the door and peered out then closed it. "Looks like they're home."

"Bitch probably bought out Anchorage again." She arranged herself in her wheelchair so she slumped sideways. "Remember, mum's the word!"

He nodded and the door opened. A man entered, glanced at him, then Kimberley. "What's going on here?"

"I'm Chief of Police O'Banion. I stopped by to see if you folks heard or saw anything unusual going on next door in the past few days."

His wife walked in, struggling with a couple of shopping bags. "Unusual in what way? Who are you?" She glanced toward Kimberley as she dropped her packages on a chair.

"That's my new boyfriend," Kimberley said, wriggling with obvious enjoyment. "We just went and popped off a quickie. Good thing you didn't get home fifteen minutes ago."

Now he was doubly uncomfortable, partly because of her remark and also because her son was still holding his hand.

"I'm Clint Clarke and this is my wife, Melissa," her son said, finally breaking the clinch. "Don't pay any attention to my mother. What's the problem next door?"

Jack took a good look at both of them. Clint was about five-ten, salt-and-pepper hair. Manicured fingernails, soft hand, a pot-belly that propped up a striped pullover shirt, loafers scuffed and run down.

In wild contrast to her husband, not a stitch was out of place on his wife and she didn't appear to have an extra ounce of flesh. Her red hair seemed to have just been done up and her movements were swift and sure as she pulled off her sweater and dropped it on the floor, ignoring Kimberley's astonished look.

"Yes," she said, "is something wrong?"

"Mrs. Clarke, an unidentified female body was just dug up next door this morning. I came to see if anybody here has seen or heard anything going on over there in the past few days."

They glanced at each other, then back at him. "I haven't," said Clint. "I don't have time to talk to the neighbors. I'm getting ready for my new job."

"What's your new job?"

"I'm taking a course in engineering."

"Mail order," said Kimberley. "He's a permanent student. Keeps him from having to go out and earn an honest living."

Clint flushed. "I'm almost done. I have a good offer here but I need to finish this course. My wife will probably teach English at the high school this fall."

"And I'm gonna help," Kimberley chimed in. "I'm gonna give talks to all her classes about the movie business." She flashed a grin at Melissa, apparently oblivious to the way her daughter-in-law's jaw worked, silent but furious.

Melissa caught him watching and recovered quickly. "I haven't seen or heard anything, so if you'll excuse us...." She rose, putting an end to the conversation.

It was clear that he wasn't going to get any information here, not today, anyway. He let himself out the door and headed back across the Morressey's yard, glancing at the windows as he passed the house. The shades were drawn.

When he got back in his vehicle he headed for the north side of town, where Oliver Jackson, the first one of Mark's men he wanted to interview, lived with his wife and six kids.

FIVE

Jack had only been gone a short time when Red's fuse began its usual slow burn. It had been a while since his last blowup, which was a welcome reprieve. I almost never understood what set him off or the reason for it. This time it was aimed at Timmy, and although I had lived with years of Red's irrational demands, I couldn't begin to understand how he could pick this day of all days to pick on a troubled little boy for no reason at all.

Red had been silent a few minutes, sitting at the kitchen table brooding into his coffee cup, when he looked up. "I want to talk to Timmy."

I frowned. "Red, I think he's asleep."

Red took a sip of his coffee. "Go wake him up and tell him to get up and come in here. I saw Jack carry him in. There was no reason why he couldn't walk himself."

I forced myself to speak calmly. "Listen. To. Me. The doctor said he's in shock and right now he probably can't walk. He can't seem to talk, either. Just let him rest."

Red jumped up from his chair and stomped to the doorway.

Silence filled the house. Alice had gone out with her girlfriends and Charlie was back upstairs, sleeping.

I followed Red into the small bedroom where Timmy lay awake, not moving a muscle. His glance moved toward me but looked right through me. I wanted so badly to pull him close and tell him everything was alright, but I could see he had blocked out everything. My insides wept for him.

Red towered over him. "Timothy, get up."

Timmy turned away, staring out the window. The sun was out, shining brightly onto his covers and making oddly shaded designs in the indentation between his legs on his blue and yellow Scooby Doo bedspread.

Red touched his shoulder. "Timothy. Look at me."

Timmy turned back and looked at his father, his expression unfathomable, then turned away quickly and pulled his covers up over his head.

Red pulled them back down. "Get up, Tim. I know you can walk."

Timmy drew his knees up to his chest, curling into himself under the covers.

I was livid. "Red," my voice shook, "leave him alone!"

Red looked back down at Timmy, swore under his breath and stomped out of the room.

I followed him out. "You go back in there and apologize to him, Red. You can see he's in trouble!"

Red stared at me for a minute, then his shoulders slumped and he turned to face the window, his face twisted with what I could only perceive as contrition. "You're right, hon. I'm sorry, really I am sorry. I just want him to grow up to be a man." His glance darted around the room, away from mine.

I was determined not to back down. "He'll grow up to be a much better man if he has a caring father figure, don't you think? How dare you go in there and demand he do something he obviously can't do? What's wrong with you?"

Red stared at me for a minute, shook his head, then went back into the bedroom and stood by the bed. "I'm sorry, Tim. You get well now, we can talk later, when you're feeling better." He patted Timmy's back through the covers, then turned and left the room.

I watched him walk out. How could he do that so effortlessly, be angry and unreasonable one second, sweet and solicitous the next? And thinking back, how long had he been doing it? I couldn't remember, but I realized it had to have been a long time.

I turned my attention back to Timmy. He had pulled the covers back down and was watching me. "It's okay, honey," I murmured, stroking his forehead. "Dad just doesn't understand right now, but he will."

He turned away from me and closed his eyes. I sat on the side of the bed, stroking his cheek and smiling down at him, thinking God, how I love this sweet baby.

Sensing from his breathing that he wasn't really asleep, I said, "Timmy, would you like for me to tell you a story my father used to tell at night when I was a little girl? I don't think I've ever told you the one about Seal and Bear. Would you like to hear it?"

He turned back to me, blinking to clear his eyes, and nodded.

I had to think back. I wasn't sure I could remember it exactly the way my father had told it, and I knew I'd never be able to re-create the theatrics he and my uncles had used when they told their stories in the ancient way.

"Okay. In the daytime," I began, smoothing his forehead, "when my father told stories, he would run around the room waving his arms, dipping and quivering with rhythm and joy because he loved to tell stories more than anything else in the world."

I stroked Timmy's hair, aware his eyes were on me and he was listening to every word.

"But it was very different in the dark of our cold Alaska nights, when our cook stove died down and there was no more heat to warm us. Then we would all huddle close together in one bed, bundled under thick fur blankets, and my father would tell this story, almost singing the words."

I paused for a moment, remembering my father's hypnotic voice, the sound of his chants, and felt my own voice falling into the ancient rhythm, speaking his words as he had spoken them to me.

"My father would speak in such a soft, low voice that the sounds of Wolf howling in the distance would begin to fade, and the ice floes crackling out on the water's edge would become only a faint, sharp whisper, lulling me to sleep."

My father's words began to come to me now, soft and hesitant, filtering into my memory while I struggled to translate them into English from his way in Yup'ik, the Athabascan language I'd been accustomed to in my childhood, but had been suppressing for years.

"Bear, big white one, wanted to catch Seal. Seal didn't want to be caught, no, not at all, so Seal ran out on ice and ice cracked and Seal started to sail away, like on a big canoe. Seal was happy, but Seal

didn't know Bear could swim.

"Big, big winds came up, pushing ice further out over water and Seal was happy because he thought he'd get away from Bear. But then he looked back."

"Do you know what he saw, Timmy?"

Timmy drowsily shook his head, fighting sleep. I stroked his arm, smiling as I clearly remembered now the ancient story I had thought was gone from my world.

"He saw Bear swimming toward him."

Timmy's eyes widened.

"But do you know what happened then?"

Timmy shook his head.

"Whale came shooting up out of water, whoosh! under Bear, and made Bear fly far, far away into sky, far over water and ice and land until Seal couldn't even see him anymore."

"Can you guess what he did?" I glanced at him. His eyes were closed and he had fallen into a deep sleep.

When I went back into the kitchen a few minutes later, Red was gone.

SIX

By late that afternoon it was pretty clear Jack wasn't going to reach Vera by phone until she felt like it. He was too busy after he'd got done talking to Mark's men and went back to the station, a big mistake because he had to spend the rest of the afternoon fending off the locals who dropped by after they heard about the body in the Morressey yard.

As usual, they were all in a hot sweat to have their say. He heard more theories that afternoon than he'd ever heard in his life, except when he'd read about the oil spill out in the Sound and everybody had wanted to blame it on somebody else.

This time they ranged all the way from pointing their finger at some unknown tourist to wondering if the Morressey boy had done it. None of them made a lot of sense to him.

After he got rid of them all he walked over to the clinic, but Doc was still busy with the autopsy. He told Doc to give him a call when he finished and headed out to get something to eat. By five o'clock he was sitting alone in a corner booth at Halibut House, eating an early dinner and thinking back over his talks with Mark's men earlier in the afternoon.

Oliver Jackson was an Alaska Native, the first man Mark had hired when he opened his construction company and he'd been with Mark ever since. His kids had been playing basketball in the back yard when Jack went to his house, a neat chrome-and-white double-wide on the edge of town. He liked Oliver's kids, they were always clean and well behaved and he stood watching them for a couple of minutes before he knocked on the door.

Oliver's wife, Maybelle, opened the door and let him in, pointing toward the living room where Oliver was sitting in a recliner, staring at the television.

Jack sat across from Oliver on the sofa and held up his hand to refuse a beer when Maybelle offered him one. Oliver said he wanted one and they waited while she brought it, then waited a couple more minutes until she took the hint from their silence and went outside.

Oliver took a swig of his beer and clicked off the T.V.

"I don't know nothing about that body. I never seen her before."

"I didn't think you did, but I have to ask. I am wondering why somebody would bury it in Red's yard, though. Got any idea who would do that?"

Oliver snorted. "Just about anybody, I expect."

"What makes you say that?"

"Red's a sonofabitch. I thought you knew that, everybody else does."

He could see the controlled anger in Oliver's eyes. "Why do you say that?"

"Ain't nobody's business but mine."

He already knew it was hard to get Oliver to talk when he didn't feel like it.

"Wouldn't surprise me any if he did it himself." Oliver filled a pipe with tobacco, avoiding his eyes while he tamped it down and lit it.

"And buried the victim in his own back yard? Why would he put it there, if he did it himself?"

"Safest place to do it, seems to me," said Oliver. "Red's smart, he knows nobody would believe he buried it there himself, in his own yard."

Jack struggled to keep his face still. "He's always been pleasant enough when I've talked to him."

Oliver's eyes flashed. "I still hope you find out he did kill that woman."

"Sooner or later you'll have to tell me why you're so pissed at Red. You might as well tell me now."

Oliver's mouth smiled but his eyes didn't. "It's personal, that's all."

Jack leaned forward for emphasis. "Talk to me."

Oliver puffed furiously on his pipe. "I'm not involved in this. Leave me out of it."

He'd have to let it go for now. He left and headed out to Klem

Bayliss' shack.

Klem had never been married as far as Jack knew. John North, Mark's third employee, stayed with Klem from Monday morning to Saturday afternoon when he got off work.

Jack had never met John's family but that wasn't unusual. Lots of Alaska Native men kept their families out of town, that was only one of the things that had been happening ever since the government and others had begun to wipe out the Alaska Native culture.

In John's case, he'd told Jack once over coffee, he kept his wife and kids at their village so the kids would grow up knowing who they were. After that, he said, it was up to them.

Klem's shack was a couple miles out of town, just off Richardson Highway. A long row of identical two-story apartment buildings, which had originally belonged to the oil companies for their employees to live in, lined the street. Some yards were full of old cars and car parts and discarded washers and dryers, a few refrigerators. Not always a bad thing. If something broke, a spare part was most likely right outside the front door.

Klem yanked the door open before Jack got the third knock in. "Took you long enough to get here. I've gotta get to the store so let's make this quick."

Jack glanced at his watch. One-thirty. "Good to see you again too, Klem."

He looked around for a comfortable chair but there was only an old green and white sofa where John lay sprawled watching a movie. He waited for John to sit up but John just glanced at him and took a swig of beer. He walked over to the kitchen table, looked around for someplace to put the magazines that covered both chairs and the tabletop, finally gave up and put them on the floor, pulled a chair out and sat far enough behind John that John would have to turn around to see him.

John, looking more like an angry bulldog waiting to pounce than usual, clicked off the remote and hauled himself up to a sitting position.

Klem was a few inches taller and a lot heavier than John and it was hard to tell what he looked like because a thick beard and mustache covered most of his face and neck.

Jack pointed toward the sofa. "Have a seat, Klem."

Klem sat next to John. "Make it fast."

Jack pulled out a cigarette and took his time lighting it, deliberately fumbling with the lighter, got it lit then laid it in an ashtray. He didn't smoke, never had ever since he tore his gut out one afternoon smoking seven of his dad's cigars when he was five and got his ass whupped for his trouble. The prop still came in handy when he was stalling for time.

He didn't like the atmosphere in this room. Until this day both men had always been as friendly as anyone ever got with the chief of police.

"So do either of you know anything about that body?" he asked, knowing the answer he'd get.

"Nope," said Klem. "Can I leave?"

He shrugged. "Stay or go. I can talk to John while you're gone."

The two men glanced furtively at each other. "That's okay," said Klem. "We'll both talk to you now."

Rule number one, Texas police academy: Never let two suspects or witnesses talk to you at the same time in the same location.

"Fine," he said, mentally kicking his training manual under the table. He hadn't come from the Dallas PD where he'd shot up the ranks in eight years flat because he always stuck to the rules.

"First, can either one of you ID the body?"

"Have to be pretty intimate with her to do that, wouldn't you say?" said Klem.

"I ain't never cheated on my wife," John said.

"I take it that's a 'no' from both of you?" He eyed the cigarette, watching the smoke go straight up in the still room.

They both nodded.

"Klem, do you know of any man in town angry enough to do that to anyone, to their wife, maybe?"

Klem snorted. "Probably all of 'em, one time or another."

He had to silently agree. "How about you, John?"

"Me?" protested John. "I ain't around my wife long enough to get that mad."

"I wasn't accusing you. I meant, do you know anyone with that kind of anger toward his wife?"

"How come you're so sure it's somebody's wife?" shot John.

"It doesn't have to be anybody's wife. I'm just asking questions here, fellas, trying to get a bead on this."

"So why don't you ask the obvious question?" asked Klem.

"And that would be?"

"Do we think Red had anything to do with it," said Klem.

Jack watched John peel something from under his fingernails with the end of an ivory-handled hunting knife.

"I was just coming to that. Do you?"

John looked up. "You talking to me?"

"Both of you, one by one. You first. Do you?"

John's tee-shirt moved as his chest muscles rippled. "I dunno. Never thought about it."

Jack turned to Klem. "What about you?"

"I'm thinking I need to get to the store before all the fresh bread's gone. Can we just put a lid on this?"

"As soon as you give me an answer I like."

A slow grin turned the crevices around Klem's eyes into laugh lines. "Okay, here's one you might like. I think Red's way too smart to pull something stupid like that. If he'd of done it, he would of put the body someplace else. How's that?"

"I've been thinking something along those lines, myself." He thought over Klem's answer for a minute. "What makes you think Red's so smart?"

Klem shrugged. "He's the guidance counselor over at the high school, ain't he? That must mean he's got some kind of smarts."

"Yeah, sometimes it does." He'd already sent up north for a background on Red.

He stood and headed for the door, then turned back. "Go ahead and buy your bread, Klem, but don't go too far away, either of you. I might think of something else I need."

"That's it?" said John, reaching for his light jacket. "We're done?"

"You're done," he said, "for now, anyway. Go on home and

take care of your wife." Then he headed for the restaurant and his dinner.

He was just finishing his coffee and pie, no closer to anything except the realization that not one person had given him a straight answer on anything, when his cell phone rang.

"So are we on now?" purred Vera. "Or are we off?"

SEVEN

Timmy slept most of the day, waking only when I brought him some chicken noodle soup and fed it to him spoonful by spoonful. It was early that evening, after Red had returned and dinner had come and gone, and the house was silent except for the faint sound of Alice's television upstairs, that it happened again. This time there was no doubt about it.

This was the time of year the whole atmosphere changed in Valdez. No longer dark most of the day, the neighboring metal rooftops shimmered under soft twilight. People had already begun to put out their flowers and a riot of vivid color and fragrance filled the town, surprising the tourists who were beginning to arrive. They could smell it, along with the faint saltwater odor from the port, coming in on Egan Drive.

I had already loaded the side porch with hanging baskets of red and pink begonias and geraniums, and the sweet odor of moist dirt and summer flowers filled Timmy's room on the first floor. From my kitchen window I could see the stark white glaciers growing faint in the distance through the oncoming half-light. This was usually my favorite time of year, but the horror of what had happened in my back yard that morning lay heavily on my mind as I opened Timmy's door.

He was sitting up in bed, smiling and waving at his window.

I glanced that way, expecting to see neighborhood kids, but there was nothing visible except for flowers hanging at the edge of the porch and the mountaintops, now dimming and shadowed.

I looked back and saw he was still smiling, still waving.

"Timmy?" I edged closer to his bedside. "Who are you waving at?"

He didn't seem to hear me.

I went over to the window, thinking maybe kids had ducked

below the windowsill when they saw me come into the room. No one was there, but when I turned back, Timmy was still smiling and waving.

I walked back to his bedside, sat beside him and pulled him into my arms. "Did you have a nice dream, sweetheart?" I buried my face in his damp little-boy neck, nuzzling, savoring the lovely, familiar smell. "What did you see?"

He stopped waving and looked straight at me.

"Xwaayi, leelk'w, at shi."

I almost lost my breath. Those were words he couldn't possibly have known, but once again, this time so clearly I could understand him, he had spoken in the language of my people, an ancient language he hadn't been taught, other than a few words. Except for the elders who still lived in the outer villages, no one used it much anymore.

My blood turned cold as I realized he had spoken the words with complete authority and in an entirely different, matter-of-fact adult voice instead of his normally high-pitched and excited little-boy voice. They sounded, to me, as though they had come straight from his mouth, and although he seemed to know exactly what he was saying, it was the voice of my father who spoke the words.

"Xwaayi, leelk'w, at shi."

Tribal relation. Grandfather. Singing.

EIGHT

Jack spoke into his cell phone. "Where are you?"

"I'm still on the ship." Her voice lowered, husky with passion. "I can meet you at your place if you're done with whatever you've been doing all day."

No curiosity at all about the murder. He shoved that thought aside now because Vera's voice had produced an immediate physical reaction, and this was one of those times when he was anxious to get back to his personal life. It had been too long and his testosterone was going full bore, giving him the clear message it was time for a little R&R.

"Be there in fifteen minutes." He grinned in spite of himself.

"Make it ten," she said.

He made it in eight.

They did their usual routine, walking through the doorway at his place together, frantically groping each other and ripping off their clothes while they made their way to the bedroom. He was sitting on the side of the bed with his jeans down over his boots, getting ready to pull them off, looking over at her already naked body and gritting his teeth to keep from diving into it with his boots still on, when his cell rang again.

Vera ran her fingernails down his back. "Let it ring."

He looked at her, at the phone, back at her, back at the phone. Her eyes grew dark and narrow as he picked up the phone.

"O'Banion."

"Doc here. You'd better get over here right away, Jack. One of your men just found a human head in a plastic garbage bag floating in the water. He said he swung by the city docks to have a few minutes alone before he went home, just to clear some of the crap out of his head. He saw the otters playing with something under the long dock, the one that's closed off at the entrance. When he took a closer look and saw the shape of the bag, he cleared the area and fished it out."

"Which one of my men?"

"Bill Nicholson."

"Bill? How come he didn't call me first?" Jack was more than a little pissed. That didn't sound like Bill.

"He didn't have time, he wanted to make sure I was still here. He was still puking when he walked in and handed me the bag. I just got him stopped a couple minutes ago. How come you can't hire any officers around here with strong stomachs? All they've done today is gag and puke."

"Do either of you recognize the head?"

"Nope, there were holes ripped in the plastic and it's already decomposed, what's left of it anyhow. Crabs got in there with it. There were a couple small ones in there still eating when I opened it. Want 'em? I don't like crabmeat."

Ah, jeezus. "No, thanks. I'll be there in a few minutes." When he turned back Vera was hunched over the side of the bed with that luscious blonde hair fanned out over her shoulders, reaching for her slacks and ignoring his pleading look.

He stood and zipped up his pants, a maddening sound at that moment. "Vera, please just wait here, I won't be long."

She sighed and walked out of the room, ignoring him. He watched her pick up her bra, her blouse, her purse. She put her blouse back on and stuffed her bra in her purse.

"Yes, you will," she said over her shoulder and slammed her way out of the house.

Ten minutes later he was in Doc's autopsy room, looking down at the severed head of who-the-hell-knew. The crabs had done a good job. There wasn't a sign of skin or eyes or hair left.

Doc watched the scummy gray water, still spreading from underneath the skull on his stainless steel table and dripping down onto the floor. "Damned if I can tell who it might be. It could have drifted here from someplace else, but it fits the body, sliced off neat as a hunk of corned beef. Must've used a cleaver or machete, something like that. It's gotta be somebody really good with a knife anyhow."

Raven Talks Back

Jack eyed the skull. "That's no help. Everybody around here's good with a knife. We'll have to send it up to the state lab and see if they can make an ID." He glanced from the skull to the two crabs still floating in the bucket under the table.

"It could take weeks if there are no dental records or DNA match," said Doc. "I heard they're building a new compound up there so I have no idea what shape their lab's in right now." He lifted the skull, lowered it into a clean plastic bag and sealed it shut.

"Then they'll send it on to the FBI," Jack said. "They might not be able to make a match even there. A lot'll depend on whether or not this woman had a criminal background. Let's just hope she's had dental work done in Anchorage." He sighed and shook his head. "I guess I'll mosey on over to the office and make some notes before I go back home."

Doc gave him a strange look. "On Saturday night? Jeezus, don't you have a life?"

He looked at his watch. "As of about thirty minutes ago, not much of one. Not this weekend anyhow."

He said goodbye and left. He was halfway to his office when he remembered he'd talked to everyone except Mark, so he swung back and headed for Mark's house. What the hell, they were friends. If his Saturday night could be skunked, so could Mark's.

He pulled into Mark's driveway, surprised to see all the lanterns around his patio lit. He should have expected it. Weekends were nearly always party time at Mark's in the summertime. He'd been to many a good one there but he hadn't been invited to this one, which pissed him off even more than he already was.

He sat in his vehicle, debating the pros and cons of crashing, finally decided not inviting him was another good reason to mess up Mark's night, added to the fact that Mark would probably get laid afterward and he wasn't going to. That was enough to piss him off too, although not enough to make him think seriously about getting married just so he could have regular Saturday night sex.

On the other hand, he'd spotted a few couples sitting at the picnic table in the back yard and they seemed content enough. He wondered, as he often did, if he'd ever find that kind of contentment, at least enough to marry the source of it. So far he hadn't come anywhere close. He sighed, climbed out of his vehicle and headed for the back, sniffing the air as he walked.

Yep, steaks again, well done. He didn't care what anybody said, to his mind there was nothing better than a thick black steak slathered with hot sauce, the hotter the better, and a big pool of it in a separate saucer for dipping, like the sorghum molasses his grandpa used to fix up every morning for dipping biscuits. Steaks and a cold beer. Yeah! He sauntered over to the cooler and pulled out a beer, ignoring Mark's surprised look.

"I'll have the usual," he called, grinning while he popped the tab and took a big swig.

Mark didn't miss a beat. He pointed to a stack of plates. Jack grabbed one and handed it to him. They almost had a routine, no need for words, invited or not.

Mark plopped a steak on it and Jack slid onto a bench by the table. He'd eaten earlier but it was too late to worry about that now, he'd already cut into the steak and dipped it into the hot sauce. His stomach sighed with pleasure while the steak slid down. The rest of him was frustrated. Steak wasn't going to help that any, but it might help take the edge off.

Half the neighborhood was there, all good people, loud and rowdy and obviously a few beers ahead of him. They traded some jokes, laughed, pumped him a little about the murder but they didn't really care, they were already half in the bag.

A couple of beers later he motioned for Mark to walk around to the front of the house with him.

By now the trees on the nearby mountains had turned deep blue-green with the oncoming night and the sky was streaked with blue and a little bit of yellow—odd but nice. They sat silent for a few minutes on the front steps while shadows fell and trees turned black against the sky, which wasn't going to get much darker. There wouldn't be a lot of bright stars that night for sure, they usually weren't even visible until late August, early September. Somebody had turned on country-western music in the back yard and when Jack glanced that way he could see several couples dancing. They'd probably get laid too.

Mark spoke first. "So what's up?" He took a deep gulp of beer. "I saw the ship come in this morning and I thought you'd be playing house with Vera tonight, otherwise I'd have invited you."

"My apologies for crashing," said Jack. "She bailed. Doc called and I had to leave. She got mad and split right in the middle of everything."

Mark laughed. "That'll teach you to answer your phone on a Saturday night."

"You ain't just whistlin' *I Can't Get No Satisfaction*, Jack muttered. The yellow sky streaks disappeared and an eagle flew overhead in a wide arc. By now they could barely see the glaciers and he was beginning to feel the slight chill. The last of the bright light slid over the mountaintop and the glaciers all but disappeared into the mist.

"So have you got any idea how that body got in Red's yard?" Jack asked.

"Not hardly. I never saw her before, whoever she was."

"Think any of your men might be involved in this?"

Mark's voice dropped. "I don't think so. They were as surprised as I was when it popped up there."

"What about Red?" They'd talked just about everything over ever since they'd become buddies several years back and Jack knew Mark wasn't crazy about Red.

Mark was still for a minute. "I don't know. He's got the temper for it, I've seen it in action a couple of times, but I don't know much about him except he works at the high school and runs the scout troop. I'm not sure I can see him going that far, bad temper or not."

"Yeah, maybe you're right." Jack was silent for a minute. "Well, buddy, I have to ask you what I've asked everybody else so far, since you're the owner of the company that found the body. Can you account for your movements in the past week?"

Mark glanced at him, surprised. "Well, yeah, sure. Want me to write it down?"

"I'd appreciate that."

"Now?"

"Monday's fine, just drop it by the office. Sorry about that, but you know how it is. You were there so I need your statement."

They shook hands and Jack left, heading for his log cabin on the far outskirts of town. It was too late for his usual after-work target practice, so it looked like another Saturday night of either CNN or some crappy B movie, or the Internet.

He walked into the house and turned on his computer, ready for a night of surfing although first he wanted to check on the town kids, see what they were up to.

He didn't think anybody in Valdez knew that part of his degree back in Texas was in computer science. He'd aced all the courses and diddled with computers a lot. There wasn't much he couldn't do with them.

His setup, in a small room off his bedroom, with three monitors, fax-scanner-printer, was very state-of-the-art. In fact, it looked like something a science fiction producer might have dreamed up, and he was damn proud of it. Plus he was a good hacker and he'd stumbled onto the private chat room the teens in town had set up a while back. They had no way of knowing he was watching every word they typed.

This night they were going strong. The usual couples had broken off into private rooms where they could have cybersex, which he checked every once in a while just to make sure it was still only the teens, since he knew all their screen names.

He switched on his secondary monitors and pulled up a couple of the other rooms and sat reading for a few minutes, as usual a little surprised at how creative the teens were, even though most of the things they described seemed anatomically impossible to him. Then again, they were young'uns.

Six different conversations were going on in the main room as he watched the lines spin across his screen. The usual stuff. Bitching about parents, which indie bands had the best websites, who had the latest pirated CD's, making plans for when summer really got going— but then his eyes caught something new. He hunkered over the keyboard, watching.

They had said something about 'the job', just a couple of words, then three of them spun off into another room he hadn't been to before. He spent the next ten minutes scrambling to track them down and by the time he got in there they were almost finished talking, but

Cyberdarth666—that was Charlie Morressey—said they'd do the preliminary check while they were camping with the troop next weekend, after everybody was asleep. Then they set it up for when they were cleaning one of the big ones while it was still empty.

Then, as if some signal had been given, they all jumped back to the main room and rejoined the conversations as if they'd never been gone.

What the hell was that about? Charlie and his two buddies, all three seniors this coming year, were still in Red's scout troop. He knew all the kids in town and so far none of them had done anything illegal, but this didn't sound legal to him. He made a mental note to keep close track of this because the oil containers were the only significant containers in town he could think of. They were usually partially full, some full all the way, but whenever one was empty they cleaned it out.

Why would three teenage boys be even thinking about them, if they were? It was impossible to get into the area where the tanks were filled, without solid identification. High barbed wire topped chain link fences surrounded the terminal and their armed guards weren't kidding one bit. Nobody could get in there without a valid electronic pass, everybody in town knew that and tourists found out soon enough. He figured it was probably nothing, but then again, with young'uns, you never could tell.

He watched another half-hour or so, but finally switched it all off after noting the same couples in the sex rooms were still at it, only four had traded partners. Well, why not. It was free, and you couldn't find safer sex than that anywhere.

NINE

No one mentioned the murder the rest of the weekend. It was almost as if it had never happened. It struck me then for the first time that everyone in the house seemed to have the same inability to really talk to each other. Timmy's was just more apparent.

On Sunday, Red went fishing and Alice and Charlie went out with their friends. I was alone most of the day except for periodic checks on Timmy, so I had plenty of time to think about what happened to him, and the possible reasons behind it.

Had my story caused him to dream about his grandfather? Was he still basically asleep when I went into his room and found him sitting up, smiling and waving at an empty window? If he was, where had that voice and those words come from? I couldn't see any way possible that I could have imagined them, unless I was subconsciously still missing my father. Did I still miss him that much, after all the years that had passed since the day of his death?

I had rushed home from college when my Aunt Lucy came into town and called to tell me my father's time was near. I arrived at the house far out in the bush with only minutes to spare but he was already too far gone to recognize me. While the men in our tribe smoked and chanted outside, I barely had enough time to lean over him and rub his hands before he took his last breath. I could only watch, devastated, as his soul left his body, taking away his songs and laughter and stories forever.

The following March, after I married Red and was pregnant with Charlie, my tribe held the *Stickdance* in Mulato, honoring all male members who had died since the last ceremony, but Red had refused to let me go.

On the last night the men were doing the shuffling dance they always performed while they sang *Hi'o Keleka,* the twelve surviving ancient tribal death songs out of the original thirteen we think they had. They told me that while the dance was going on, my mother quietly fell over dead beneath the ceremonial spruce pole, onto the tribe's handmade gifts to the dead and the living who had attended the ceremony.

Did I ever forgive Red? I tried to suppress the rage I felt at the time, but it still simmered beneath the surface, I couldn't deny that.

After I got over the additional shock of my mother's death I felt very much alone, my heritage relegated to the past where, Red insisted, it belonged. He never understood the concept of blood ties, and would never listen whenever I tried to speak of it after my mother was buried.

And so I silently paid my respects to my parents during those early morning moments when I still heard their voices calling to me through the fog, then was immediately jolted back into a culture still foreign to me by the noise of the dishwasher and television, especially when the shrill sounds of Saturday morning cartoons played in the background for the amusement of my half-Alaska Native, half-Caucasian children.

Monday morning Doc called to tell me Timmy had an appointment in Anchorage at three o'clock that afternoon. This gave me just enough time to call the airport and book two seats, and then get Timmy and myself ready, since Red refused to go.

Timmy walked on his own into the Valdez airport terminal, a long, two-story building on the outer edge of town, but for the first time in several years he held tight to my hand. We'd almost made it to the loading gate when I heard Hopscotch's voice.

"Hello! What have we here?" he called in his soft British accent. His brown leather jacket flew open as he rushed to catch up with us. As always, his WW1 flight helmet completely covered his head, his clipped mustache hid the top of his lip, and his goggles swung from a long chain around his neck, although he usually kept them on when he walked around in the airport.

The town people called him Hopscotch because of the way he flew the small planes in and out of the Alaska passes and I thought, as always when I saw him, he had to be one of the nicest, most gentle people God ever put on this earth.

I first met him when I went back to work part-time at the airport after Timmy was old enough to go to school. We had tea together one afternoon, hit it off, and then after that we always ate lunch together whenever he wasn't flying. We were just friends. I never thought of him as anything else.

"Hello there, Ace." Hopscotch stooped to pat Timmy's head, as always, but he glanced up at me, his eyes questioning. "He looks a bit knackered this morning. What's going on?"

I'd been around him long enough to understand most of his British expressions. He was saying Timmy looked tired.

"Didn't you hear what happened over the weekend?"

He shook his head. "I've been in Anchorage all weekend. Managed to get a skin full Saturday, I'm sorry to say, but I'm over it now. I just got back this morning. I've been in the office catching up on paperwork. What happened?"

I eyed Timmy. "Let's talk about it later, okay? Right now, Timmy and I are heading for a doctor in Anchorage."

"Is he sick? No wonder he looks so peaked." Hopscotch ruffled Timmy's hair again. "We'll get you off to the doctor soon, Sport." He looked up. "High ceiling today, we'll have a fast flight. When's your appointment?"

"Three," I said, relieved to hear he'd be flying.

"What's the address?"

I told him.

He nodded. "I keep a car at the airport in Anchorage. I'll drive you there and back to the plane. No arguments. I have time to kill and there's only the one flight back in today."

I already knew better than to argue with him. He might be soft spoken, but when he said he'd do something, it was done.

He knelt in front of Timmy. "If you're very, very good for your mum, we'll nab you an ice lolly when we're done. Okay?"

Timmy licked his lips. Popsicles were his favorite junk food. I saw Hopscotch's questioning eyes over Timmy's head, but I just mouthed, "Later."

The floor-to-ceiling window in Dr. Randells' office looked out over Cook Inlet, where you could see for miles, a beautiful, tranquil sight. The colors in his waiting room and his office were the same as outside—soft blues and grays, a few pastels on the walls, thick gray carpeting, and in one corner, a small table and chairs stood next to several shelves full of toys.

Timmy eyed them as we were ushered into the office but he followed me and sat in front of the doctor's desk. I wanted to cry at the picture he made, a very small boy in such a large chair. His glance kept wandering toward the toy cars on the lower shelf.

"Go ahead, Timmy," said Doctor Randell. "You can play with the cars. Your mother and I will just sit and chat for a few minutes."

Timmy climbed off his chair and walked slowly toward the toy shelves, then sat on the floor, his head bent as he inspected the cars and trucks one by one.

Dr. Randell leaned over his desk, and began rolling a ballpoint pen between his hands. "I spoke to Dr. Martin this morning," he said, keeping his voice low. "He filled me in. How has Timmy been? Anything new happen the rest of the weekend?"

I told him Timmy was still refusing to say anything to anyone, although most of the time he seemed aware of what was going on around him.

"He hasn't spoken at all, then? Not even to you?" He was watching me closely, his dark eyes slightly narrowed.

My fingers dug into my palms. If I told him what Timmy had said and how he'd said it, he was going to think I was the one who needed therapy. If I didn't, he might not be able to help Timmy.

Still, I fought it, shrinking from trying to find an explanation because there was none, but I knew I had to tell his doctor everything.

"He spoke once when he was having a dream, while he was sound asleep. And once while he was awake. But..." My voice drifted off and the words floated in front of me.

He waited for a minute, then said in a soft voice, "But?"

I knew my face was flushed. I could feel it. "I don't know how to explain it without sounding like I'm crazy. I know that's what you're going to think and I won't blame you."

He smiled and made a couple of quick notations on his yellow lined tablet. "Whatever it is, you can tell me. Just take your time."

I drew a deep breath. "The first time, while he was asleep, he spoke with a man's deep voice and he was almost singing the words to something that sounded like—again, I know this is crazy—one of the old Athabascan hunting chants my father used to sing. I couldn't make out the words but I'm almost sure it was one of those chants."

He stared at me for a few seconds. "Has he been taught your language?"

I shook my head. "We live in the city and nobody there uses it. I've taught him a few Athabascan words here and there along the way, for sea lion, seal, bear, things like that. He knows the word for ice cream, I make it every once in a while in the old way and he loves it, but..." I knew I was floundering but I couldn't help it.

"Look, here's the thing. I understand the language, although I've forgotten some of it now. My parents taught me when I was little, but Timmy has never been taught. None of his friends know the language—not many people do and it's dying out fast. They don't teach it in school. In fact, they're not allowed to use it there even if they do know it."

"Couldn't he have learned it from someone else, one of his friends, maybe?" He was watching me closely now.

"I don't see how. Timmy's always somewhere nearby. He's been very protected. I always know where he is and who he's with and most of the time they play in our yard. Only a couple of his playmates are Alaska Natives and they haven't been taught the language either, it's just too hard to learn. You have to live with it every day for it to stick with you." I paused, wondering if his friends would still play in our yard.

"So I don't see how he could have known them, Dr. Randell. Hunting chants are way too difficult. I doubt I could do them myself now, although I did know them at one time. And the voice he used—the chant was in a man's voice, and it came out of his mouth." My words were almost running together now. "I don't understand what's happening."

He wrote something then looked up. "What about the second time he spoke? What did he say?"

I had pulled a tissue from my pocket a few minutes earlier. I looked down and saw it was in shreds, tiny white pieces fluttering toward the floor like seagulls over the Sound on a lazy day. "You're going to think I'm insane, I know you are."

He smiled and the measured reassurance in his eyes frightened me even more. "Mrs. Morressey, please just tell me what happened and what he said."

Confusion swept over me and my eyes closed while the scene played out in my mind as though it were happening all over again.

"I went into the bedroom and he was sitting up, smiling and waving at someone in the window...but there was no one there." I opened my eyes.

"Are you absolutely sure of this?" More notations on his pad.

I couldn't speak so I nodded

"Did you ask him who he was waving at?"

"Yes," I whispered. I could still see Timmy at that moment, his look of delight, almost pure love.

"I went over to the window in case some kids were hiding, but no one was there and he was still smiling and waving when I turned back. That's when I asked him, and that's when he...when he..." I couldn't hold the tears back any longer. They'd been hovering on the surface all weekend and now they rolled down my cheeks. I dabbed at my eyes with a piece of the tissue.

"That's when he..." Dr. Randell handed me another tissue.

"He said a few words. Clear words. I knew exactly what he was saying and so did he. And just like the first time, it came straight from him. I swear it was from him!"

He glanced at Timmy. "What words, Mrs. Morressey?"

I tried to keep my voice from shaking but it was useless. "He said, in perfect Athabascan language, 'Tribal relation. Grandfather singing.'"

He stopped writing. "And his voice, this time?"

"It was the same voice as before. It wasn't his voice at all. But the words were all coming straight out of his mouth, just as they did before."

"Did you recognize the voice, Mrs. Morressey? Had you ever heard it before?"

"Yes," I said. "It was my father's voice."

The expression on his face changed and he was silent for what seemed an eternity, looking first at me, then Timmy, then back. He leaned over the side of his desk, pulled out a manila folder, removed the pages from his notebook and slid them in.

"I'd like to talk to Timmy for a few minutes now, and then we'll discuss possible treatment. Timmy," he called, "would you mind coming over here for a few minutes?"

Timmy pulled himself up, still holding a small red truck, and climbed back into the chair. Dr. Randell spoke softly, trying to draw him out, but after fifteen minutes during which Timmy only stared through him as if he weren't there, he turned to me.

"Well, at least he can walk. From what your doctor said when we discussed Timmy this morning, that's an improvement. Now," he turned to Timmy, smiling. "We need to work on getting this young man's voice back. Timmy, would you mind going with my nurse for a few minutes? She's a very nice lady, you'll be safe, I promise you. I need for her to weigh you and see how tall you are. Then you can come right back. Would you do that for me?"

Timmy looked down at his truck and nodded.

Dr Randell pushed an invisible buzzer. His nurse appeared and guided Timmy out of the room.

He gave me a long, measured look. "I have to tell you, I haven't had a case quite like this, but I've heard of them. I'll be consulting with another child psychologist but for now, I can definitely tell you that your son is suffering from PTSD, Post Traumatic Stress Disorder. He's deeply traumatized because of the body, and worse, its condition. Pretty nasty, I heard."

"It was. I saw it and it made me sick."

"It'd make anybody sick, but a young child and as you say, protected—he's been traumatized to the point where he can't speak. Make no mistake about this, in case anybody's wondering, he really can't. He's disassociated from almost everything at the moment and it's probably going to take a month or so, maybe more, but I think we can help him. There are new treatments for childhood trauma, one in particular I think might work to relieve what's going on in his mind right now, but we need to take this slowly."

I dreaded the "however" I knew was coming.

"However," he said, "this voice phenomenon, the different voice you say sounded like your father's. Are you absolutely sure your imagination wasn't running away with you?"

He held up his hand. "No insult intended, Mrs. Morressey, but you had a shock too, and it could have affected you a lot worse than you think. Isn't that possible?" He watched me closely, as he'd been doing all along, clearly expecting me to agree that yes, maybe I had been imagining things.

"Forgive me, but I'm not imagining anything. I know what I saw and heard. I just don't know what the explanation is. I don't know if there is one." I stopped to dab at my eyes.

"I only know what I heard my son saying, and I saw his face while he was saying it. An expression of joy is the only way I can describe it. For some reason my son really thought he was seeing his grandfather at that window. He told me, in clear Athabascan, that his grandfather was singing to him!"

"Using his grandfather's voice," said Dr. Randell.

"That was the voice I heard, yes."

I watched him fighting to hide his expression. "Mrs. Morressey, do you believe his grandfather was speaking through him? I've heard the fables, stories passed on down to Alaska Native children, mysterious things, talking animals, spirits that walk about in the heavens, that sort of thing. I wonder if this isn't influencing you somehow."

"Are you asking me if I'm inventing a brand new fable?"

He flushed. "Well, this is very unusual, you have to admit that."

"I do. That's why we're here."

"Okay then." He pressed his buzzer again. "Please make Timmy another appointment for Wednesday morning." He glanced back at me. "I'll need to see him three times a week, for right now." He caught my dismayed look and added, "We'll start to spread it out as he progresses.

Meantime, don't press him to talk if he doesn't want to. Children with this disorder are depressed and withdrawn, you've already seen that. We'll start on Wednesday, I'll see you again Friday, and we'll go from there."

"Will I be in here with him?"

That quick smile again. "Of course. If it begins to interfere with his treatment though, I may need to see him alone from time to time. We'll see how it goes. Sometimes it goes quickly, sometimes not. It all depends."

"On what?" My hand, clammy and cold, reached for my throat.

His mouth spread into a faint smile that didn't quite reach his eyes. "On whether or not something else is bothering him."

TEN

It didn't take long to get the corpse's ID. The lab up north did a dental check first and got back to Jack Monday afternoon.

The murder victim, much to his surprise, had been identified as Carolyn Crumbe, one of the English teachers at the local high school. When he heard that and called Doc right away, Doc was as surprised as he was. Neither could imagine her involved in anything that might have resulted in such a brutal death.

Jack had met Carolyn several times at various school functions whenever he was obliged to go and she'd always struck him as the mousy type. Medium brown hair pulled back into a tight pony tail, no makeup, hard to figure eye color, he'd never really tried because they'd always been almost hidden by thick bifocals. He thought she was probably early forties, although she seemed much older.

There was one thing he clearly remembered, though. He'd never seen her without something long-sleeved on, and her stockings were always, now that he thought about it, thick and dark. He'd figured, in passing, she had a fairly nice body, but it was hard to tell with all those heavy sweaters and whatnot, so he'd never given it much thought.

When he and two of his men shot over to her apartment with a search warrant and the landlady let them in, there was no doubt in anybody's mind. They had found their crime scene.

Inside, they found blood spatters, dry and caked by that time on everything, including the walls. It had pooled and dried on the furniture and seeped deep into the carpeting. And nobody in the neighborhood had seen or heard anything. Carolyn Crumbe hadn't even been missed.

Beth Anderson

ELEVEN

I left Timmy home with Alice when I went back to work Tuesday and told my boss I was going to have to temporarily cut my hours short because of Timmy's appointments. It was the worst possible time, the beginning of tourist season as well as the scriptwriters' conference held in Valdez every summer, and I worked at the ticket counter. It couldn't be helped. My son came first.

I had gone to work at the airport right after I left college and could barely wait to start my new life. A degree in accounting would have meant I could go to work for the oil company if I stayed in Valdez. This had been my father's plan for me and I intended to follow it, but when I came home and saw there was a permanent opening with the small airline that flew in and out of Valdez, I jumped at the chance. Soon I had a good job and my own small apartment in a town I loved. I was happy on my own. Then I met Red.

I was thinking about him when I walked into the dark lunchroom Tuesday afternoon to have tea with Hopscotch. This was the same room where I fell under Red's spell one early fall afternoon when the cold, dark days were fast coming upon us.

He had got off the plane on his way to an appointment with the school board and come into the lunch room to get a cup of coffee and ask directions. I took one look at that thick red hair, his muscular arms and deep-set, smoldering eyes, dark with apprehension over his job interview and something else I took as loneliness, and suddenly the oncoming winter didn't seem so forbidding.

From that moment on, nothing else mattered. Not family guidance, not background, not ethnic differences. There was no doubt in my mind this was the man I wanted, even though I knew little about him. I can still hear myself trying to explain to my mother and Aunt Lucy over their objections. I loved this man. Had to have him.

All that mattered was being with him, closed into his arms, weak with the aftermath of our turbulent lovemaking which had begun almost immediately, then making plans for the home we'd have and the children in it. I had told him then that someday I wanted a heated greenhouse for my flowers. It had taken me all this time to save for it.

Hopscotch was already in the lunchroom. He beckoned for me to come sit with him, where my tea was waiting.

"How's the little chap?" he asked after I was settled into my side of the booth.

I lifted my cup, inhaling the steam. "I don't know. He still doesn't say a word to anyone. He's walking around the house now, but he won't go outside."

"Alice watching him today?" He bent to tear the wrapper from a brownie, intent on peeling it just so.

"Yes, and she's fine with him right now, he minds her." I smiled. "So far, anyhow."

"Any more problems?" He held his brownie out to me. "Bite?"

I shook my head and watched him take a precise bite into the corner, as always. "He won't look out into the back yard and he won't look at Red at all. I don't know what's with that, although..."

He glanced up from the wrapper he had been folding into perfect squares. "Although?"

I felt my face go hot as realization swept over me and I looked down. "I shouldn't have said that." I sipped my tea, thinking back. "It's nothing, really, but he seems very afraid of Red for some reason."

Timmy had been afraid of Red from the time he was a small child and it had only gotten worse as time progressed, although I hadn't realized the extent of it until that minute.

"I wouldn't call being afraid of your father nothing." He popped the last of the brownie into his mouth and chewed for a minute. "How does Red treat him?"

I didn't know how to answer without sounding disloyal to Red. Normally my conversations with Hopscotch never got personal where family or marital matters were concerned. He was mainly a nice, safe friend. *An escape*, said a little voice inside. I shrugged off the voice and forced myself to smile.

"Red's pretty strict. Sometimes too strict. Timmy's a very sensitive child. He's more like my side of the family than Red's. At least I think so. Red's people are all dead, I never met them and he never talks about them."

Hopscotch's eyebrows shot up. "You don't know anything about them?"

I shook my head. "Actually, no. He did say they lived down south, but he never said exactly where, and he won't elaborate."

"I see," said Hopscotch. "Timmy's more like your side of the family as far as you know. Is that it?"

"Something like that." In the semi-darkened room his eyes, as they looked across the table into mine, seemed to shine and the laugh lines around his eyes deepened.

"He's a lot like me, anyhow," I said. "He's more sensitive, things affect him. The other kids, well, they're tougher, more like Red. They bounce back, nothing seems to bother them for long. But Timmy..." I paused again.

Hopscotch tilted his head toward me, listening.

"Timmy's more easily hurt. He retreats into himself a lot, although nothing like these past few days."

"Good thing we're getting him to a doctor then." Almost automatically he reached for my hand and squeezed it. His fingers stroked the back of my hand so softly I could barely feel it, but I did feel it, and the sensation, almost like a warm shock, crept up to my elbow and beyond. Hopscotch was a toucher, a sweet, friendly man. He'd done that before, but something about it was different this time.

This time he was looking into my eyes and I had the feeling he could tell how much his touch was affecting me. So gentle, so caring, so very nice...

I felt tears pushing their way out, quickly looked away to stop them, and saw Jack standing at the door watching us. I drew my hand away, feeling suddenly guilty, waved at him and he ambled over to our booth, staring straight at Hopscotch.

"Mind if I sit in?" Without waiting for an answer he pulled a chair from a nearby table and turned its back toward the booth, straddling it. "I just got some surprising news."

I glanced at Hopscotch, then Jack, definitely feeling tension as they eyed each other.

"What's the news?" asked Hopscotch. "Or is this personal and I should leave?"

"Not personal." Jack stared at Hopscotch's hand. "We just found out who the murder victim was."

"Who?" we both said at the same time. I glanced around to see if anyone was listening but there were only two strangers at a table on the other side of the room, too far away to hear us.

"Carolyn Crumbe."

I gasped and saw Hopscotch's face go pale.

"Carolyn Crumbe," he said. "The teacher?"

"I don't know anyone else by that name, do you?"

Hopscotch coughed, then recovered. "She's the only one I know of. Damn it all," he muttered under his breath. "This is a pickle."

Jack nodded. "I can understand that reaction from anybody involved with her, considering how she died, so how about giving me a complete rundown of your movements over the past, oh, say, week and a half."

I was baffled, watching Hopscotch's flushed face as he struggled to answer.

"I suppose I could, mate, although about all I do is go to work and then back to my place."

"Okay." Jack gave him a strange smile. "Write it all down and don't forget to name everyone who saw you just going to work and then back to your place, as well as anywhere else you might have been."

Hopscotch glanced at his watch. "It'll have to wait, I'm afraid. I have a flight leaving in a few minutes." He looked back up at Jack. "If that's all right with you."

Jack nodded, and then moved aside as Hopscotch slid out of the booth and left the lunchroom.

"What on earth was that all about?" I asked, unnerved by the anger I felt coming from Jack in waves.

His eyebrows arched and rose. "So you didn't know he's been dating Carolyn? I thought you two were close friends. That's what I've been hearing, anyhow. Who's that coming in, do you know?" He pointed toward the door.

I turned and looked at the doorway where two people stood peering into the room, but out of the corner of my eye I saw Jack lift Hopscotch's cup and drop it into a small bag he had pulled from his pocket.

"I don't know who they are, Jack, and why did you do that?"

Jack gave me a wide-eyed, innocent look. "Do what?"

"Take his cup."

"Forget you saw that, Raven. Just forget it and don't mention it to anybody. Not even Red, do you understand?"

"But Jack," I protested, "if you're starting to think he's—Jack, Hopscotch wouldn't do anything like that. He's not capable of it. I know him, he'd never hurt anyone!"

He smiled but his eyes were narrowed and dead serious. "I understand that's how you feel, Raven, but I've got a murder investigation going on. Until I eliminate people one by one, everybody who knew Carolyn is a suspect. I know Hopscotch is your friend and he may seem like a nice guy, but I still have to do my job, so just let it go and I'll do what I have to do." He smiled again and stood to leave. "Okay?"

"I guess it has to be, but I'm telling you, Jack, you're looking at the wrong person."

Jack's eyebrow shot up. "Then who's the right person, can you tell me that?"

"I don't have any idea. I knew her, but not enough to know anything about her." I stopped to ponder his news. "I still can't believe a woman who would have tattoos all over her body was our quiet little high school English teacher."

His lip twisted into a sardonic grin. "Well, she was. I guess they didn't do a physical before they hired her, or maybe she had one done by a doctor back where she came from. I know Doc didn't do it. He was as floored as I was when he saw all the scars. I'm running a background on her right now. I just came by to pick up something and asked where you were. This a usual thing, do you have coffee with him a lot?"

I shrugged. "Tea, actually, and all the time, if you want to know. Hopscotch and I are good friends."

His eyes were impassive. "I've heard that, but I'd like to hear it from you. How good?"

I felt the back of my neck heating up. "Very good friends, anyone here can tell you that, but it doesn't mean anything."

He started to walk away, then turned back. "I hope not," he said, "for your sake."

TWELVE

That afternoon Jack called Mark. The phone rang six times. "What, you can't answer the phone now? You and Susan having a nooner or something?" he said when Mark finally picked up.

"Check your clock, cowboy, it's after four now." Mark chuckled. "What makes you so sure it'd be my wife anyway? Maybe she went shopping and my girlfriend's here."

Jack thought about that for a few seconds. Nah. Susan was a former LA model and a real sweet looker. Second best-looking woman in town, after Raven. Nobody in their right mind would ever cheat on either one of them.

He laughed. "No way, buddy. I know you, and I know what time it is. Look, have you got a couple of minutes? I want to run something past you, or do you have to start dinner?"

He sat back, swung his feet up on the coffee table and picked up his beer, enjoying his little dig while he took a sip. There was a price to pay for regular sex. Mark did all the cooking in his house. All the more reason not to get married, if that was the way things went.

"Sure, I guess so," said Mark. "What's up?"

"We may have a juvie problem going on in town, although I'm not sure. Here's what I've got so far—." Jack told him what he'd seen in the chat room.

"So now I know how you spend your nights when Vera's not around," said Mark, after he stopped laughing. "What, you think these horny kids are planning an oil heist or something?"

"I don't know what they're planning." Jack chafed a little at Mark's tone. "I'm thinking maybe we ought to follow them to the campsite Saturday night and see if we can find out what they're up to."

"We? On Saturday night? You out of your mind? Jeezus, Jack, Susan's invited people over and you know I hate camping!"

"I'm not saying bring your sleeping bag and marshmallows, we're not staying there. I just want to see what they're up to. Meantime, I'll keep tracking their conversations late at night. Maybe I'll find out beforehand and we won't have to go."

There was a long silence. "Who all was talking?"

He thought back. "Red's boy, the older one. Calls himself Cyberdarth666 on their chat line. He's the one who said they'd have to check it out while they're camping this weekend after everybody's asleep. And two others, both town kids. Kit Carlyle, Roger's boy, the skinny one, although hell, he's no skinnier than I was at his age. His screen name's Devildust69. All the women in town are worried about him, it seems."

Mark snorted. "Yeah, I know him. What're they worried about?"

"Nobody ever sees him eating, not even at school. The dispatcher said she heard it from one of the mothers in town. They want to feed him. There's one more. Spoiled as hell, has his own convertible, plenty of money, flashes it around all the time. Jason Matthias, Jed's youngest son."

"Yeah, I know him. Tough-ass kid," said Mark. "Nearly ran me down with that car once. I can't believe he hangs out with a scout troop."

"Well, he does, and you'll crap when you hear his screen name." Jack scraped his boot on the ridge of his coffee table, trying to pry it off his foot.

"Lay it on me."

"ShoeSize13."

Mark laughed. "Nothing like advertising, is there. Well, I'm gonna have to pass, buddy. Sorry about that, but you know Susan."

Jack held his bottle up to the light. Empty. He was still thirsty. He hauled himself up and headed for the fridge, grabbed a beer and went back to the sofa.

"Yeah," he said after he took a long swig, "I know Susan. I'll get Bill to go with me. I didn't want to, his wife's a terrible gossip and the younger rookies are even worse when they get going, but I'll have to take the chance."

"I'm sorry, ol' buddy, but I'd never hear the end of it if I left a party to go play Sam Spade."

"I keep telling you to come be one of my officers."

"Nah, not for me. Susan would never stand for it and I like my life just the way it is. I have no interest in police work, that's your gig. Building's mine. Nice, easy life, I'm the boss and nobody tells me what to do. I don't want anything to screw that up."

"Can't say as I blame you. Maybe I'll see you afterward."

"Come on by, but if the light's off, don't knock." Mark chuckled and hung up.

He could understand that. If he had a woman like Susan, his lights would be off by six p.m.

THIRTEEN

Wednesday morning Timmy and I sat in Dr. Randell's office for ten minutes while he and I chatted, trying to get Timmy to relax, but Timmy's white knuckles still gripped the sides of the leather chair exactly as they had when we first came into the room. Dr. Randell caught it and spoke directly to him. "Timmy, we have a game we play here sometimes."

Timmy's eyes closed halfway, dark with mistrust, and I watched the little v between his eyes form a frown, growing deeper by the second.

Dr. Randell rose and motioned for me to go sit in a chair by the window while he headed for the play area. "Could you come over here, son? I have a play house with little people in it. I'd like for you to sit here on the floor and pick out some of them to play with. Could you do that for me?"

Timmy's eyebrows rose slightly but he got up from the chair and knelt by the house, a nicely constructed little wooden two-story home filled with miniature furniture. He glanced back at me and I smiled to encourage him. A whisper of a sigh escaped from him as he picked up a male figure and moved it slowly from room to room. I found myself wondering where this was going to take us.

When Timmy looked away I glanced at Dr. Randell and saw him watching me. I flushed and turned to look out the window, watching a ship far in the distance as small as the toys Timmy was lining up in a row. Then, because I couldn't help myself, I turned back to watch.

First the man, then a woman, then three children. He put the rest of the dolls aside and frowned with concentration as he moved two of the children over by the father.

"Only two, Timmy?" asked Dr. Randell in a soft voice.

Timmy picked up the third child and studied it, turning it over and around several times.

"Where's that one going, son?" Dr. Randell's hypnotic voice floated through the room. "Is he going with the others?"

Timmy looked straight at the doctor, raised his arm, reared back and threw the doll all the way across the room. The clatter it made and the look of fierce anger in his eyes as it bounced off the wall shocked me even more than the fact that he'd deliberately thrown it. I'd never seen that look in his eyes before and he wasn't in the habit of throwing his toys. At that moment he seemed to have forgotten anyone else was in the room.

His movements became slow, careful. He picked up the two other doll children and walked them, one in each hand, down the stairs, out of the house, across the floor. He propped them against Dr. Randell's desk, then pulled himself up and went over to the corner, picked up the third child and brought it back to the house, moving it carefully past the father, making it tiptoe up the stairs and into a room. He sat it on the floor, then turned around and glanced my way.

"Has the child been bad, Timmy?" Dr. Randell's voice broke into the silence. "Is that why you threw him?" His hand moved over his notepad, illegible marks, black on yellow.

Timmy ignored the question and picked up the female doll, walked it out of the house and across the room to the toy shelf, where he propped it next to a toy airplane. I almost lost my breath watching this tableau in the silence that filled the room. The mother had left the house.

His mouth pursed in deep concentration as he picked up the child and walked it down the stairs, out of the house and over behind Dr. Randell's desk. He set it down, then moved back to the house. I glanced at Dr. Randell. He was watching every move. The father was alone in the house now and the child was gone.

Timmy stared at the male doll for several minutes without moving. Then he crawled back over to the extra dolls and picked out a female. Brown plastic hair, blue dress, black shoes, all painted on, all part of the doll. He walked it into the living room where the male stood, then picked him up with his other hand and walked them both up the stairs and down the hallway, into the bedroom. His movements were silent, his eyes dark. He put the male face up on the bed, then lay the female down beside him and moved the male over until it was close to the female. He turned toward Dr. Randell, his eyes glittering.

Dr. Randell's soft voice broke through the silence. "Who is that, Timmy?"

Timmy ignored him and crawled behind Dr. Randell's desk, grabbed the child and tiptoed it toward the house. He walked it up the stairs, barely touching the steps, walking it everywhere except the room where the two dolls lay. Finally he walked it to the bedroom door, moved its arms to indicate it was opening the door, stood motionless for a minute then backed up and closed the door. He crept it back downstairs out the door and looked straight at me, his eyes bleak and fathomless as he tossed it back into the corner where it had landed earlier.

"Do you want to say anything, Timmy?" asked Dr. Randell. "You don't have to. You might feel better if you did, though."

Timmy turned toward me, opened his mouth, and again I heard the voice of my father.

"Cookie."

He had spoken. Just one word, but he said it, I knew he had...hadn't he? I felt my mouth tighten and my eyebrows draw together. Why a cookie? He'd eaten breakfast just a short while ago. Why my father's voice? None of it made any sense.

"Are you hungry, sweetheart?" I asked, thinking back to what he'd eaten for breakfast. Oatmeal, orange juice, milk. He'd helped himself to a couple of cookies just before we left the house and shoved them into his front pocket. They were still there, I could see the lump in his jeans pocket.

Timmy shook his head. I glanced at Dr. Randell to see if he'd heard, but he was bent over his notepad writing something. He put the pen down and stood, adjusting his shirt cuff.

"Good job, Timmy. Thank you. I'll see you again in a couple of days." His glance, warm and friendly, swept past me and rested on Timmy. "How about you go out to my nurse and tell her I said you could pick out any lollipop you want. We have some new stickers too.

Tell her I said you could choose one."

Timmy headed for the door. "I'll talk to your mother for just a few minutes," said Dr. Randell, "then she'll come get you and you can go home."

Timmy stopped at the door, turned back and stared at him for a few seconds, shook his head, then left the room without another glance, pulling the door shut behind him.

Dr. Randell's eyes seemed dangerously hooded as he glanced at me. "Mrs. Morressey, who do you think that doll was?"

"Which one?"

"The one lying in bed with the male doll."

My face grew hot. "What are you getting at, Dr. Randell?"

"I'm wondering if it could represent your husband and your daughter."

Horrified, I jumped up and leaned over his desk. "How dare you suggest such a thing! Red would never do that!"

He flushed slightly. "I didn't say he would, Mrs. Morressey, but in my profession, we know it's always a possibility. I asked you who you thought it was."

"Well, I don't think anything like that." I eased myself back into my chair, smoothing the crease in my slacks. "I took the one with the boy doll over by your desk to be my daughter."

He made a notation on his yellow pad. "You're probably right, but we have to explore all avenues because it's more than possible that something else is bothering him. I mentioned that last time you were here. Anyhow, it's just one possibility of many. He could have seen something on television he didn't understand. It could be any number of things. It could even be you, and maybe he saw something he shouldn't have without you realizing it."

He rose. "At any rate, I think we're making progress. We'll have to follow up, but I think he may have just told us something important."

Relief washed through me as I stood, facing him. "You heard it, then?"

Dr. Randell frowned. "Heard what?"

At that, I could barely speak. "What Timmy said."

His frown deepened. "I heard your question, but Timmy didn't make a sound the whole time he was in my office. What are you trying to tell me?"

Cold perspiration burst under my armpits. He had to have heard what Timmy said. There was no way he could have missed it. I looked around the room, finally forcing my puzzled gaze to settle back on him.

"Mrs. Morressey? What did you think you heard?"

I could barely breathe. *Think I heard? He didn't hear it? How can that be? It was perfectly clear.*

He sat on the edge of his desk, looking at me. "I only meant he may have, in some way, told us something about his conception of some family interaction with the dolls. What did you think he said?"

He said "cookie," Dr. Randell, and the voice I heard was the voice of my father. I have no idea what to think.

I couldn't make a sound. I'd already been through this. He didn't believe me then, he wouldn't believe me now. How could I help Timmy if I didn't tell his own doctor about the voice? I didn't know. I only knew somehow Dr. Randell had become the enemy. Maybe not Timmy's, but definitely mine.

"Mrs. Morressey?" Dr. Randell leaned toward me. "What did you think you heard your son say just now?"

I drew a deep breath. "Oh, I thought I heard him say he was hungry." I forced a smile. "You know how kids are, they grab something to eat and then fifteen minutes later they're hungry again. In fact, he has a couple of cookies in his pocket right now, so if he was hungry you'd think he'd remember them." I heard myself chattering desperately, trying to mask the truth.

My dead father just spoke to me again, Dr. Randell. Here, in this office.

Dr. Randell frowned again, his favorite thing when he was talking to me, it seemed. "Did he eat breakfast?"

"Yes." I stopped, my mouth suddenly dry. I had broken one of my father's rules, one he had insisted upon and one I had always, before today, followed.

Never lie, daughter. Lying is against our tribal code. It will always come back to haunt you if you lie.

Dr. Randell had picked up the yellow pad and begun writing again. I rubbed my hands together to warm them; they were cold and damp, maybe he could see that. His eyes became hooded again while he wrote for a minute without glancing back up at me. "Have you heard any more of those strange voices since the ones you told me about before, Mrs. Morressey?"

I shook my head. "No."

Except just now, Dr. Randell, when Timmy opened his mouth and my father said "cookie".

Panic washed through me again, I couldn't stop it, but I couldn't let him see it.

He rubbed his forehead. I stared at his hand and the room grew dark. Hovering directly in front of my face I saw a man's hand covered with blood, holding a knife.

Whose hand? Whose knife?

The image vanished as quickly as it had appeared and the room was light again. I glanced out the window to see if clouds could have covered the sun for an instant but no clouds were visible anywhere.

"Well," he said, "sooner or later we'll get to the bottom of everything that's troubling him." He gave me the same smile as the first time we sat in this room talking. "He should be done picking out his sticker by now. I'll see both of you Friday." He stood, an unspoken dismissal.

Both of us. Crystal pinpricks of fear shot through me. Either he thought I was insane, or I was insane. But I'd heard the voice and the words as clearly as anything I'd ever heard before, and whose hand had that been? What was happening to me? What was happening to my son?

"We'll be here Friday." I stood and headed for the door, then turned back. "Dr. Randell, please—"

"Mrs. Morressey," he interrupted, "your family has suffered a tremendous shock and it's only natural you'd all be affected by it. We'll work on this together, but our first job is to get Timmy speaking normally again, don't you agree?"

I nodded, trembling with fear and anger as I walked out of the office.

He did speak again, Dr. Randell. Or my father did.
I closed the door and went to retrieve my son.

I was silent as we flew low in between the Chugach Mountains, filled with wonder once again, as always when I made this trip, at how small the mountains looked from the plane, but how massive and forbidding they were when you stood at the bottom, looking up.

The fog had come in early and I watched it moving, swirling, misty gray cirrus clouds of it this time. It sifted across the valley below in layers, and the somber wails of my ancestors came to me through the noise of the plane's engine.

We're here, daughter. We're always here. If you listen carefully, you'll learn secrets we know, but you have yet to discover.

On Friday Dr. Randell tried once again to initiate a conversation with Timmy, but he was having none of it. He refused to play with the dolls again in spite of my urging and sat in the chair the whole time, staring at the front of the desk. Dr. Randell shrugged, told me some sessions would be like that, he'd see us again Monday.

The flights to Anchorage and back to Valdez were strained. Usually, Hopscotch would invite us to go up front, but this day he didn't. In fact, he barely had a word to say and both landings were bumpy, almost frightening, and unheard of when he was the pilot.

He wasn't meeting me in the lunchroom on my breaks, either. He'd been coming to work when his flights were due and leaving immediately afterward, with nothing but a short salute and an almost embarrassed half-smile my way.

That afternoon, after I took Timmy home and came back to work, I watched until I saw Hopscotch heading out toward the parking lot and ran to catch up with him.

He stopped to kneel and adjust something on his boot and I almost bumped into him. He looked up and his eyes flashed a quick, guarded welcome. "Hello, mate."

He'd never called me that before.

We stared at each other for a long, silent moment until he pulled himself into a standing position and fumbled with his goggles, reminding me of a flushed, nervous politician tugging his collar when someone asked a question he didn't want to answer.

"Coffee, tea, or...?" I said, trying to make a joke so I could see him smile again.

"Raven, don't, please." His voice had a strangled tone I'd never heard coming from him. Remote. Detached. He turned and began to walk away.

I was stunned. He was actually getting ready to walk away from me and I had no idea why. I reached out to touch his arm and he stopped without turning to look at me.

"Hopscotch, what's wrong? Why are you doing this?"

"I can't talk to you anymore." His words were muffled, almost surreal in their simplicity.

I felt my jaw drop. "But why?"

"I just can't. I can't explain why. It's best we don't talk anymore. Raven. Believe me, please believe me, I'm doing this for you."

"For me?"

He nodded. "Just let it go, Raven. I'm not good for you. It won't work."

What wouldn't work?

I watched him walk away.

FOURTEEN

She doesn't know.

Hopscotch headed for his car, walking fast. His feelings toward Raven had been growing almost past the point of no return for a while now, but she was married and he'd kept his feelings hidden because of it. The problem, as he saw it, was that she was unhappily married, desperately so from what he could gather. She didn't seem to realize that either.

She could have been happy with him, he would have made sure of it. But now... He stood by his car with his hand on the door handle, looking past the mountaintops and up at the sky. Now it was too late. Now everything was going to come out, all of it. He should have never continued seeing Carolyn, he'd known she was bad news after the first night they spent together. But she was a substitute, a diversion, that was all.

How could he tell Raven?
Just tell her.
How much?
Everything.
I can't put that on her.
You've got to tell her, you know you do. Whatever happens, happens.
What if she tells Jack?
Would she do that? Do you really think she would?
She won't have to. He's going to find out when he runs a search on me. Dammit!
Then tell her first, before you're extradited back to Minnesota. You owe her that much, at least.

He swung slowly around and walked back to where she was still standing, watching him.

"Raven, luv, I'm afraid I do have to talk to you after all."

She glanced at her watch and gave him a tentative smile. "I'm relieved to hear that, but I have to go inside now, I'm almost late."

He smiled. "And I'm leaving soon for my last flight to Anchorage. I'll be there all weekend."

"Okay then, how about Monday, when we're both here?"

He tipped his head, half-smiling. "Monday will do it."

"Monday, then." She held out her hand. "Friends?"

He took her hand. "Always friends, Raven."

Monday would do. He'd have at least that long.

FIFTEEN

Saturday morning Red and Charlie left on their overnighter with the scout troop. I wanted to object because the nights were still cool but I knew it was pointless, they were going whether I wanted them to or not. I packed their food and helped them find their equipment, then watched them leave.

    I had a lot of thinking to do while I cleaned the house and started the laundry, still worried about Hopscotch. He'd been my best friend for so long that I knew I'd be lost without him and our teatimes together. What could have happened to make him so strange all of a sudden? Was it Carolyn's murder? Could he somehow be involved? I couldn't even begin to imagine such a thing, but then I'd never known he was dating her, either. He'd been very quiet about that.

    Then again, I thought while I sorted the white clothes from the dark and punched my instructions on the washing machine, since when did he have to tell me anything about his love life…if it was a love life. I stopped with the soap only half poured, wondering at the twinge I felt at the thought. Had I become more emotionally involved with him than I'd realized?

    About two that afternoon Red came home by himself. He walked into the house and beckoned for me to follow him upstairs. I knew what was coming. He would head for the shower while I undressed. I would stand waiting with my back to the bathroom door, nude except for the high-heel gold slippers and turquoise fake feather boa he'd brought home one day just a little over two months before, and insisted I wear them. When I objected, he had remarked, in an offhand way that if I wouldn't do it, someone else might.

    I didn't give that too much thought. We'd never had problems with our sex life before and I felt this was just a passing thing that he'd tire of soon enough and we would get back to our usual routine. When we were first married and for many years after that, the sex between us had always been sweet and loving and glorious. Even three children later it was still that way, but for some reason I could not fathom and he refused to discuss, everything had begun to change between us over the past year until suddenly he was into staged sex.

    This day I definitely wasn't in the mood for that nonsense. I had shopping to do. But Red would win, he always did, although I didn't at all like what was happening. I just wanted my marriage to get back to normal.

    I heard the shower stop and listened to him climb out and yank the towel off the rack. I knew the sound and sequence of every movement as he dried himself. Hair...face...ears...neck…left arm, right arm, fingers, fingernails, for heaven's sake, as though we had all day and Timmy and Alice weren't downstairs. Body...front and back, legs...feet...I listened to his careful, measured toweling between every toe as my own tapped with weary impatience.

    The sounds stopped and I tensed as he turned the knob and shoved the door open, clicked it shut and padded toward me. I wasn't allowed to turn around and look at him, that was one of his rules. This time I heard him slide his knife out of its leather sheath. That was new and I didn't like the sound of it. I felt my shoulders growing tighter. I had groceries to buy and he was in Jack the Ripper mode? Why? What was I supposed to do now?

    I didn't know.

    He walked past me, looking at me the whole time, but not with passion. He was watching me to see what I'd do.

    He laid the knife on the dresser top, still watching me. The knife was close enough that he could get it if he wanted to, and he had pointed it straight at me. It glinted in the afternoon light, threatening, ominous. His eyes, when he looked my way, held a dark, feral look, void of expression.

    "Don't move till I tell you to," he said in a guttural whisper.

    It was unnecessary for me to pretend I was afraid. I *was* beginning to be afraid. Someone had used a knife on a woman here in

Valdez only a few days ago.

"You can't tell your husband about this," he warned, easing into his favorite scenario.

"Oh, I won't, I promise," I said, trying to brush against him so he'd get on with it, and trying to concentrate on the contents of our refrigerator, making a mental list.

Milk...apples...butter...lettuce...but no tomatoes, we never had decent tomatoes in Valdez unless someone from the lower forty-eight shipped them to us...

"Lie down," he ordered, trying, no doubt, to excite me with impending danger. He was excited enough for both of us and the thought of that knife on the dresser pointed at me, after what had happened to Carolyn, made me nauseous. I didn't want to lie down but this was his fantasy so I did as he said. He crouched above me and I could feel him hard against me as I lay on the floor face down, turning my head so I could watch the knife.

I forced my voice to sound tremulous, reciting the next line. "You're not going to tie me up, are you? I have money, I'll give it to you if you promise not to hurt me."

Tie me up? He was the only one in his scout troop who couldn't tie a decent bowline knot. Any three-year-old in my family could tie one, but not Red. His forté was charming one of the boys into tying it for him.

His breathing became labored as he kneeled above me and his arousal increased. "I don't want your money. You know what I want."

This was the signal for me to turn around and face him. I turned and saw he was actually holding a piece of clothesline as if he were getting ready to loop it around my wrists. This was new, too. He must have brought it upstairs with him.

This wasn't funny. I didn't like anything about it. He really was scaring me at that point, but I could feel his member standing straight up, the veins beginning to swell against my stomach. This would be over soon and then he'd leave and I could get on with my day.

He dropped the rope on the floor beside me and my movements stopped. I almost couldn't breathe. Another new twist, one I detested. I felt his muscles shudder with the strain of impending climax as his breathing became shallow and he spent himself on me.

He smiled, pulled away from me and moved to the side of the bed, where he lumbered to his feet, retrieved his clothes and headed for the bathroom. "That was good, hon," he said back over his shoulder.

A few minutes later he came out, fully dressed. He walked to the dresser, watching me out of the side of his eyes and slid the knife back into its sheath. He attached it to his belt and pointed at the knife, smiling again.

"Never know when I might need this," he said, and walked out of the room.

Still unsettled, I dressed and returned to the kitchen and my grocery list. When I went out the front door a little later, I found myself staring up at the mountainside, so close to my home, yet so far away. Somebody was watching me. Again. I knew it.

SIXTEEN

Saturday night came fast, but not nearly fast enough for Jack. Everybody in town had been nagging at him like a rubber band hanging out of a cat's behind, but he didn't have anything to tell them. That didn't stop them from bugging him.

Vera's ship hadn't showed up yet, although he figured it was due in soon. He was glad to escape when he left the office after he told the late night rookie to call him on his cell if anything went down. He'd made his arrangements for Bill Nicholson to go with him and he headed across town to pick him up.

As always, he looked at everything as he drove through town. The weather was a little warmer every day and the town was already full of shaggy beards and torn jeans on motorcycles, campers parked everywhere, even in restaurant parking lots.

On top of that, the scriptwriters' conference was about to begin, which would mean more tourists running around yakking, videotaping, closing the bars at night, doing everything but writing their damn scripts.

Summertime, his favorite time of year.

Not this year.

Bill was one of his oldest and most reliable officers. He lived on the outskirts of town in a small house just big enough for himself and his wife now that his kids were all grown and living in the lower forty-eight. Bill's wife waved goodbye from the living room window when he climbed into Jack's vehicle and ten minutes later they parked and entered the campground, sneaking in on foot through an overgrown side path.

"Hell of a way to spend a Saturday night," Bill bitched. He'd tripped over a fallen branch on the way in and bent over, rubbing his ankle and swearing under his breath. "We could kill ourselves out here."

Or worse. The bears were out of hibernation now.

"Well, nobody's said anything online the past couple of nights," Jack said. "If they had, you could be home having a beer and watching television with your wife. Right now we'd better keep quiet." They hunched down on a log in a thicket of pine trees, close to the campsite and the water's edge.

The sky was the color of burnt pewter, everything surrounding them murky and dark beneath the trees. An owl swooshed overhead and sped off, heading for his nest. Jack envied him. At least the owl was doing something rational.

They spent the next half hour watching tent lights go out one by one. Finally Jack heard Bill's heavy sigh. "Okay," Jack said, "we can whisper, but keep it low. I don't know why the kids got so quiet this week unless they changed their minds." Something landed on the back of his neck and he slapped it away.

"They're probably on to you," said Bill. "Kids are smarter than us, everybody knows that."

"Yeah, well, they might think so, but I've got a few years on them."

"Maybe, but these kids have criminal minds. That makes up for the extra years."

"Oh, I'm not so sure they've really got criminal minds," Jack said.

"If they don't, what the hell are we doing here? It's cold, my ankle aches, I'm thirsty and bored, and they're all in there under the covers, either laughing like hell at us or sound asleep by now." Bill shifted a little. "I bet they knew you were watching and decided to set you up. Wouldn't put it past the little shits. They're warm in there and here we are—"

Jack heard a slapping sound. "Slap softer, can't you? It's just mosquitoes. Jeezus, you're such a wimp. Let me tell you, back in Texas—"

"Yeah, I know, Chief, they're ten times bigger."

A few minutes passed. Bill sighed again. "Jack, why the hell am I really here?"

Jack grinned. "I didn't want to get lonesome."

"Bullshit." Bill rubbed his ankle again. "Why, really?"

"The truth is, I need a seasoned pair of eyes with me and I can't trust anybody else to keep quiet, and I hope your wife does."

Bill grunted. "She will. I told her, not one word to anyone."

A few minutes later a light flickered on in Red's tent. The other tents were dark, no sound coming from any of them. Everything was quiet except for the soft slap, slap, slap of water hitting the shoreline a hundred yards away. Five minutes passed and Red's light went back out.

Jack shifted. Didn't make any difference, the log was damp and cold and slippery no matter how he sat and a cool breeze had sprung up. He made a mental note to give those asshole kids the biggest ticket he could write first chance he got.

"I'm still waiting for the background on Carolyn," Jack said to pass the time after they'd been quiet for a few more minutes. "Maybe that'll give us some idea what was going on with her."

"That's gonna be a while, the way things move up north."

"Yeah. You'd think they'd move a little faster, but we're too far downstate to count, I guess."

Bill shifted to one side. "It's a sure bet something was going on, unless it was a random killing."

"Nah, had to be somebody really mad at her. That was no random kill, that was personal. You saw her apartment when we went in there."

"Yeah, and nobody around there heard anything. I'm not convinced of that. Somebody had to have heard something, with all that going on."

"Go back Monday morning and ask them all again. Maybe somebody'll remember something new."

"Will do."

Moonlight reflected on the water, a triangular slice of white. Red lights blinked on and off across the Sound where the oil containers stood, reminding Jack of red eyes in dark photographs, eerie and threatening.

"What about the blood spatters?" Bill asked, scratching his leg.

"Anything back on those yet?"

"Nope. Still at the lab. I'm waiting to see if there's more than one blood type, in case the killer cut himself."

Bill swung around toward him. "I never thought of that."

"Then you just learned something, compliments of the Dallas criminal justice system where I saw it all the time. Knifers sometimes cut themselves if they're in enough of a frenzy, and this one was for sure."

"Makes you wonder sometimes why you got into this business, doesn't it."

"I gotta admit, this is a bad one."

"Yeah. This kind of thing makes me wonder if I ought to just open my own gift shop downtown. What've we got now, eight, ten?" Bill chuckled. "What's one more?"

Jack thought about that for a few minutes, wondering if he ought to maybe open his own business somewhere, but he couldn't think of anything else he'd be profitable at. Not that police work was all that profitable, but he got along and he managed to save some money every month. That and his pension would set him up real nice some day, if he lived long enough to collect it.

They lapsed into an uncomfortable silence again. Jack fought to keep his eyes open for the better part of fifteen minutes until they both spotted three shadowy figures creeping out of two of the tents. "There they go."

Bill started to pull himself up.

Jack reached over to stop him. "Let's give 'em a couple minutes, see what they do."

The three boys were dead silent, walking single file along the path to a small ridge that separated the water from the campsite. One reached over the edge and yanked on something that looked like a rope but it was hard to be sure.

"They got a boat down there?" whispered Bill. "I didn't know they had one."

"I didn't either. They must've bought it last fall and kept it in a garage somewhere." Jack wasn't about to take his eyes off the boys. He watched them climb over the ridge and disappear from sight.

Raven Talks Back

"We going over there?"

"Yep." Jack moved his hand to let Bill know he wanted him to follow while he inched low across the tundra. It was hard as hell, the ground was solid and what little growth was there was damp and slimy-cold. He heard Bill slip and fall flat on his face, swearing under his breath.

"You better plan on giving me a day off to make up for this," he whispered.

Jack grinned and kept moving.

They stayed low to the ground and made it to the water's edge. Jack lifted his head slow and easy. He might have saved himself the trouble, the kids were already paddling across the Sound and sure enough, heading straight for the shore where the oil tanks were housed.

"Are they crazy?" whispered Bill when he crawled up to the ledge and saw where they were headed. "They're trying to get in there that way? They'll get shot sure as hell. Don't they know that?"

Jack kept his eyes on the boys. "Everybody else in town does."

"You going to call the guard's office?"

"Naw, not yet. Let's just watch and see if they try to get in. If they do, I'll call, but these idiots have to know about the searchlights."

The boat was still headed for the tanks. They watched the paddles dip, lift, dip, lift.

"Jeezus, Jack, call the guards. They're gonna get killed!"

"Not yet, hold on." The boat had made a soft turn, avoiding the moon's reflection.

They got within five hundred yards or so of the shore when blue searchlights swept across the shoreline and out over the water, just missing them. The boat stopped, moved sideways with the water's movement for a few seconds, then the boys turned back around and headed for the shore where Jack and Bill lay waiting.

"Let's go," said Jack. They scrambled across the damp tundra as fast as they could and hid in a clump of pine trees while the boys pulled the boat in, tied it back up again, creeping across the campground and into the tents without making a sound.

Jack and Bill looked at each other and without another word headed back into the woods in the direction of Jack's vehicle.

"What the hell can they be up to?" said Bill as soon as they climbed in. "They can't really be scoping out those oil containers, can they? Any idiot knows you can't get to 'em."

"I don't know, Bill, but they said, 'scope it out', and that's what they did."

He pulled his vehicle away without turning on the lights and drove down the road a hundred yards or so before he switched them on and headed into town, then dropped Bill off at his house a few minutes later, declining his offer for a sandwich. "I'm too beat," he said, trying to fight off a yawn. "I need to get home and just get some quality sleep."

Bill yawned. "Yeah, me, too. See you later."

Jack nodded and headed home.

He lay awake a long time trying to piece together whatever those boys were thinking.

They couldn't get in the terminal. It was impossible. Whatever they were thinking before, they sure as hell weren't thinking it now because now they knew. It couldn't be done.

SEVENTEEN

Sunday morning I woke around four a.m. from a recurring dream I'd been having throughout my life whenever I was overstressed. Animals always called to me in the night in that dream, waking me with their forlorn sounds, but this was different. I found myself jolted awake, listening.

I reached for my robe, glancing out the bedroom window at the moon traveling through the sky far to the west, then went downstairs. I made myself a cup of tea and wandered out onto the front porch, blowing into the tea to cool it as I pulled the screen door shut. A white mist of steam rose from the tea and I pulled my robe closer.

The front porch was mainly a large roof overhang, with white latticework on one side where red roses and pink hollyhocks grew, weaving themselves between the openings. A few years back I'd bought a small white wrought iron table and chair for the concrete slab so I could sit out there when it was raining. I always loved being outdoors at night in the summer, especially when the air was sweet with flowers and upturned earth in my garden.

This night it was cool and I wasn't about to go anywhere near my back yard. In fact, I had a bit of an uneasy feeling just sitting in my chair. The upturned earth out back lay untouched where Carolyn's body had been found. My sun room, along with everything else in my life, it seemed, was on hold.

I had taken a couple of sips of tea, mentally planning the new flowers I wanted to plant in the side rock garden by the garage, when I heard it again, a soft, keening sound that didn't seem to be any animal I'd ever heard. It appeared to have come from the street.

I set my cup on the table and hesitantly walked a few steps to the edge of the overhang to look.

Kit Carlyle stood in the middle of the street a few yards to the left of our driveway, staring at me. He raised his arms as if to reach out to me, then they dropped back down to his sides. He wore only a white t-shirt and cutoff jeans and tennis shoes.

"Kit," I called, "I thought you went camping with Red and the boys. Where's your jacket, aren't you cold?"

He didn't answer. He seemed to be staring at something past my shoulder. I turned slightly to see what he was looking at but saw nothing out of the ordinary.

When I looked back at him, he'd moved a little closer. The temperature had dropped all of a sudden and the fog almost enveloped him. Still, it was Kit, he'd been in our house countless times...so pitifully thin...

I pulled my robe closer, "Charlie's not here, he's at the campground. How come you didn't go with them?"

I could have sworn Red had mentioned him being at the camp with Charlie earlier. This was so strange, the whole thing felt surreal and yet I knew it wasn't because I had made a cup of tea and I was wide awake, drinking it and talking to him.

He didn't answer, but through the haze, with the moon almost below the mountaintops now, I could see his dark eyes, his look of mute appeal.

I motioned to him. "Come on in, Kit, I'll make you a sandwich and then give you a ride home."

I'd always had a soft spot for him and had been trying to help put some weight on him, but never with any success. I barely knew his parents, odd in such a small town where everyone seemed to at least somewhat know of everyone else, but they had always kept to themselves and Kit had been withdrawn every time I'd seen him.

He looked past me again as though he didn't hear me. I turned all the way around this time, definitely jumpy now, straining to search every inch of the back yard that I could see, but nothing was there. When I turned back, Kit was gone.

Gone? I shivered. He couldn't possibly have disappeared that fast, and yet he had.

I walked rapidly across the front yard, all the way to the edge of the street, looking right and left, everywhere, but he wasn't there and neither was anyone else.

Maybe he was hiding for some reason. I peered into all the front yards but definitely didn't want to go any further than my own. As it was, even before there had been a murder in this town I'd always had to watch out for bears or moose or raccoons when I sat outside. They did come into town at night from time to time and they could be dangerous if you surprised them. Tonight I again had the definite feeling someone or something was watching. Still, nothing moved. Kit had simply disappeared.

I gave up and went back to bed, where I fell into a deep, dreamless sleep. I didn't wake again until a little after seven, when the first sirens pierced the air over Valdez.

EIGHTEEN

Jack's cell blasted him out of a sound sleep early Sunday morning. Thinking it was the alarm, he knocked it off the bedside stand. When he leaned over to pick it up he saw it was six-forty-five and the caller was Vera. He shot up, wide awake.

"I'm back," she said. "We got in last night and I couldn't wait any longer. I'm off-duty for a few hours. Are you awake?"

"Actually, I was thinking about you in my sleep."

"Want company?"

He heard the familiar half-smile in her voice and grinned, thinking this wasn't going to be one of those Sunday mornings when he'd sleep late out of boredom after all.

"Sure do. Little Jack here wants company real bad. Got anybody special in mind?"

She laughed. "Somebody special will be there in a few minutes. First though, are you absolutely sure you're not busy today?"

"I'm sure. Make it ten minutes. The front door'll be unlocked. Don't stop to tip the doorman, just come straight on into the bedroom."

She snickered and hung up. He jumped out of bed and unlocked the front door, then crawled back under the covers, waiting for his ship to come in. Sleeping in nothing but his skin was going to come in mighty handy this morning.

He had first laid eyes on Vera down at the docks on the outside of town, where he went sometimes when he was at loose ends to watch the sea otters play. Everybody in town did it, one time or another. Great therapy without all the group hugs. Friday afternoon was always a good time for it, so he had headed over there on his way home.

She was standing on the ship's deck leaning over the rail,

Raven Talks Back

looking around, when he had glanced up and spotted her watching him.

He thought for sure some guy on that ship was lucky as hell and spent the next few minutes alternating between watching the otters and her, most of the time her. She appeared to be doing about the same thing and he started wondering if she was on that cruise alone.

After a few more minutes she walked down the gangplank and casually made her way over to where he sat on a log, tossing rocks out over the water. She sat beside him without looking his way at first, but he caught her glancing at him out of the corner of her eyes a couple of times and he could smell her perfume. Faint, but whoa doggies, look out!

"So," he said, getting the preliminaries out of the way, "are you traveling alone?"

"Sort of." The falling sun hit her hair just the right way and he figured it had to be natural because bleached hair could never look that good. "I'm the new entertainment director on the ship."

The perfume. The hair. The body, now that it was close enough for him to get a really good look. He'd been hankering for some heavy duty entertainment for a while. It'd been a long dry spell, except for a couple of straying wives in town who'd been making mating noises his way, but he wasn't having any of that.

"I'm Vera," she said. "Vera Cruze."

He nodded. "Jack O'Banion here."

"You're a cop." She eyed the badge on his shirt pocket.

He shrugged. "That's what I hear."

"Been there long?"

"Long enough, I guess. They made me chief of police."

He was quiet for a couple minutes, tossing a few more rocks out over the water and plotting his strategy. She picked up a small rock and threw it sideways. It bounced three times before it sank. He couldn't get his to bounce once.

"So," she said, "where's your wife and kids?"

He grinned inside. Evidently he wasn't the only one plotting strategy. "I'm not married."

"Never?"

"Not even once."

"You're the first chief of police I've ever met who wasn't married. How come you're not?"

"Just lucky, I guess. You?" He eyed her.

"Not even once," she said, eyeing him back.

He raised both eyebrows and glanced at her empty ring finger. "Not even attached to anybody? How'd that happen, a good-looking woman like you?"

She looked him straight in the eye. "Just lucky, I guess."

Without another word he had reached for her hand, led her to his vehicle, and taken her home with him by unspoken mutual consent. She hadn't gone back to the ship till Monday.

He was lying in bed after remembering that first time when he heard the front door open. When she walked into the bedroom a few seconds later her clothes were off.

"That was fast," he said, crooking his finger at her.

"I'm desperate." She grinned and walked to the bedside, looking him over. "Hmmm. Is that a Glock .45 under there, or are you just overjoyed as hell to see me?"

Before he could answer she yanked off the covers with one quick motion and climbed onto the bed, straddling him with her breasts hanging over his face.

Oh, those breasts. So lush and full, and her nipples stood straight out just the way he liked them. He was more than ready for a trip to the moon.

He reached for a nipple. His cell phone rang.

She sat up. "Son of a bitch!" Sparks flew from her eyes while she reached for his cell and handed it to him. "*Here*. I might as well do something useful today."

He punched the talk button. "What?" he shouted.

"You need to get over to the scout campsite right away," said his night deputy. "We've got another one."

His eyes were on what was in front of him and so was his mind. "Another what?"

"One of the town kids got killed there sometime last night. They just found his body a few minutes ago. "

"What?"

"I said—"

"Never mind that. What kid? What happened?"

"They said—"

"Who said?" he interrupted, trying not to scream. Vera had climbed off before he could stop her and stomped out of the room.

"The scoutmaster, Red. He said it's Kit Carlyle and his head's gone. There's a rock where his head was, same as last time."

He jumped out of bed, grabbed his clothes and shouted into the living room. "I gotta go, honey, I'm sorry."

He might as well have not bothered. She was gone.

He raced to his vehicle and switched on his siren. When he rushed onto the campground four minutes later, everything was in chaos. Red stood by the tent he'd seen one of the boys leave and go back into last night, guarding it to keep anybody else from looking inside. His face was whiter than Jack had ever seen it, even whiter than the morning Carolyn's body showed up in his back yard.

Scouts in various ages and stages of undress crawled in and out of the other tents. Some of them ran aimlessly around the campsite picking up things, dropping them. One was trying to light a fire that wouldn't light. Red's boy, Charlie, stood next to his father, shaking, his teeth chattering.

Jack headed for the tent. "What happened here, Red?" He lifted the flap and looked inside while he waited for his answer. It looked like Kit's body—the stone where his head should have been sure didn't, though. Nasty, chilling sight, blood pooling on the ground beside his cot.

He stared at it for a couple of minutes, sickened even more than he'd been when he saw Carolyn's body because this was a kid. Every bad thought he'd ever had about Kit shot through his head, fighting with waves of regret. It'd be a long time before he'd be able to drop off to sleep easily at night again after seeing this happen to a kid in this town, on his watch.

He closed the flap back to wait for Doc since it was clear Kit didn't need his help now.

Red rubbed his eyes. "We just woke up a little while ago. I tapped on top of all the tents like I always do and yelled at the boys to get up. Everybody did except—"

He glanced back at the tent flap. "When Kit didn't come out after I called him twice, I opened the flap and that's when I saw—." He drew a deep breath. "Jeezus, I can't believe this. Another frickin' nightmare! How could anybody get in there and do something like that without anybody else hearing it?"

Maybe they didn't. "Did you call Doc?"

Red shook his head. "I just called your office. I didn't know what else to do and jeezus, Jack, we don't need a doctor, the kid's head is gone!" He gagged and Jack watched the color fighting to return to his face.

"Did anybody touch anything in there?"

"Just me. When I opened the flap to call him the second time, I went in." Red stopped and took a deep breath. "I didn't touch anything inside, I just backed away and told one of the boys to find my cell so I could call you."

The camp had turned silent. All the boys huddled close by, listening, shaking, crying and wiping wet noses on their sleeves, all of them in shock.

"Okay," said Jack. "See if you can't get something warm in these kids and I'll call doc." He turned to the boys. "Don't anybody leave or come anywhere near this tent. Just stay put where you are till I say you can move."

Some plopped down on the ground and put their heads between their knees, arms hiding their eyes. The others stood deathly still. Nobody made a sound.

Red got the fire started and made a pot of coffee and one of the boys busied himself making hot chocolate. The sirens Jack had been hearing spilled over on them as four of his men pulled into the campground and jumped out. Doc arrived a minute later.

Jack spent the next half hour with Doc in the tent, examining Kit's body and fighting the urge to hurl at the sight of the neat slice where his head had been. Hell itself must have smelled like this crime scene and the rock, lying crooked above his neck, had a face like his worst nightmare. Two white eyes ringed with black, black pupils, its mouth a wide, screaming red circle.

Raven Talks Back

Doc stuck his thermometer in the usual place. "According to this and the temp last night, I'd have to say he was killed sometime around three-thirty this morning, maybe a little earlier." He wiped it off and slid it back in its holder. "Has anybody called his parents?"

Jack stuck his head out through the tent flap and told one of his men to get over to the Carlyle home and tell them what happened and they could meet Doc at his office in an hour or so, he'd see them there. He didn't want them out here at all if he could help it.

He had two of his other men take digitals of the body and the location while he took measurements and drew sketches, all the time worrying about the kids in the background showing up in the photos they were taking.

After he was as done as he could be, Doc covered Kit's body so the kids couldn't see it and Jack wrapped the rock in a new tarp he had in his trunk and marked it. Some of the blood got on his clothes. He wiped off as much as he could and closed the tent flap with some tape until they could go over it again after the kids were gone.

After they got the body in the van and Doc drove off, he and Bill scoured the area but only found camping paraphernalia and some gum and candy wrappers. He bagged and marked them and found himself tasting chocolate for a quick, nauseating second before he turned back to the boys.

They were all sitting on the ground now except for Charlie and Jason, off in a corner talking in low voices, looking back at him. One of the smaller boys grabbed his shirt sleeve when he passed close by. "Was Kit's head really cut off, sir?" His voice quivered and Jack didn't want to answer him, but the kid had called him 'sir'.

"How about we talk about this a little later, son." He reached over to give the boy a quick pat. "Try not to worry. I know it's awfully bad right now, but you're safe." The boy closed his eyes, sighing.

The news had spread like fireweed up on the mountainsides. Parents rushed into the campsite grabbing their kids, hugging them, looking to him for some guidance. He held up his hand for attention while his men stood at the pathway to prevent more people from coming in.

"Everybody, listen," he shouted over the noise, "I don't want folks trampling around here and maybe destroying evidence. Everybody except parents, stay outside the path. Parents, I don't want you walking around either. Stay where you are until I speak to your boys, then you can take them home. You'll have to leave their gear where it is for now. Everybody try to remain calm."

He headed first for the small boy who had asked the question earlier. He looked like he needed to be in his own home, safe from whoever had done this. It was going to be hard, talking about it to all of these kids, but he had to if he was going to find out who killed Kit Carlyle.

And almost certainly—unless this was one hell of a copycat murder—who also killed Carolyn Crumbe.

NINETEEN

I sat straight up in bed when I heard the sirens, wondering what on earth was happening. They almost never sounded like that or went on so long. I grabbed my bathrobe and was heading downstairs when the phone rang. I ran the rest of the way and picked up the phone.

"Raven, did you hear what happened out at the campground?" I could tell from my neighbor's voice it was something horrible.

"No." I couldn't move. The campground. "I just heard the sirens. What happened?"

My neighbor's voice was shaking so badly she could barely get the words out. "One of the boys—they got up and found one of the boys dead."

My heart pounded as I sank into a chair. "Dead? Who?"

"I don't know."

"I have to hang up, I'm going out there."

I ran back upstairs, threw on my clothes, grabbed my purse, headed for the front door, remembered Timmy, ran back up to Alice's room and leaned over her bed, shaking her. "Alice, wake up, you have to wake up!"

Alice rolled over. "What's the matter?"

"Something's happened out at the campsite, I have to go out there right away. Watch Timmy and give him some breakfast when he gets up."

"You mean like cook him something?" Alice rubbed her eyes. "What happened?"

"I don't know yet and I don't care what you give him. Cereal, a breakfast bar, it doesn't matter, I have to go. You need to stay awake, Alice. You don't have to get up, but I want you to take care of Timmy until I get back."

Alice nodded and rolled back over, her eyes beginning to close again.

I ran downstairs, out the back door into the garage, jumped into my car and ground the gears pulling out of the driveway. I sped to the stop sign at the end of the street and went through it without stopping.

One of the kids was dead out there. *Please, God, don't let it be Charlie.* I headed down the street behind our house, out onto the highway. The words ran though my head over and over while I raced down the road. *Dear God, please, please, please don't let this be true.*

But I had heard the sirens. I knew it was true.

If only I'd argued a little more, asked them to put it off another month, even another week, it might have made a difference, but my father had always said, "You can't fight the fates, daughter." I could still hear him trying to console me the time I rolled off of a Caribou skin he'd fashioned into a small sled for me when I was only seven, and broke my arm crashing into a tree on the slick ice.

And now…

Someone at the campsite is dead.

I stepped on the gas and made it to the campsite faster than I'd ever driven before. When I pulled into a space and saw Red and Charlie talking I ran to them, hugged them both and burst into tears.

"Thank God you're both alright," I said when my crying slowed. "What happened, Charlie, who was it?"

"Kit," he mumbled.

"Why—how can that be?" My mind shot back to Kit, looking at me across the yard, his sudden disappearance.

"When did that happen? What happened? This can't be right, Charlie, I saw Kit early this morning and he wasn't at the campsite, he was at our house, on our street!"

"He was here all night, Mom. He couldn't have gone anywhere, somebody killed him here early this morning."

"Killed him? Here? Oh, that's crazy, Charlie! What are you talking about?"

He took a deep breath. "They did it just like the other one in our yard. Somebody cut his head off and took it with them. The doc said, I heard him, it happened around three-thirty this morning. He was here then, Mom. They did it here, not at our house. You're thinking about some other kid or else you had to be dreaming."

I looked up at Red and saw shock in his eyes. Mountains, tents, trees, dirt, clouds, fog, glaciers spun around me, the world grew dark and smoky gray-blackness fell over me.

I dropped to my knees. I had seen Kit. I had! Doc had to be wrong. Kit wasn't dead at three-thirty. He was with me a few minutes after four.

TWENTY

Jack had been talking to one of the boys when he'd glanced up and seen Raven arrive a few minutes earlier, then turned his attention back to the kids.

After about ten minutes he realized he was wasting his time talking to the younger ones. None of them had seen or heard anything, they all said they were asleep and he believed them, but he hadn't talked to Charlie or Jason yet. He turned to see if they were still with Red and Raven. He watched for a minute while Red patted Raven's face with a handkerchief and walked her over to a bench and helped her sit down, the first time he'd ever seen Red do anything with such tenderness. He looked away and waved for Jason to come over.

He was going to have a big problem with Jason and Charlie and he knew it. He'd seen them with Kit last night when they headed off across the water, and he'd watched them come back. He couldn't let them know that and he didn't expect either one of them to admit to it.

He plunked himself down on a wet bench with Jason Mathias, the kid with the red convertible. About five nine, medium-length blond hair, gray-blue eyes, and, Jack figured, from online conversations he'd seen, size 13 shoes. He glanced down at Jason's feet and revised his generous estimate because they were only about size ten. So much for truth on the Internet.

He turned on his tape recorder. "Let's get straight to it. I need to ask you some questions."

Jason shifted his hundred eighty some-odd pounds, unwrapped a piece of bubblegum, plopped it in his mouth and dropped the wrapper on the ground. "Shoot."

"State your name."

Jason's eyebrow rose. "Jason Mathias."

"Do you know anything about what happened to Kit?"

"Nope. You do get straight to it, don't you."

He wasn't about to get into a pissing contest with this snot-nose kid. "Did you hear anyone go into Kit's tent at any time?"

"Nope." Jason chewed his gum, his jaws working.

"He had his own tent? Slept by himself?"

"Right."

"Why?"

"I don't know, I never asked. Maybe he wanted privacy."

"Do you know why he wanted privacy?"

"Nope." He shrugged. "I didn't care."

"All the other boys are in double tents though, isn't that right?"

"I guess." *Cocky snot-nose kid.*

"Did you leave your tent at all after you went to bed?"

"Nope." Jason looked away, then back. His eyes were wide open, completely innocent.

Jack had to grudgingly admire the fact that Jason could lie so easily to a police officer during a murder investigation. The kid was damn good, didn't even blink when he lied. He stared at Jason for a long minute. "You're sure of that?"

"Yep."

"Did Charlie leave the tent?"

"Nope."

"You're sure?"

"Yep. He sleeps like he's hibernating, never gets back up."

"You know this for sure? He couldn't have got up and been quiet about it?"

Jason shrugged. "I suppose, but I never heard anything."

"About how long have you known Kit?"

Jason put his finger to the side of his nose and frowned a little, mocking him with his wiseass eyes. "Hmmm...around two years, I guess."

"You hung around with him that whole time?"

"Off and on."

"How did you meet him?"

"Um...Charlie and I both met him the first day of school. What difference does that make?"

"During that time, did Kit have any enemies you know of?"

"Enemies? You mean the kind who'd kill somebody like that? Hell, I don't know."

"Did anybody you know of dislike him?

That seemed to take Jason aback. "Well, lots of guys, I guess. He got all the hot girls."

That wasn't what Jack had seen online a few nights before.

"So you and Charlie went to bed when Kit did, is that what you said?"

"You asked me all this before."

"I'm asking you again. Did Charlie leave the tent at any time last night?"

"Not that I know of. I went to bed and went straight to sleep. I didn't wake up till Red called us."

"So you didn't leave your tent at all after lights out, is that correct? Not even to go to the bathroom?" He was giving Jason one last chance to tell the truth.

"That's what I said."

Jason wasn't biting. Not even a nibble. *Tough, cocky, snot-nose kid.*

"And you didn't hear anything after that? No noise at all?"

"I sleep pretty sound." Jason grinned. "Pure mind, pure heart."

Jack wanted to slug him. Jason was lying, he knew it and Jason knew it, but right then, Jason had him. "Okay, I've got your statement."

"Then we're done and I can get my stuff and leave, right?"

"You're done and you can't take your stuff. Leave it here till we call you. You can pick it up later."

Jason shot straight up. "You can't do that! It's illegal without a search warrant."

Jack shrugged. "Call the ACLU and file a complaint. This is a crime scene, I'm chief of police here, I'll have a warrant soon enough, and I intend to go through everything. You got anything to hide, tell me now."

Jason shrugged. "I didn't do anything. Help yourself."

"All righty, then. You go on home with your folks. I'll be in touch later on. I might have more questions."

Jason muttered something under his breath and headed for his parents' car.

Jack fought hard to keep his poker face. Damn straight he had more questions. A lot more. He could feel the wet slats soaking into his underwear and a quick thought of Vera shot into his mind. He pushed that thought back and turned toward Red's family, where Charlie was watching him.

He beckoned for Charlie to come.

Charlie got up and ambled over.

"Sit down, Charlie." Jack flipped his recorder back on and indicated the spot Jason had just vacated. Charlie sat, taking a sip of the coffee his dad had just handed him.

"State your name, please."

"Charlie Morressey."

"Jason tells me you and Kit might have gone outside with him after lights out, is that right?" He'd done this plenty of times back in Dallas. Sometimes it worked.

Charlie's face turned white. "He told you that?"

"That's what I just said."

Charlie mumbled something under his breath.

"Mind repeating that a little louder this time?"

"I was just wondering why he said that."

"Maybe because it's true? Could that be it?"

"We might have taken a little walk, but not for long. We were only gone about a half hour. Not even that long." His freckles stood out against his pale skin and his hands worked.

"Where'd you go?"

"No place, really. We just walked around."

"Why, after your father thought you were in bed?"

Charlie shrugged. "I didn't see anything wrong with it, we were just walking, for chrissake."

"What did you talk about while you were just walking?"

"I don't remember." Charlie looked down at the ground.

"Did you argue about anything?"

"Nope, we were just having a good time."

"Look at me, Charlie. What, exactly, were you guys doing?"

"Nothing." His eyes wavered. "Messing around, looking at stuff."

"What stuff?"

"Stuff, that's all."

Jack waited to see if he wanted to elaborate. He didn't.

"How long have you known Kit?"

"A few years, why?"

"Close friends, were you?"

"Pretty close. We hang out."

"How'd you meet him?"

"At Jason's house, someone brought him to a party there. What's that got to do with what just happened?"

"Did Kit have any enemies you know of?"

"Shit, no, everybody liked Kit. He was more fun than anybody."

"What does that mean?"

"I don't know, he just—well, he knew a million jokes, kept us laughing all the time. I don't know why anybody would..." His glance followed Jack's over to the empty tent and he shuddered. "I mean, do that."

"Did you secretly dislike him?"

Charlie swiveled back toward him. "You trying to pin this on me?"

"Not at all. I'm just trying to get a bead on why anybody would want to kill him."

"I don't know why, but it wasn't me and it wasn't Jason."

"How do you know it wasn't Jason?"

"I just know, that's all. Jason wouldn't do that."

"Because he liked Kit a lot, is that it?"

"Yeah," he said. "That's it. He liked Kit a lot."

"What was Kit like, besides funny?" Jack leaned toward him, giving him a friendly, curious look. "What else do you know about him?"

Charlie looked off into the distance. "Actually, not a whole lot, if you're talking about what he did when he wasn't with us. We just liked him. I can't believe this happened. Who could have done something like that?"

"I believe I asked you first," said Jack. "It's possible whoever killed your English teacher might be the same one who just killed your friend. Any ideas?"

Charlie stared at him, apparently shocked by the question. "You mean, were they both messed up with the same person? How do I know? They could have been, I guess, it's not that big of a town."

"Did you ever see Kit with her?"

"In school?"

"After class. Away from school."

Charlie flushed. "I don't know what you're talking about. I never saw them together anyplace, if that's what you mean."

"So in your opinion, it would have been impossible for Jason to be involved in this, am I right?"

"Well, hell, I don't think so, but I guess I don't know. I just know after we came back—"

"From where?"

"From our walk, after we came back we all went inside the tents and went to sleep."

"As far as you know."

"Well, yeah. But I'm a light sleeper." His face colored. "I guess I shouldn't of said that."

"I don't know whether you should or not. Is there any reason why you shouldn't? We're just having a friendly conversation here."

"I guess," Charlie mumbled.

"So you say you're a light sleeper. Did you hear anything during the night then, an animal, anything like that?"

"I don't know. I don't remember hearing anything. Not like my mom did anyhow, that's for sure."

Jack's head shot up. "Your mom? What about her?"

Charlie dropped his head into his hands. "Oh, shit."

"What about your mother? What does she have to do with this?"

Charlie looked at Raven and Red, who sat sipping coffee, watching them. "It's just that she started telling us she saw Kit early this morning in our front yard and we told her she was dreaming. She swears she saw him, though."

"When?"

"Just a couple minutes ago, when she first got here. Didn't you see her almost pass out?"

"I meant, when did she say she saw him?"

"I don't remember. Ask her."

"I'll do that. Meantime, is there anything else you want to tell me?"

He frowned. "Like what?"

"Like what you were really doing outside after lights out."

Charlie scratched his chin, where Jack could see a faint beard trying to grow. "I told you, we just walked around, talking."

"Were you arguing about anything?"

"Nope. I didn't hear anything else all night either. Can I go now?"

Jack sighed inside. Sooner or later Charlie would know he was there watching the three of them on that boat. "You can go on home, Charlie. Leave your stuff where it is, don't touch anything, just go. You can pick up your gear later. We'll let you know when."

Charlie stood to leave, then turned back. "Are you going to talk to my mother and father?"

"I'll talk to them in a bit. You go on now, I'll see you later."

"Yeah, well, I can't wait." He walked away without looking back.

Jack leaned back with his hands behind his head and stared up at the clouds, thinking. Then he snapped to. "Charlie," he called, "come back a minute, I need to ask you one more thing."

Charlie stopped and turned back. "Yeah?"

Jack patted the bench. "Over here."

"What do you want now?"

"Did your father leave the camp after you got there?"

Charlie didn't want to answer that one. Jack could tell he didn't by the look on his face.

"Well, not last night, not that I know of."

"When did he leave?"

Charlie heaved a long sigh. "Early in the afternoon, if you have to know."

"I have to know. Do you know where he went?"

Charlie's face was beet red by that time. "Home," he mumbled.
"Do you know why?"
"Well...yeah."
"So, why?"
Charlie half snickered. "For his nooner."
Jack was speechless for a minute.
"His nooner?"
"You better never let them know I told you that," Charlie warned.
"I won't."
Charlie relaxed a little. "My dad always thinks we don't know, but we do. We followed him home once."
"Who followed him?"
"Me and Kit and Jason."
"How did you know what he was doing?"
Charlie's face had turned dark red now. "Well, he went in the house and they went straight upstairs to the bedroom."
"How do you know that?"
"We snuck in the back door and Alice told us they were upstairs, so I went up there and...uh...well...oh, hell. We listened at their bedroom door."
Jack fought to control his face. "Okay."
"It's the joke of the whole troop," Charlie volunteered, "except for the younger kids, they don't know anything about it." He glanced nervously over at his parents. "You better not tell them I told you about that, he'd have my—" He stopped, flustered. "I mean, they'd both be mad. So don't. Please don't."
"I said I won't. Now get on out of here."
Charlie left and Jack gave himself a few seconds to think about Charlie's information. Whatever was going on in Red's household, looked like it wasn't holding up his sex life any.
He was surprised how much that bothered him.

TWENTY ONE

I watched Jack trying to hide the fact that he was staring at me while he talked to Charlie. His glance moved up the mountainside, over glaciers you could see from the campsite, down the dirt pathway, past the tent nobody wanted to look at, and finally came to rest on me. As upset as I was, it was evident to me that even though he seemed to be looking everywhere else, he was tracking me with his peripheral vision. He finally looked straight at me for a few long seconds like he was puzzled about something, then shrugged, as if he decided whatever it was, he wasn't going to worry about it.

I knew I'd have to tell him about Kit's visit early that morning, and that Kit had definitely been with me, even though they were saying he was already dead by that time. They had to be wrong, unless Kit somehow made it back to the campground very quickly and then it happened.

But my bedroom window had been open and I hadn't heard any cars going past on the highway. Without a ride it would have taken him a good half-hour to walk that distance. I thought back, trying to re-live the scene in my mind, already blurring, and I began to wonder if somehow I had dreamed the whole thing. But no, it couldn't have been a dream. I could still feel the sudden swoosh of icy air when I saw Kit.

Could I have seen his ghost? I'd heard stories from my parents about those in our tribe who claimed they'd seen ghosts, and to them the unexplainable was very real. I'd never put much stock in those stories, just chalked it up to legend. Such things never happened to me.

...But what about the voices in the fog? I heard those voices, I know I did. I always had.

...And what about my father's voice? I was hearing that now, too, loud and clear.

No. I had to have somehow dreamed Kit was in my front yard,

some kind of ESP event that happened because he was being murdered and I somehow sensed that something was horribly wrong.

Either that, or I was losing my mind and none of those things had really happened.

After he finished speaking with Charlie, Jack pulled himself up off the bench, brushed his backside and walked over to where Red and I sat. I was getting nervous by that time because I couldn't quite fathom the expression in Jack's eyes. Sad, serious, half-quizzical, his eyelids were narrowed, although not in a threatening way, but I felt threatened just the same.

"How are you doing?" he asked.

"A little better now, I guess, thanks." My dizziness had disappeared, leaving deep sadness and exhaustion in its wake. "This is unimaginable. I can't believe it."

"Me either," said Red, "and I know how this looks."

I glanced at Red. His eyes were streaked, as if he'd been rubbing them. It was damp and chilly everywhere, even though the sun was out, shining directly into Jack's eyes.

Jack tipped his hat down over his forehead to shield them. "How what looks?"

Red gave a disgusted snort. "You think I'm crazy? This is the second murder in a location I'm responsible for."

Jack stared at him. "The first one didn't happen in your yard."

"It might as well have. Whoever did it buried her there."

"I'll give you that."

He turned his attention back to me. "Are you sure you're alright? If you are, I'd like to talk to you alone for a few minutes." He nodded toward the bench where he'd been sitting with the boys. "How about over there?"

Red grabbed my arm. "Raven..." He glanced at Jack, back at me, then gave a heavy sigh. "Go ahead, talk to him if you want to." His eyes bored through me as though he were willing me to say something, or not say something, I didn't know which.

I followed Jack.

He picked up his jacket and laid it on the bench. "Sit here, Raven." His eyes crinkled into a gentle but wary half-smile.

I sat, knowing I had to tell him. He was going to think I was crazy, but I had to tell him.

I watched him switch on his tape recorder. "Please say your name."

I gave my name, eyeing the recorder.

"You told your family you saw Kit early this morning, is that correct?"

"Yes."

"What time was that?"

"About a quarter after four." A small frown formed on his forehead while he waited for me to say more. I didn't want to, but his silence was making me nervous. "I know it was four when I heard the noise the first time, and it had to be at least a quarter after four when I heard it the second time."

"What noise was that?" His voice was low, almost hypnotic.

"It was like..." I thought back. "I can't really say it was an animal sound, at least not like I'd heard before, but..."

"What was it like?" he prodded.

"I don't know, almost like an animal's cry, but different. Softer, somehow. It sounded...almost lonely. That's the only way I can describe it."

"Could it have been a human cry?"

"I suppose it could." I looked down at the ground, trying to remember. A bug crawled over a leaf, moving in slow motion, inch by inch.

"Raven? Are you okay?" His voice seemed to come from far away.

I nodded. "I think so. I was just trying to figure out what the sound was. I couldn't go back to sleep so I got up..."

"Because you couldn't go back to sleep, or because you wanted to find out what the sound was?" He leaned forward, watching me.

The bug crawled away, reflected in Jack's pupils, a slow motion movie through a very small lens. I saw his eyes. Saw the bug. Heard the bug's feet as it took a step. Heard it breathing. The bug blended into

Jack's eyes and now they were only two black dots in his face...

I shook my head to clear it. "What did you just ask me?"

"What, exactly, made you get up? Because you couldn't get back to sleep, or was it the noise you heard?"

"A little of both, I guess. I was wide awake and I wanted to know what was going on outside..." A quick flash of the dirt pile in my back yard shot into my mind.

"And?"

"And...it...the sound was like something moaning, only low, but it almost seemed to fill the whole house, like the sound wind makes when it rushes through. Almost as though I were feeling it rather than hearing it." I looked back up at Jack, appealing to him to understand. "I don't know how else to explain it."

"Was your window open?"

"Yes."

"Okay. You got up and then what happened?"

"I walked downstairs and listened but I didn't hear anything else. I thought maybe it was my imagination, maybe I'd been dreaming. I've had dreams like that before and heard almost the same sounds, but this was different. I went downstairs to the kitchen and made a cup of tea, walked outside with it, but I didn't hear the noise anymore. Oh, wait—"

"Yes?"

"I did hear it again and then I went outside."

"Why would you go outside when you heard noises you didn't understand? Weren't you afraid, that time of night?"

"Not really. I often go outside at night just to sit and think. I went over to my chair and I was going to sit there for a few minutes and drink my tea. That was when I saw Kit."

Jack rubbed his eyelid. "Was he alone?"

I nodded. "He was just looking at me. No, wait, he reached out to me, then..."

"Then what?"

"Then he stared at something behind me and that did scare me. I turned to see what he was looking at but there wasn't anything so I told him to come in, I'd make him a sandwich and drive him back to the campground."

Jack hunched forward. "What did he say?"

I shook my head. "Nothing. It was weird. He just kept looking behind me, so I turned around again to see what he was still looking at and when I turned back..." The scene replayed itself over again in my mind, everything exactly the same every time.

"When you turned back, what did he do, Raven?" His voice was low, his words seemed to roll slowly out of his mouth like cold gravy on a winter night.

"He was gone."

"Gone? That fast?"

"Yes. I looked around for him, but he was just...gone. I went back upstairs after that and went back to sleep. I didn't wake again till I heard the sirens a little while ago."

Jack frowned. "Did he look okay to you, or could you see that well? We had some fog this morning, it only started to disappear when I got here a little while ago. Maybe it was one of the other boys?"

"It was more hazy than anything else, but it was him, Jack, I swear I saw Kit this morning after four o'clock. He couldn't have been dead at that time, he was at my house, trying to tell me—" I stopped.

"Tell you what?" His frown deepened.

"I don't know. He never said anything. He just reached out to me. He looked like he was trying to tell me something, but he never actually spoke. I—Jack, I don't understand this, I really don't. All I can tell you is that Kit was at my house about a quarter after four, maybe a few minutes later. In fact, it had to have been closer to four-thirty because I stopped and made my tea before I went outside."

"Did you drink it?"

"I don't know. I can't remember. I started to, on the way out the door, I know that much, but—"

"Where'd you leave the cup?"

"I don't know. Maybe in the kitchen sink."

Jack closed his eyes and rubbed his forehead as though he'd suddenly developed a headache. He raised his head. "Raven, do you take anything at night to help you sleep?"

"No. I've never taken sleeping pills."

"Tranquilizers, antidepressants, anything like that?"

I could only stare at him. "You don't believe me."

"I didn't say that."

"But you don't, do you?" He seemed uncomfortable. I couldn't blame him.

"I believe you saw something." The frown between his eyebrows deepened. "But it was foggy."

"It wasn't that foggy, Jack. No, wait. Yes, it was foggy. And he was sort of hard to see. It was misty everywhere, now that I think about it. But Jack, it was him, I know it was Kit. This all happened a little after four-fifteen, I swear to you, Kit Carlyle was standing in my front yard reaching out to me!"

"But he never said anything."

"That's right."

Jack sighed. "Raven, if he was there, it had to have been much earlier. Doc Martin told me he was killed around three, three-thirty. You couldn't have seen him at the time you said you did. It had to have been earlier, if..." His words drifted away.

"You're saying 'if I saw him,' aren't you? You don't believe a thing I've said, do you?"

He looked at me from under his lowered eyelids. "I want to believe you, Raven. I'll ask Doc to recheck his time frame. Maybe he was wrong, maybe it was later than four."

"He has to be wrong," I insisted. "Kit Carlyle was in my front yard around four-thirty this morning and he was alive."

"All right, then." He stood and switched off his recorder and slipped it into his shirt pocket. "You can go now, tell Red I said he should take you home. I'll be by later to talk to him, maybe we'll know more by that time." He patted my shoulder, guiding me toward Red.

I turned back toward him. "Jack, you have to believe me. It was well after four, I remember looking at my watch just before I got all the way downstairs. Something's really wrong here."

He started to turn away, then swung back around, took his tape recorder out again and clicked it back on. "Raven, what was Kit wearing when you saw him this morning?"

I thought back. "A white t-shirt, I remember thinking he must be cold with no jacket."

"And?"

"And? Oh, jeans. Cutoffs, frayed above his knees."

He stared at me a minute. I stared back, trying to imagine what he was thinking.

"Did he have shoes on?"

I nodded. "Tennis shoes."

"Socks?"

I struggled to remember. "I'm not sure, but I don't think he did. Just the tennis shoes, at least that's all I remember seeing."

"Did you look in the tent when you got here?"

I shuddered. "No."

"Did anyone tell you what he had on this morning?"

"No, we didn't talk about that."

"Okay. You go on home and get some rest, Raven. I'll be talking to you again soon."

Red took me home. Before I went into the house, I looked out front. My chair was pulled out where I'd been standing and a partially empty cup of tea sat—now I remembered—exactly where I had laid it when I saw Kit out in the street.

TWENTY TWO

Red and Raven were the last to leave other than Jack and his men. He watched them drive off, feeling sick inside. Raven had described exactly what Kit was wearing when he lifted the tent flap and saw the body.

She had to be wrong about the time. Either that, or...he shook his head to clear the bad thoughts trying their damndest to pile in on him but they wouldn't go away. Could she have—? No. God, no. It wasn't possible. There was no way Raven could have had anything to do with either one of those murders.

And yet, he had to consider the possibility. You could never tell for sure what was in somebody else's heart and mind. He didn't like what was in his.

He headed for the tent to look around again, now that everybody was gone.

The tent was bare except for the cot. Not even an overnight bag. Usually kids' tents were full of junk, dirty socks, unrolled sleeping bags, comic books, pop cans. He didn't find any of that in this tent, even though all the others he'd looked at earlier were piled high with crap. No scraps of paper in this one, no extra clothes, nothing. Apparently Kit traveled light. Whatever he had with him, he had on when he was killed, right down to his tennis shoes, and it looked like he'd slept in his clothes, with his shoes on.

Maybe he didn't have extra clothes and that was why he slept alone in his tent. Maybe he didn't want anybody to know. Jack had seen kids like that in Dallas, who would do anything to keep the other kids from finding out how bad off they were.

He spent another half hour poking around every inch of the interior, but finally gave up. Whatever the reason for Kit's murder, it wasn't in this tent. He pulled off his latex gloves and left, instructing his men to do a thorough grid search and call him when the area was ready to be cleared.

Then he headed over to Doc's office so he could talk to Kit's folks, if they were there.

Kit's mother, a heavy set woman with thick graying hair, somewhere in her mid-to-late forties, sat on the leather sofa in Doc's reception room, staring at the opposite wall. She looked up when he walked in, her dark eyes weary and red from crying.

"I'm so sorry for your loss, Mrs. Carlyle." He reached over to take her hand.

She pulled away. "You should be. Why haven't you caught the guy who killed his teacher? It's the same guy, isn't it? It has to be."

"We're doing everything we can. We're working on it every minute. We just have little to go on."

"You don't have anything to go on. It looks to me like all you've been doing is driving around town."

She was about right, although he was expecting information soon on Hopscotch as well as everybody who'd been on the first scene.

"Ma'am, AST, the Alaska State Troopers we're working with up north, are having work slowdowns right now, new systems being installed, that kind of thing. Give us time and we'll find whoever did this to your son, that's a promise."

She gave him a raised-eyebrow look and turned toward the door, where Doc was inside working on her son's body. "My husband's in there." Her voice came out soft and disjointed, parts of her words slurring and disappearing as soon as she formed them. "I couldn't look." She turned back to him, her face expressionless. "Did you find my son's head?"

"No ma'am. Not yet."

"Well, don't put yourself out any. It'll probably wash up in the Sound like the other one did. I heard about that. Nice. Real nice. Quick police work."

He cleared his throat. "Do you think you could answer a few questions, Mrs. Carlyle?"

She eyed him. "Like what?"

"Did Kit, as far as you know, ever see Carolyn Crumbe away from school?"

"What are you talking about?" Her face crinkled with distaste.

"I'm just trying to find out if there's any connection between Kit and his teacher, since they were both—"

"Is the word you're looking for maybe 'beheaded'?"

"Ma'am, I'm trying to establish some kind of connection, if there is one. Did she ever call at your house for Kit, did he ever meet her anywhere other than school?"

"I'd like to know what you're getting at."

"It's just that there's got to be a connection other than the classroom and I'm trying to figure out what it is. Did Kit talk about her to you?"

She almost smiled. "Oh, okay, I get it. You're trying to find out if Kit was doing his teacher, that's it, right? I don't think so. I heard Hopscotch has been, though. Have you talked to him?"

"Did Kit know Hopscotch?"

"Oh, God." She put her head in her hands, then lifted it again. "Everybody in town knows Hopscotch, you know that. Or you should."

"I meant, did Kit know him personally? Did they ever talk, have a meal together, anything like that? Has Hopscotch ever been in your home?"

"No, no, no, and no. Not that I know of."

"So you don't know of any connection between Kit and either of those people?"

She shook her head.

"What about his friends, Mrs. Carlyle? Has there been a problem with anyone recently?"

She looked away again. "I don't know." Her voice was low, not clear at all now. "Kit's friends never came to the house."

That surprised him, but not a lot. Maybe something was going on she didn't know about. If there was they'd find out, but it had to be sooner rather than later. He didn't want any more murders in his town.

He left her sitting alone and went into the back room where Doc was cleaning up.

Kit's father stood by the bathroom door with his hand on the doorknob and his head bowed, fighting a case of dry heaves. Jack felt sorry for him and told him so. Kit's father didn't respond, just shook his head, turned and left the room.

Jack followed him out. "Folks, if either of you think of anything, anyone who might have had reason to do this to your son, please call me right away. We'll find out who did this, but I could sure use your help. I'd like to send a couple of my men over to search his room now, is that okay or would you rather I get a search warrant first?"

Mr. Carlyle spoke. "It doesn't matter either way. I want to know if there's anything in there myself. Tell 'em to come on over, they can look all they want. We won't go in there or touch anything."

Jack pulled out his cell, called two of his officers and told them to get on over to the Carlyle house right away and no, they didn't need a warrant, they should thoroughly check Kit's room, then canvass the neighborhood. He shook Mr. Carlyle's hand, offered his condolences again, and watched while the Carlyles let themselves out the front door.

"Bad stuff," said Doc, wiping his hands when Jack went back into the autopsy room. "He's pretty broken up. Physically sick, actually. Can't blame him a bit."

"She's kind of strange though, isn't she," said Jack. "She seems more mad than upset."

"A little, but maybe that's just her way of coping right now, Jack. It's not every day your kid gets murdered."

Jack looked at the table where Kit's body lay under a green sheet. "Do you have any idea how anybody could have done that without Kit making any noise? He had to make some noise somewhere along the line, didn't he? I know you couldn't do that to me and me stay quiet."

"Not necessarily. The killer could have chloroformed him, something like that. That's my guess but I can't say for sure till we locate his head. Even then, it depends on how much decomp there is on the skin around his mouth and nose. We may never know for sure."

Jack's eyes were fixed on the green sheet. "Why the hell would anybody want to kill him? What could he have done that bad, to make anybody do that?"

"Got me, but he must've made somebody mad."

Jack thought for a minute. "Have you got anything new on the time of death?"

Doc nodded. "I was a little off earlier. I did a liver temp reading once I got him in here. Close as I can figure now it was two, maybe two-thirty or so."

"You're positive it couldn't have been after four?"

He shook his head. "No way. Rigor set in sooner than I thought. Why?"

"Raven says he was at her house after four this morning."

Doc's eyebrows shot up. "She must have been dreaming."

"Why would she be dreaming about a dead kid?"

Doc shrugged. "I don't know. Maybe she's psychic. A lot of Alaska Natives are, or they say they are."

Jack stared at him. "You don't really believe that stuff, do you?"

Doc shrugged again, picked up a couple of instruments and slid them into his sterilizer. "Nobody's ever proved anything one way or the other to me. Could be she's having a breakdown, although she's always been pretty stable. I couldn't blame her if she is though, with all she's had on her mind lately."

"True. It can't be any fun finding a dead woman in your back yard."

"Yep, and now this one, plus her youngest kid's got problems right now. I've been talking to the psychologist in Anchorage. Timmy's regressed and he's got PTSD. The shrink thinks there might be something wrong with Raven, too."

Jack's head shot up. "Come again?"

"This is confidential so don't get me in trouble, but she's been hearing things that didn't happen, according to him. Maybe she's seeing things too. I just wonder why, all of a sudden."

"So do I," said Jack. "Look, we know the cause of death on Kit but send a blood sample up north anyhow."

Doc switched on the sterilizer.

"I was going to. I didn't spot any needle holes or anything like that but then again..." He shrugged.

"I want to know exactly what his blood shows," said Jack. "Have it tested for everything you can think of."

TWENTY THREE

When I got home I checked my watch against all the clocks downstairs before I went upstairs. They all showed the same time. When I passed my bedroom door I glanced at the clock on my night stand. It was the same as the others, so I knew that much at least was okay. I had the time right.

When I went back downstairs and walked into Timmy's room he was lying on his side facing the wall, curled into a ball again.

Alice followed me in. "He's been like that for a couple of hours. I can't get him to even open his eyes, ever since—"

I wheeled around to face her. "Ever since what?"

She gulped. "Nothing happened to him, but everybody was calling here and they kept calling, and is it true, Mom? Kit's actually dead?"

"I asked you what happened to Timmy."

She rolled her eyes. "I didn't mean to scare him. Mom, somebody actually cut off Kit's head?"

"Alice. What. Happened. To. Timmy."

She chewed her lower lip. "Well...I didn't think..."

"You told him about Kit."

She took a step backward. "I guess so..."

"Why did you do that?" I heard my voice rising but I couldn't stop it.

"Well, I—"

"You what? Did he ask you what happened?"

"Well, no, but he looked like he wanted to know."

Red spoke from the hallway. "Know what?"

At the sound of his voice both Alice and I turned toward the door.

"She told Timmy about Kit and he's been like that ever since." I pointed at Timmy. Out of the corner of my eyes I saw Alice flinch.

Red walked over to the bed. "Timmy, open your eyes."

Timmy's eyes slowly opened, but he stayed curled against his pillow.

"Get up."

Timmy's eyes closed again and he sighed, pulling himself even tighter.

"Leave him alone, Red. *Now!*" My voice seemed to come from someone else and sounded, even to me, threatening.

Red took a step back. "I'm sorry, honey. I was just trying to—"

"Never mind what you were trying. Alice, go to your room and stay there."

"But Mom—"

I took a step toward her. "I said go to your room!" Avoiding Red's eyes while Alice stormed out of the room, I went to Timmy and sat beside him, stroking his head.

"It's okay, honey," I said. "You're safe here. Nobody's going to hurt you, ever, I promise. I won't let them."

He opened his eyes, looked at his father, gave me a raised-eyebrow look of disbelief and closed his eyes again.

I hated to do it on Sunday, but I went downstairs to call Doc Martin and tell him what had just happened.

"You have an appointment in Anchorage tomorrow?"

I said yes.

"Well then, let him sleep. Try to get him to eat, or at least drink something warm if he's not eating. But otherwise, leave him be. That's all I can tell you, besides lock your doors."

That jolted me, but he was right. This was a small town and there was a dangerous killer loose somewhere out there. I hung up and checked all the doors, then went into the living room where Red sat flipping through channels with the remote.

I stood between him and the television, something I'd never done before. "Red, we have to talk."

He gave a disgusted snort and snapped off the television. "What now? Does baby Timmy need a new pacifier?"

Cold shock rolled through me. "Don't you understand anything

I've told you? Timmy is sick!"

He fingered the remote, moving a little to the left so he could see the blank screen. "Sick in the head, maybe. Sounds like you both are. He wants to sleep, you want to see things. Maybe we can get a two-for-one deal with the shrink, ya think?"

I lowered myself onto the sofa, trying to control my fury. "I saw what I saw and Timmy is definitely sick. Red, how on earth could Kit have been killed at that campground?"

He smiled. "Are you asking me if I killed him? See any blood on me? Look real close now, maybe you'll have a vision." He held out his hands and wiggled his fingers, mocking me with his eyes. "Any blood on these hands?"

I stared at them, bubbling inside with fury at his nasty arrogance. "No, but I don't understand what's going on."

He flipped the television back on. "Nothing's going on here, Raven. Could I just watch my race now?"

"After we discuss how I'm going to get Timmy to his doctor tomorrow. If he can't walk, I can't carry him."

Red shrugged. "Get Hopscotch to help you. I hear he's falling all over himself at the airport doing things for you."

I was stunned. "Hopscotch is a friend, Red, that's all."

He started clicking again, switching channels. "So call your friend. Or you could put your baby in a stroller, since he refuses to walk."

I heard the sound of the remote, click...click...click...but deep in my mind, Red was not sitting in that chair, in our home, taunting me and clicking the television to block me out, ignoring his son. All I saw at that moment was his face the night we were married, when passion had overshadowed any misgivings I might have had over entering into a marriage with a man I barely knew.

As I lifted the phone to call Hopscotch, something hit me with excruciating clarity, something I had never put into words, even in my mind, until this moment.

What Red and I had all this time was not love. Passion, maybe. Not love. It couldn't be. I hadn't even liked him for years, but I'd been blocking it from my mind and my heart. I set the phone back down, staring at him as if I were seeing him for the first time.

When had this happened, that I hadn't realized it before? How could it have happened, after building a home and having three children together, all of the things that were supposed to cement a marriage? I had no idea.

I picked up the phone again and dialed, listening to it ring on the other side, but Hopscotch wasn't there or if he was, he wasn't answering. I glanced back at Red, aware that all of a sudden he looked completely different. His eyebrows were raised, his eyes were wide open with amusement and his mouth had opened up into a wide smile.

He put down the remote and got up, walking toward me as if he'd never said any of those ugly things, then he put his arms around me and pulled me close.

"I'm so sorry, Raven. I don't know what got into me, honest, I don't, honey. I don't mean to be that way, it's just that sometimes it feels like Timmy's the only one you ever think about."

My voice was muffled against his chest. "He's not the only one I think about, Red, but he's a small child with some big problems."

He nodded. "I know, poor little guy, he doesn't deserve half the things I've said. Tell you what, baby, if Timmy's not walking by Monday, I'll go with you, help you with him. I'll carry him all the way if I have to." He tipped my chin so he could look into my eyes and smiled again. "That okay, hon? Can I do anything else to help you?"

I looked down at my fingernails. "We'll see how it goes."

He smiled. "That's my girl. Anything you need, just let me know."

He walked back to his chair, picked up the remote, still smiling, and turned the television back on.

I could only stare at him, afraid to trust this sudden switch. Again, it was as if he were two different people and he seemed to be able to switch them both on and off as easily as he did the remote. How long had he been doing this? Why hadn't I noticed it before? I must have noticed it. How long had it been simmering quietly in the back of my mind?

How long had I been fooling myself?

And now, could I seriously be thinking Red might really know something about those murders? Was that possible? Why would he have done such horrible things, if he had?

And even more ludicrous, if my gut feeling was right, why had I just checked the doors and windows, when Red was living right here in this house with me?

He had to be the reason why I felt evil surrounding me, coming at me in rolling waves, shimmering black dust devils that swirled across the room and crawled up my arms and throat, cutting off my breath, while the ghosts of Carolyn and Kit hovered in the shadows of my mind.

TWENTY FOUR

At the airport Monday morning Hopscotch lifted his head with great difficulty and saw Raven standing at the doorway watching him. He beckoned and pointed at the tea he had waiting for her.

It wasn't going to be easy to tell her. He didn't know if he could. He'd started tossing Scotch down again Friday night, he remembered that much, and evidently hadn't stopped Saturday night, as he usually did. Just kept going until sometime Sunday, because he woke up Sunday evening and discovered he was parked somewhere off the highway outside of Anchorage, apparently heading back in toward the city. Filthy, stinking, aching all over, and he had to have just one more drink to kill the ache.

Just one more hair of the dog that bit him good.

His head was still feeling the effects. The whole thing scared the living hell out of him. He couldn't recall ever blacking out before, but this time he had, finally.

Time to stop, mate. Time to stop.

He'd been toying with the idea of quitting for a long time, but the craving always overtook him when he was least expecting it and drowned out both his objections and his common sense. He knew, had known ever since he left Minneapolis, that somewhere, someday, he'd be caught.

But there was always that sudden craving for Scotch to slam down his throat, where it traveled with lightning speed to his fingertips and back up his arms, through his body, down his legs all the way to his feet and back up again.

The craving. And the bad, bad realization that only another drink could calm it and make it go away.

Just go away.

He always promised himself, just one. But somehow after one, two didn't seem like such a big deal. Anything after two was pretty much lost to the high he couldn't feel any other way. Now, when his life depended on keeping his wits about him, even one was too much and he knew it, but he hadn't given it a second thought Friday night.

Just one. One small drink and he'd stop, but he hadn't and now he had no idea what he'd done or where he'd been all weekend. Just trying to remember made him sweat.

He remembered climbing in his car and driving late Friday night but he couldn't recall much of anything past that, other than the panicked feeling when he woke and didn't know where he was or how he got there.

Raven settled into the seat across from him, took a small sip of tea and looked at him, her eyes questioning.

"What?" he asked.

"I'm waiting."

"For?"

"The reason why you said you couldn't talk to me anymore."

"Oh. That."

"Yes. That." She took another sip.

He bit into his cookie, chewed for a minute, staring at her. God, she was so soft and lovely...

He took a deep breath. "The thing is, Raven—"

"Yes?"

"I got into a bit of trouble several years back."

"What'd you do?" She eyed him, sipping her tea.

He sighed inside. "I skipped parole and came up here."

"Parole? What for?"

He shook his head. "It doesn't matter now."

"Oh. I see." Her eyes said she didn't see at all, but she put the cup down and tried to smile. "Well, at least it's not like you've been breaking the law up here."

"It's not as simple as that."

"Why not?"

"That's a hard question to answer right now. I just think it's not good for you to be seen sitting here drinking tea with me every day like we have been."

Her face scrunched down into a frown. "Hopscotch, I don't understand this at all. I haven't done anything wrong and neither have you. We're just having a friendly cup of tea. I don't see what that has to do with anything in your past."

"Raven, I've been breaking the law just by being here. I was trying to live my life, do my job, keep out of trouble, but now, with this murder investigation going on—look, I knew Carolyn, I even dated her some. That's bad enough all by itself, but the thing is, unless I get very lucky, they're going to find out about the parole and if they do, I'll probably be extradited to finish out my sentence."

She had given up any pretense of sipping her tea. "How long would that be?"

Another ten years and probably more now. "I don't know, Raven, but I'm trying to protect you. I shouldn't even have told you this much. I didn't want to, but I thought I owed it to you to tell you something, at least."

She leaned back. "What are you going to do?"

He shrugged. "Just hope the statute of limitations has passed. I don't know how that works, but it's all I can do, other than disappear again. I'd like to avoid that if I can." He looked down at his watch, back up at her. "Your break is about over and I have to fly out in a few minutes."

"Oh, you've got the morning flight this time?"

"Yes, unfortunately, and I've got a few things I need to take care of in Anchorage, so I won't be flying back until tomorrow. Why?"

He saw questions in her eyes, but she only said, "Oh, nothing really, except Timmy's regressed and can't seem to walk again, but maybe he'll be okay by noon. It's no problem, don't worry about it." She glanced at her watch. "Okay, I'll go to work, you go to work. But you can't avoid me that easily, you know. We both work in the same place." She slid out of her seat and reached for her purse. "Thanks for the tea. We'll do this again, and don't worry, I'm not afraid."

I am. He forced a nonchalant smile. "I'll see you around, then."

She stuck out her hand. "I hope so."

He took it, fingering her wrist lightly with his thumb, sending shockwaves all the way up to his neck this time. "It'll all work out one

way or the other, my dear. Please don't worry about me."
She turned and left, obviously perplexed.
He finished his tea and headed for the plane, surprised to find his headache was gone.

Beth Anderson

TWENTY FIVE

Monday morning Jack headed for the station, hoping something had come from AST so he could begin making some real progress. He had to. They were itching to swarm down to Valdez and take over the case. If they weren't in such a mess with their computer system they'd probably have already been there. When he walked in the door Ryan, his youngest rookie, waved a handful of papers in his face. "This just came in over the fax."

Jack took the papers and sat down at his desk, leaned back and put his feet up on the desktop. Five seconds later he slammed them back down on the floor and hunched forward with his mouth open, reading as fast as he could, trying to digest everything all at once.

His grandma had a favorite saying whenever something really floored her. "Lord God Miss Agnes!" This was a Lord God Miss Agnes minute if he ever saw one. He dropped the papers on his desk and yelled into the outer office.

"Nicholson, I need you in here, on the double!"

Bill rushed into Jack's office. "What's goin' on, Chief?"

"Get this." Jack waved the pages at him. "Hopscotch isn't Hopscotch Montgomery. He's not English and he doesn't have a pilot's license, at least not one obtained legally."

"You're kidding me!" Bill plopped down into the chair across from Jack's desk.

"Nope. According to AST, his name is Harry Maloney and he's wanted by the State of Minnesota for breaking parole after a murder conviction and early release."

"A murder conviction? What the—Hopscotch?"

"Just listen. In 1984, when he was twenty-four years old, Harry Maloney was up for twenty-five to life for the murder of his wife and assault of his mother-in-law and father-in-law.

"Apparently he got off easier than he should have. There was a hung jury first time around and the seventy-six year old judge who heard the second case bought the temporary insanity defense." He looked up. "I could almost understand that if it was Texas and a guy caught his wife in bed with a couple of men, but this was Minnesota."

"Anyway, he wound up with twenty-five, did fifteen, behaved with the shrinks, got paroled early because he had so much good time and the shrinks swore he was totally rehabilitated. He reported to his parole officer like the good boy they thought he was, and then disappeared almost as fast as he reported in. Looks like he had his plans all set before he left prison, and Valdez had to be the town he picked out."

"I can't believe this," said Bill. "Where the hell did he get that thick British accent?"

"According to the report, he grew up in Minneapolis, never was in England or anywhere else to speak of, never was in the service, was married at twenty-one to a nice hometown girl, but she wound up not so nice after all. Had these two boyfriends all along and her parents knew it. According to the trial evidence, they didn't like Harry and wanted her to divorce him."

"Jeezus," said Bill, grinning. "Two boyfriends? And she was in bed with both of them? Hmmm."

Jack frowned at his tone of voice. "Yes, and instead of taking care of it the easy way and let her have her divorce, Harry did it the hard way with a .38, then he took a tire chain to his in-laws and disappeared after that.

"They caught up with him in North Carolina a couple of months later, extradited him back to Minneapolis and Harry finally went to prison. Behaved himself while he was there and studied English—not our English, their English, according to his cellmate, who said he wanted to kill Harry because he drove him nuts practicing his British accent day and night." Jack glanced up and saw Bill trying hard not to grin.

"According to this, while he was perfecting his accent he read everything he could find on airplane mechanics and flying. His cellmate told the investigators he said he wanted to be a pilot." Jack

126

slammed the papers down. "Sonofabitch! No valid license—I wonder how he pulled that off—and he's flying planes out of here."

"So we arrest him and send him back to Minnesota, right?"

"Hell no, I don't want to do that! I want to arrest him for these murders and fry him right damn here, but we don't have a death penalty and come to think of it, neither does Minnesota."

"Want me to go pick him up?" Bill shook his head. "I can't believe Hopscotch is a killer. He always seemed like such a wimp."

"He's a wimp wanted in Minnesota for breaking parole on a murder conviction and he could have done the same thing here. We know he was dating Carolyn. I don't know what his connection is with Kit, but see if he's at the airport and go pick him up if he's there. I want to find out where he was Sunday morning."

Five minutes later Bill told Jack Hopscotch was on the plane to Anchorage and due back in Valdez in six hours.

Jack called Anchorage PD and told them to meet the plane, apprehend Hopscotch and hold him until his officer got there, then told Bill to drive up to Anchorage, pick him up and bring him back down to Valdez.

After Bill left, he headed for Kimberley Clarke's house to see if Kimberley or anybody else in the neighborhood had been up around four a.m. Sunday morning and seen or heard anything. There was always that long shot. The Clarke house was as good a place as any to start.

TWENTY SIX

Timmy and I made it to the airport in time to go into the lunchroom and have a quick snack, since he hadn't eaten much lunch. He was picking at the wrapper on a chocolate donut and I was sipping a cup of tea when my boss slid into the booth next to me.

"Did you hear about Hopscotch?"

I went cold, lowered my hand slowly and set my cup down. "What about him?"

Don rubbed the puffy lids under his eyes, a nervous habit I'd noticed before. "Looks like he's in trouble." He peered at me. "You don't happen to know anything about him getting arrested in Anchorage, do you? They called from the airport there and told me."

I shook my head, fighting the nausea that gripped my stomach. "No, I didn't know about this."

He shrugged, massaging his right arm as if it were sore. "I have no idea what happened either. I knew earlier Jack was looking for him, but not why. It must be something serious for them to arrest him as soon as he got off the plane. Now I have to reschedule all my pilots and find a new one. Dammit!"

"What on earth could have..." I glanced at Timmy. His freckles stood out from his face like candy sprinkles on an ice cream cone. He stared up at me, closed his eyes and gave a long, resigned sigh.

I pulled him close. "It's alright, honey, somebody's just made a mistake. I'm sure he's okay. Maybe he just didn't pay a traffic ticket or something, right?"

He opened his eyes. The café went dark for an instant and I heard the voice again.

"Kaxeél' yeedát."

I thought back, struggling to remember the words.

He had just said, "Trouble now." But how did he do that? I

looked up at Don, fighting to hide my panic.

He frowned. "What's wrong, Raven?"

"Did you hear Timmy?"

Don drew back a little. "He hasn't made a sound since I got here. Say, are you okay?" He reached across the table and patted my hand. "Ah, hell, we're all jumpy, seeing shadows everywhere, rumors about flying all over the place, everybody in town talking about—" Mercifully, he stopped.

"I'm sorry, Don." I tried to smile. "I guess I'm jumpy too. I thought I heard Timmy say something and he hasn't talked ever since...ever since..." My son's eyes had closed again and he shivered.

Don nodded. "I know." He glanced at his watch and smiled as Timmy opened his eyes again. "Your flight's leaving in a few minutes, son. One of these days we'll have to give you your own pilot's wings, you're flying so much here lately."

Timmy didn't respond. I gathered up my purse and slid out of the seat, pulling Timmy behind me. "We'll see you later."

Don nodded. "Take care of that little fella. The rest will take care of itself."

It didn't seem to me anything was taking care of itself, but I let it go and we boarded the plane.

TWENTY SEVEN

Clint was outside digging in his garden and his wife was talking to him when Jack pulled up in the driveway. He couldn't miss the barely hidden look of annoyance on their faces as they watched him scramble out of his vehicle.

"Howdy, folks. Nice afternoon for gardening, isn't it."

Clint dropped his trowel on the ground and stood. "Well, it was. Is anything wrong?"

"I'm just stopping by to ask if you folks were up and about early Sunday morning."

Melissa grimaced. "For once we weren't. One of us usually has to get up and help Clint's mother with her night diaper. She loves to wait till it's too late and then call us, she's made a career out of that, but she hasn't bothered us at all the past couple of nights. Why? What happened now?"

Evidently they didn't know, although he didn't see how they could have missed the sirens. "Neither of you were up at all for any reason? Go to the bathroom, get a drink of water? I'm mainly wondering if you heard any strange sounds, like somebody calling, anything like that."

They both looked at each other, then back at him. "Not me," said Clint.

"Nor I," said Melissa. "Why? I asked you if something else happened around here."

"Is your mother home? I'd like to talk to her for a minute, if you don't mind."

"She's inside watching TV," said Melissa. "Go on in if you're sure you want to." Her eyes flashed. "Not that she'll tell you anything. She's having one of her off days, I'm sorry to say. I'll stay out here, I've had enough of her babbling."

"If she says she needs a diaper change," Clint said, "run for your life. She wanted creamed corn for lunch again today."

Jack gave a quick salute, wondering why they'd send him in alone to talk to Kimberley, considering what they thought of her state of mind. He headed for the door and let himself in to find her hunched over in her wheelchair, watching a game show.

"I win again," she said without looking at him. "That's ten thousand dollars so far today." She raised her head. "Hi. What's up?"

He couldn't help but smile. "Hello, yourself, Mrs. Clarke."

"Kimberley," she reminded him.

"Yes, sorry. Kimberley. I just dropped by to see if you saw or heard anything in the neighborhood late Saturday night, early yesterday morning."

She glanced at the television, then turned back. "I heard sirens very early yesterday. What happened?"

"Just asking."

"Asking what, exactly?" She didn't appear to be having an off day to him. In fact, she seemed sharper than either of the two outside.

"Kimberley, let's talk seriously for a minute. They're outside, they can't hear us. Did you by any chance get up early yesterday morning before dawn and take a ride up to the window in that thing?" He indicated her wall chair.

"Maybe I did, maybe I didn't. Why?"

He'd sure as hell hate to be a trial lawyer trying to get anything out of her. "I need to know if you were up around four a.m."

She grinned. "Probably."

"Your family doesn't know that."

"Neither of them knows whether anything happens around here at night after they kill off a liter of wine." She smoothed her slacks, watching him. "I get up all the time, go up in my chair and look outside. It's a lot nicer at night. I sit and look out that window and think how I could just reach out and grab a star if I wanted to. If there were any out, I mean."

He'd often had that feeling himself back in Texas when the skies were clear. What his grandma called a magic moment, stars that big and bright, almost close enough to touch. However, early Sunday morning in Valdez it had been foggy.

"So you were up. About what time, did you say?"

She raised her gaze to the ceiling, thinking back. "About four, maybe a little after. Are you going to tell me what happened, young man, or do I have to get a crowbar and pry it out?"

"There's been another murder, but not around here."

She nodded. "So exactly what am I supposed to have seen, or is it heard? Which?"

"I don't know, ma'am. Strange noises, anything like that."

"All night noises are strange around here." She thumped on the arm of her wheelchair, frowning. "Are you going to call me Kimberley or not?"

"Kimberley," he affirmed. "Now, about that noise?"

She looked at him from under lowered lids. "What noise?"

"The noise you might have heard outside yesterday morning around four o'clock." He could see her gaze wavering. He knew what was coming.

"I did tell you I used to be a movie star, didn't I?" Her face scrunched into a frown as if she might be trying very hard to remember something, but couldn't.

"Yes, Kimberley, you did." He leaned toward her. "But I need to know if you heard or saw anything outside Sunday morning about that time."

"About what time was that?" She was listing in the chair now, plucking at her slacks, pulling a thread out of the chair cushion, looking everywhere but at him.

"Kimberley, did you or did you not hear or see anything next door at any time very early Sunday morning?"

Her eyes brightened. "I thought you said nothing happened here."

"I'm not sure anything did. I'm just trying to find out, so how about it, are you going to help me out?"

She straightened in her wheelchair, fiddling with the controls. "I saw the woman who lives there out on the front porch next door about four, four thirty."

"Are you sure about the time?"

She nodded.

"What was she doing?"

"I could barely see her through those holes in her latticework. It was a little foggy, too, but I could see that she was just standing there."

"Was anyone else there?"

Kimberley snickered. "You mean was she maybe cheating on her husband or something?" She took a close look at his face and grinned. "No, nobody else was there."

"Did she go out to the street?"

She looked up at the ceiling again, moving her eyes from left to right. He looked up and saw she was following the movements of the ceiling fan.

"Yes, I believe she did. Not all the way, though. She kept looking behind her."

"What else did she do?"

"She just stood there for a few minutes, then turned around and went back into the house. I only stayed up there a little while longer, then I had to get back in bed before the bitch got up and caught me."

He smiled inside and rose to leave.

"Oh, by the way," she said, "can you do me a favor?"

"Sure," he said, edging rapidly toward the door, thinking about the creamed corn.

"Tell my son's wife I need her in here."

He nodded and opened the door to step outside. He heard her laughing to herself as he closed it.

He delivered her information and watched them stomp toward the house, then he headed across the street.

Nobody else had heard or seen anything but they were full of questions about Kit's murder. So was he, because he suddenly realized the cushion Kimberley had been picking at was the same shade of green as the thread he'd found on Carolyn's body.

Could Kimberley somehow be involved in either murder? No, that was stupid.

Then again, he knew she could walk. And he knew now that Raven was telling the truth, she was outside after four a.m.

He headed back across the lawn to talk to Red and made a

mental note to call AST and find out if they had a profiler on staff, even though he'd rather not. This was his town and his case.

But there were two murders now.

Beth Anderson

TWENTY EIGHT

Timmy and I took a taxi to Dr. Randell's through a light rain. When we walked into his office the shades were drawn and the room was lit only by one small bulb in his desk lamp.

The doctor's eyes crinkled into a smile. "How are you today, Timmy?"

Timmy looked around the room, his eyes dark with apprehension.

"We're going to try something a little different today. I want you to sit quietly in your chair and I'm going to talk to you. You don't have to respond if you don't want to, but if you feel like it, you can."

He got up, beckoned me over to the door and said in a low voice, "I'm going to try hypnotherapy. Would you mind waiting in the next room?"

Timmy jumped up from his chair, ran to me and grabbed my hand. He shook his head rapidly, begging me with his eyes not to leave him there alone. I was a little off-balance because of the look in his eyes and the clammy feel of his hand, but I said, "I'll be in the next room, honey. Dr. Randell's going to talk to you for a few minutes, okay? I'll be right outside the door, so don't worry."

Timmy sighed, climbed back in his chair, and I left the room.

In the hallway, shadows moved past on the walls, an eerie sight, but I looked out the window and saw they were caused by moving clouds, now dark and ominous. I found a seat on a bench by the door to the doctor's office, counting them as they moved swiftly by. One... Two... Fifteen... Sixteen...

No words filtered under the door, no voices, just deep, moving shadows everywhere.

Twenty four... Twenty eight...

A scream pierced the air.

"Xat tulawdidin! Áa akooxdlixéeti!"

The room went dark, I blinked and saw the back of a man's neck for an instant, then it disappeared and the room was normal again. I jumped from my chair, rushed to the door and pulled it open. Timmy was leaning back in his chair, his eyes closed, perfectly relaxed while Dr. Randell spoke in a low monotone. He saw me standing in the doorway and motioned me back out the door.

I couldn't move. He got up from his desk and walked over to me. "Mrs. Morressey," he said, his exasperation apparent, "we're not finished. Please."

"But—why was Timmy screaming?"

His eyebrows shot up. "Screaming?"

"He was screaming in Athabascan, 'I don't feel good! I'm afraid!'. I heard it coming from in here. What did you do to him? You can't possibly say you didn't hear it this time!"

"Mrs. Morressey, was it Timmy's voice?"

Sweat broke out on my neck, running down into my collar. "No, no, it was the same voice, not Timmy's, but it came from him, I swear it did!"

"It was your father's voice, wasn't it?"

"It always sounds like my father's voice." Icy perspiration under my armpits made me shiver. "Dr. Randell, what's happening to us?"

"What's happening to you? I don't know, but I do know Timmy was perfectly quiet. Give us a minute now."

He walked back to his desk, tapped the lamp and it lit the room. "Timmy, when I snap my fingers, you'll wake and you won't remember anything you heard here. One... Two... Three..."

Timmy's eyes blinked open and he ran to me, burrowing his face in my skirt.

As we got ready to leave, Dr. Randell motioned for me to come back to his desk. He sat behind it with his hands folded in front of his face, forming a tent. His eyes were so cold I shivered under his scrutiny.

"Raven, I can give you a referral to an adult psychologist if you want someone to talk to."

I stood before him, twisting a strand of my hair, confused. I'd do anything on earth to help Timmy, but no one would ever believe I was hearing voices and they were real, that I was seeing flashes of someone and that was real. I knew they had to mean something but I didn't know why these visions were coming to me. I said I'd think about it and we left.

All the way home through the clouds and rain I tried to remember whose neck I'd seen in Dr. Randell's office but I couldn't re-create it in my mind because it had been over so fast. I couldn't even remember his hair color. The vision had left as quickly as it had appeared, leaving me mystified and more afraid than I'd ever been before in my life.

TWENTY NINE

Red answered when Jack knocked on the door. "I was just watching CNN to see if we were on it," he said. "So far, looks like we're not."

"Sorry about that," said Jack. "I'll try to do better. Is it okay if I come in? I need to ask you a few questions."

Red switched the television off and pointed to a chair. "Sure. You might as well make yourself comfortable."

He sat. Red offered him a beer. He said no and Red got one for himself, popped it open, then sat across from him on a comfortable-looking easy chair. A green one. All of a sudden everybody in town had green furniture. Matter of fact, so did he.

"Shoot," said Red.

Jack pulled out his tape recorder, secretly pleased when he saw Red's thick eyebrows lower into a quick frown, which just as quickly disappeared. "State your name for the record, please."

Red gave his name while Jack looked around. Raven was nowhere to be seen.

"First, Red, did you see or hear anything different Saturday night at the campground? Any movement after lights out?"

Red shook his head and took a sip of beer, eyeballing him over the top of the can.

"Nothing at all?"

Red shook his head again.

"You need to answer yes or no. The recorder can't hear you move your head."

"The answer to both is no."

"Did you get up during the night?"

"No. I went to bed and went straight to sleep."

"Didn't turn your light on again for any reason?"

"Nope, I fell asleep right away."

"Did you know the older boys sometimes sneak out of their tents and go walking around after lights out?"

Red sat up straight, frowning. "Who said that?"

Jack smiled. "One of the older boys."

Red lit a cigarette, taking his time. Finally he spoke. "Yeah, I know they do. I hear 'em when they go and I always listen for 'em to come back. Why?"

"Do you know where they go?"

Red shook his head. "Not far, they just walk around to prove they can put one over on me."

"Did you hear them Saturday night?"

"No. They didn't do it that night."

"You're sure of this?"

"Pretty sure."

"You said you went right to sleep."

"Well, I might not have right away."

"Do you know of any reason why anybody would kill Kit?"

"I have no idea. He was a pain in the ass, but nothing that would warrant anything like that."

"A pain in the ass how?"

Red closed his eyes for a few seconds, thinking. "Nothing you can put your finger on. Just…closed. Very secretive."

"Do you know of any connection between him and Carolyn Crumbe?"

Red's jaw worked. "No."

"Did you ever see them talking together?"

"I don't remember ever seeing them together at school or away from it. I'm in my office most of the time."

"For the record, what do you do at the school?"

"I'm the guidance counselor. You know what I do."

Jack smiled. "The tape recorder doesn't. What, exactly, are your duties there?"

Red frowned. "I talk to the kids. Counsel them. Talk to the parents sometimes."

"Where did you train for that?"

Red's eyes flew open. "Excuse me?"

Raven Talks Back

"Where did you go to college?"

Red leaned back. "I don't understand what that has to do with these murders, but I went to school in Florida." He pointed to a framed certificate on the wall by the stairway. "Go check it out for yourself."

Jack nodded. "I have noticed you have a bit of a southern accent now and again. Where in Florida?"

"University of Miami."

"Where's your wife?"

"Off to see her shrink. Well, Timmy's, but it might as well be hers. She's been acting kind of funny lately."

"Funny how?"

"I don't know, just weird all of a sudden. Swearing she saw Kit when he was already dead, things like that."

"Can you think of any reason why anybody would kill Carolyn, bury her corpse in your back yard, then kill a high school kid right under your nose, more or less?"

"Are you trying to connect me with those murders?" Red demanded, half jumping out of his chair. "Look, I counsel the high school kids and run the scout troop and that's it."

"Maybe, but it looks to me like somebody has a hell of a hard on for you, Red. First, your property, then, as you said yourself, your campsite. I'm wondering why."

He could see Red wasn't buying his friendly concern so he switched topics. "Did you ever talk to Kit regarding problems at home, anything like that?"

"Kit never came into my office for anything. I never had a problem with him myself and I don't know of any he had anywhere else."

"Even so, he must have made somebody pretty angry for them to do that. There has to be some connection between him and Carolyn."

"You think the same person did both murders?"

"The MO's were almost identical, wouldn't you say?"

Red shrugged. "I'm not a cop, that's not my gig. You tell me what you think."

"Have you seen Kit's parents since their son's death?"

Red's color deepened. "I didn't want to bother them. I'll go over there tomorrow, that's time enough."

Kit was in Red's scout troop and had been under Red's care when he was killed, but he seemed almost detached from anything connected with it. Maybe there was a reason for that. But then that would shoot hell out of his Hopscotch theory.

Maybe. He wasn't ready to let go of either one. He pulled himself up out of the chair. "I guess that's about it for now, Red."

Red snapped the television back on. "Okay. I'll just get back to my shows."

Jack left and headed back to the station to call for a profiler and book Hopscotch if Bill hadn't already done it.

Then after that, he was going to go home and do a little target practice, scrounge around in the fridge for something to eat and get to bed early and get some sleep, if he could.

"He give you any trouble?" Jack nodded toward the cell where Hopscotch lay on his cot, staring at the ceiling.

"Negative," said Bill. "He stuck out his hands in front of himself at the Anchorage police station and said, "I hear you're looking for me, mate."

"He say anything else?" Jack glanced back at the cell again. Hopscotch was lying very still, probably listening.

"Nope. Didn't make a sound all the way here. Been quiet since we got here, too."

"You book him?"

"Yep. I called Minneapolis and told 'em he's here whenever they want to come get him."

"Are they coming right away?"

"Nope. They said they'd pick him up when they could, but they're not in any hurry. They've got something else going on right now, didn't say what."

"Okay, that'll do it then. I'm going home now. Get him something to eat, then you go on home and tell your wife I said she should treat you nice."

Bill chuckled. "I'll tell her."

Jack drove out to the lawn and garden store on his way home and bought his usual two hanging plants, both filled with red geraniums to hang outside the door on his sprawling two-bedroom log cabin out on the edge of town. This was his yearly tribute to his grandmother, who had loved them and had them everywhere, every summer while he was growing up in her home. These geraniums were a real sweet reminder of her every time he pulled into his driveway. No need to worry that folks might think red flowers hanging outside his front door looked mighty odd for a bachelor living by himself, either. Hardly anybody ever came down this road anyhow. He had his privacy and plenty of peace and quiet, a real switch from his daytime job and he liked it just the way it was, red geraniums and all.

He also liked to do his target practice in his living room so nobody would know anything about his fast draw status, which was pretty damned excellent the last time he took in one of the Single Action Shooting Society conferences down in Oregon. His favorite vacation. Better than Vegas. Last time he'd brought back two first-place trophies and a brand new brass SASS belt buckle he'd bought and paid for himself and never worn. Yet.

It'd been a couple of years now. He'd been thinking about going back this summer because it was always wild fun, a crazy, cowboy-type conference where he called himself Roger Hoss for his SASS alias, and he could cut loose in his 19th century cowboy outfit and shoot from horseback, like he'd always pretended to do with his buddies in his grandma's yard, back when they were kids and only had sticks for pretend horses.

At SASS, he could yell and laugh and raise hell all day and all night. In fact, he could do almost all of the things he wouldn't be caught dead doing in Valdez. His guilty pleasure, more or less. His secret week or so where he could forget about everything but having fun.

Looked like it wasn't going to happen this year, though. Not with what was going on in Valdez, so for now he did his practice in the house, just in case. It was better everybody believed he was the soft-talking, easygoing fella they all thought he was. If he had to shoot fast he could, and a lot faster than most. Nobody needed to know that ahead of time.

He switched on the light when he entered his living room, tossed his hat on a side table, and still standing, removed the long, gleaming .357 cartridges from his Vaquero, then headed for the lock box in his computer room where he kept his gear. Protective glasses, check. Cardboard target, check. Simmunitions, check.

He propped the target up on a chair by the wall and stood replacing the .357's with six .38 Special Simmunition rounds, their blunt, stubby blue paint-filled 'bullets' looking incongruously out of place as he stood smiling down on his gun with affection.

His baby, this magnificent piece of steel. He ran his hand over it, loving it as if it were a gorgeous woman hot under his hand, waiting for him. It was a beautiful thing, this five-and-a-half-inch Ruger Vaquero .357. Black checkered grips, high gloss stainless steel barrel, he'd had it for years back in Texas and carried it with him everywhere he went. Big ol' feel-good cowboy gun, he couldn't imagine not having it on him day and night.

He went through the kitchen, passed the fridge, gave a longing look at the beer but grabbed a soft drink instead. Pulled the cap, took a big gulp, set it down and he was ready, ass-deep in questions but no answers. Maybe he'd think of something he hadn't before. He walked over behind his sofa and took aim.

Pop!

...Why would anybody chop up Carolyn that way? Green thread and a naked skull, nasty photos of the murder scene that tell us nothing about the motive but plenty about the killer...

Pop!

...Smeared bloody boot print in the middle of her kitchen...whose boot? Who knows, everybody in town wears 'em. Half a palm print that might or might not be the victim's...hands still missing... Now Kit dead on top of that, no clues there either unless the killer dropped DNA somewhere and we haven't found it yet...

Pop!

...No clue when anything'll get done up north...half the damn town dropping by to see if I've caught the killer yet and why not, it's been four days already...just one day since Kit was killed though. No

Vera this weekend...
Pop! Pop! Pop!
And what the hell are those kids up to?

This wasn't doing him a bit of good, he'd just missed the target three times in a row, almost unheard of. He lowered his gun, pissed because he was even thinking about three—no, two now, teenage kids when he had two murders to solve, but he still had to find out what they were doing.

Whatever it was, on top of everything else he had to figure out a solid way to stop them before they got too far into it if this was anything like it sounded. He sighed heavily. And what if he found Charlie and Jason had murdered Kit? Anything was possible.

He packed his gear away, cleaned his gun and headed back to the fridge to grab the beer, glancing at his watch. Eight-thirty. The kids would be on their chat line for sure.

Every kid in town seemed to be online, typing at top speed about Kit's murder. His eyes blurred watching the lines race across the page but nobody seemed to know anything he didn't, and neither Charlie or Jason were online. He sat there for an hour or so but got nothing useful from any of the kids except more questions and a lot of panic.

When he went outside for a minute before he headed for bed, he heard the deep foom, foom of a ship heading out from the dock on its way to God knew where, and found himself wondering how long it'd be before he saw Vera again.

When Jack got to the office the next morning he got a call from the captain on Vera's ship telling him she hadn't reported for work and nobody had seen her come back on board.

A worried frown creased his forehead. He told the captain if they hadn't located her by evening he should call back and they'd take a look around Valdez for her, but they couldn't start an official search until twenty four hours had passed in any case.

He'd felt like disappearing himself from time to time, but it didn't sound like something Vera would do. It was possible she'd picked up somebody on board the same way she'd picked him up and just hadn't surfaced yet. No reason why she couldn't, there were no strings on their relationship.

Anyhow, for now he had to concentrate on what was going on in Valdez. AST had told him they'd send somebody out of Anchorage that they'd recently hired who'd had FBI profiling training in Quantico, somebody named Mac O'Toole, as soon as possible.

That didn't sound too promising. He knew AST didn't usually have profilers on hand and as soon as possible could mean anything between now and the next century, even if they were itching to get their hands on his case. A profiler wouldn't be wasting his time to investigate anything, though.

He spent the rest of the morning getting everything together in one large file and going over it all again, trying to figure out what he could have missed.

He might as well have left it scattered on his desk where at least he could see it all at once. Didn't matter either way. Whatever was going to solve this case wasn't in that folder.

Jack heard a commotion in the outer office a little after two that afternoon. He checked his watch, saw he'd missed lunch again and tried to ignore his growling stomach while he headed for the front desk to see what was going on.

What was going on was a female about five-foot-four, green eyes, dark blue suit, white blouse. His rookie and one of his officers were elbowing each other, both trying to stand directly in front of her. He nudged them out of the way.

"I'm Chief O'Banion. What can I do for you?"

"You asked for a profiler?" She whipped out a badge, flashed it at him and held out her hand. "Special Agent Mackenzie O'Toole, AST. Everyone calls me Mac."

Jack tried to hide his surprise and shook her hand. "I'm glad you're here, Mac. I was just leaving to get a bite to eat, we can talk at the restaurant, then we'll come back here and go through my file, what there is of it."

Raven Talks Back

He guided her toward the door, glancing back at his men. "Back in a bit, fellas."

A few minutes later they were sitting in Halibut House with fish baskets and coffee between them.

Mac took a bite. "So you've got two unsolved murders down here. This is the first time you've had something like this, isn't it?"

"Yes, and I need help." He dunked a French fry into his catsup. "I have a couple of suspects, but hell, it could be anybody in town. We just arrested one of them when we found out he skipped parole on a murder conviction in Minnesota. He's sitting in my jail right now."

Jack filled her in on Hopscotch's background. When he was finished she asked about the workmen at the first crime scene. He told her their alibis had checked out but he was running backgrounds on everybody anyhow.

After they talked about the case a while she took the last sip of her coffee and leaned back, eyeing him. He looked up at the wall clock and discovered they'd been talking for almost three hours.

"How about we go visit the scenes where the bodies were discovered?" he said. "The apartment where the first victim was killed is still sealed, we can get in there. Is there any place else you particularly want to see right now?"

"I don't really want to see anything. I don't work that way."

He tried to hide his surprise. "Oh. Well then, where are you staying?"

"The Aspen, over on Meals Avenue. I haven't checked in yet though."

He grabbed her gear when they pulled up at the Aspen. "I'll leave you at the desk. Pick you up in a half hour, okay? I have a couple phone calls to make, then we can talk more if you want."

"I definitely want," she said.

He followed her inside and waited while she checked in. Just as he got back to his car, his cell phone rang.

"O'Banion."

"Chief—" Bill's voice sounded strained.

"What is it?"

"Where are you?"

Jack tried to ignore the bad feeling in the pit of his stomach. "I'm over at the Aspen, checking our profiler in. Can this wait?"

"Negative. I'll be there in five minutes. Meet me outside."

"Wait—what's going on?"

"Tell you when I get there." The line went dead.

Five minutes later Bill pulled to a stop, rolled down the window and stuck his arm out, waving him over to the passenger side. "Get in. We didn't want to tell you this over the phone so I said I'd find you and tell you myself."

"Tell me what?"

He motioned to the passenger seat again. "Get in first, please, Chief."

"I've got my vehicle here. What the hell's going on?"

Bill couldn't quite meet his eyes. "Vera's head floated up under the dock a little while ago, Chief. Some tourist found it, they've got him over at the station, but I don't think he's involved. He was just looking out over the water with his family and they only got here this morning."

Jack couldn't move. He stood looking down at the ground while flashes of everything he knew about Vera ran through his mind. He forced his head back up.

"Dammit all, Bill, this ain't right. This can't be right. Are you sure it's Vera?"

"Doc says it is. Come on, get in."

Jack climbed in, leaned back and closed his eyes. "Drive."

He heard Bill shift gears. "That's why I'm here."

He kept his eyes closed all the way to Doc's office. Vera was dead. No rhyme or reason for it he knew of, but somehow she'd gotten mixed up with what was going on. Maybe he was a target in all this, he didn't know, but this cleared up one thing for sure.

It was a good thing AST was here to help him, even if she wasn't going to be all that much help, because now there were three.

THIRTY

Alice burst in through the kitchen door while I was making supper. "Mom, there's another one!"

I was distracted, trying to chop mushrooms and stir tomato sauce at the same time. "Another what?" I reached past the mushrooms for the slotted spoon.

"Some woman's head floated up over at the wharf while ago, Laurie saw it. They think it's somebody who works on one of the cruise ships!"

I dropped my knife. "One of the cruise ships?" A deep chill swept through the room and I found myself thanking God it wasn't someone who lived in town. Ashamed but relieved, I glanced into the living room where Timmy had been sitting on the floor watching television. He had turned toward us and was listening to every word.

"Someone from the cruise ship?" I said.

Alice helped herself to a container of yogurt and shrugged. "I heard it's Chief O'Banion's girlfriend. It's all over town, and I heard some state trooper or something is here now, too."

Jack O'Banion's girlfriend? From a cruise ship? I never even knew he had a girlfriend. Nobody had ever said anything about that to me, but then I'd never been one to listen to gossip.

How odd though, that he had someone I never knew a thing about and now she was dead. When was this going to end? What could I do now to protect my own family from this carnage?

"Alice."

Alice was intent on scooping yogurt out with her finger. She looked up. "Yeah?"

"From now on, I don't want you going out anywhere alone."

"Oh, M-o-m—"

"Don't 'oh Mom' me, Alice, I meant what I said. You don't

walk out of this house alone, not even out the door, until whoever's doing this is in jail."

"But Mom," she argued, "if none of us can walk out the door alone, who goes out first?" She had that superior 'gotcha!' smirk on her face I'd been seeing more and more of lately.

"It's not going to be you. I forbid you to leave the house alone, as of this moment. And," I added before she could stop me, "all that middle of the night sneaking back and forth by you and your girlfriends has to stop."

Her smirk wavered a bit. "Well, what about Charlie? He does that all the time."

"I'll deal with Charlie. Meantime, you go ahead and call all of your friends and tell them what a horrid mother you have, who won't let you go out alone so someone can—" I took a quick glance at Timmy. He was rocking back and forth with his eyes closed, humming to himself. I listened closely, and to my dismay realized it was again one of my father's chants, this time a different one, but still the same deep voice.

I rushed over and knelt in front of him. "Honey, don't you worry. Someone will be watching out for you every minute of the day and night."

He shook his head.

"Yes. Timmy, look at me."

He kept his head down. I pulled him into my arms. "You're safe, love. I won't let anything happen to you."

I watched the life in his eyes grow dim again as he drew back into himself. "Honest, honey, cross my heart," I said, holding him close.

He just shook his head again, pulled away from me and trudged up the stairs as though he were carrying a fifty pound bag of concrete. I heard his bedroom door close, then nothing else.

By the time I had dinner ready he was asleep and I couldn't wake him enough to get him to come to the table. In spite of Red's sullen anger, I let Timmy sleep. He needed that right now more than anything else.

After dinner I sat alone outside, watching eagles fly over the tall pines toward the campground as a cool breeze rolled in. I pulled my sweater close, seeing once again, in my mind's eye, Kit's face out in the street.

Could that really have been only two nights back? It seemed an eternity, something that had happened a long time ago to someone else, maybe in a novel I'd read or some late night television show.

It wasn't television. Death was everywhere. Vibrations flickered around me like intermittent power surges, prickling my skin as the sun's rays shot up one last time behind the trees, turning them a bright, vibrant gold around the upper edges, but dark, so dark underneath.

Was Kit ever really here the night he was killed? My mind said no, it was impossible, he couldn't have been. But I had seen him. I knew I had. It was too real to be...no, I had definitely seen him.

Who could have done such a thing to him? And why had he come to me, of all people, in the middle of the night?

THIRTY ONE

When they got to Doc's office, in spite of the fact his feet didn't want to move, Jack climbed out of the car.

"Come on." Bill grabbed his elbow. "I'll go in with you."

They headed back into the room where Doc did his autopsies and stood by the table, staring down at the lump he had covered with a white towel.

Jack lifted it. It was Vera all right, but her face was swollen and her eyes were bulging and wide open as if she were staring, surprised, at her killer. Bill's hand gripped his shoulder.

"This is tough, Jack. I'm so sorry. I know she was your girlfriend."

"That she was," Jack agreed. He turned away and stomped into the bathroom, scooping cold water over his face for a couple of minutes, fighting the urge to bawl. A few minutes later he headed back into the room, glad to see Doc had re-covered Vera's head.

He'd been lectured over and over as a rookie that you couldn't let personal feelings enter into your actions during a criminal investigation no matter how bad it was. Like most officers when something bad does get to them, though, he wanted to let himself be mad, that bad, ice-cold, boiling-hot mad that no law enforcement officer could afford to let happen. But he was a professional and had been a long time. He couldn't allow himself to waste time being mad. Not now.

It was almost nine before Jack had time to call Mac. The phone rang a few times before she answered with a sleepy "Hello?"

"Mac, I apologize for running out on you like that, but there's been another murder. I just left the M.E.'s office."

He heard a rustle that sounded like covers being thrown to the floor. "Why didn't you call me? Never mind, pick me up in five minutes."

"I was just heading back to the station."

"I'll be outside waiting." He heard the phone click off.

"Has the victim been I.D.'d?" she asked when she climbed into his vehicle five minutes later.

"I identified her. It's a woman I've been seeing for a while. She worked on one of the cruise liners that docks here every couple of weeks. Her name's Vera Cruz. They called this morning to tell me she was missing. Now we know why."

She glanced at him, her eyes alert and curious. "Seriously dating?"

He shrugged. "Sort of, but not really. No commitment."

"But you liked her."

"Yeah." He looked over toward the docks where the sky glowed softly from the boat and restaurant lights. "I did."

"I'm sorry," she murmured. "That's tough."

"That it is." He swung around a corner, filling her in on what little he knew before they reached the station.

After they exited the vehicle she turned back to him. "You haven't mentioned any background on Vera."

"Tell you the truth, I don't know much about her. She never talked about anything but her job. We got her Social Security number from the ship's captain today, that's all we have so far."

She brushed back some hair that had fallen over her eyes. "I'll contact the Anchorage office and have them run an I.D. on her, maybe that'll tell us something. What about the other victims?"

"The juvenile lived here, so did the first victim. We've questioned people all over town, some of them twice but nobody knows zip."

"Did you request a background on the teacher? Not just the one where she worked, those can be faked if you're smart enough. Have you requested one from up north?"

He nodded. "Yeah, but I haven't received anything except the background on Hopscotch. I'm waiting for everything else I asked for."

"Well, I'll see if I can't speed things up just a little." She started to enter the building, then stopped and looked back. "Was there any connection between all three victims? Did they know each other?"

"I couldn't make a connection between the first two, other than that Carolyn was a teacher in Kit's high school and he was one of her students, but Vera didn't spend much time in town. In fact," he felt his face coloring, "she spent most of her time when she was in town with me, for the past few months anyway. I don't know about before that."

She looked past him into the office. "Well, there is some connection, even if it's just that they all had the same shaped eyes, or they all parted their hair the same way, or they were all wearing the same color the day they were killed. It could be anything, the way killers' minds work. You never know what's set them off until you hit on the connection—if you ever do."

He opened the door for her. "I'm thinking because this is such a small town they were probably all involved in some way with the killer."

"Not necessarily," she said, "although it would help. The problem with serial killers is, it's an internal thing that only they know about and sometimes they don't even know. Look at Dahmer. He said himself that he knew what he was doing was wrong every minute but he never understood why he did it, only that he had to. A lot of them are like that."

He ushered her into his office. "You're pretty sure we have a serial killer."

She opened her computer. "As far as we're concerned you do if there are two or more victims with the same M.O., and you have three. Our job is to find out what kind of serial killer he is and stop him before he can kill again."

She switched on her computer and typed in some instructions, watching as it connected with her office in Anchorage. "Okay," she said, "let's get down to the real work now. We don't want any more murders in this pretty little town."

THIRTY TWO

Wednesday morning was one of those cold, foggy summer mornings prevalent in Valdez and I could barely see fifty feet ahead. I thought the plane might not take off but it did, and I was nervous for the first time ever while flying out of this airport. Hopscotch had always been the pilot before, when the fog was this thick.

My hands gripped the armrests while I watched slate gray mist stream past the windows and found myself seriously considering whether or not Hopscotch could have killed Carolyn and Kit.

My aching heart said no. Logistically, I had to admit it was possible. He was dating Carolyn. What if he hadn't been in Anchorage early Sunday morning, but had been hiding in the mountains by the campsite somewhere? If that were so, it was possible he had killed Kit. But why would he do something like that when he barely knew the boy? And why Jack's girlfriend?

In a few minutes we rose above the fog, but although warm sunlight flooded the small cabin, I was chilled to the bone and my feeling of unrest only grew. When the plane landed in Anchorage forty-five minutes later and we walked through the airport toward the taxi stand, I was still distracted, wondering if life in Valdez would ever be the same again.

As Timmy and I entered Doctor Randell's office a few minutes later I saw it had been redecorated over the weekend, which only added to my off-kilter feeling. Now the walls were covered with a pattern of several soft shades of mauve and the doctor's desk was in the center of the room, facing the door. I settled into a new chair by the window and Timmy headed for the toy shelf.

Dr. Randell motioned for me to keep silent. "Timmy," he asked, "would you like to play with the toy house again today?"

Timmy had knelt in front of the toy shelf and was slowly

fingering the small dolls lying by the dollhouse. He didn't respond. Instead, he picked up one of the dolls he'd played with before and his back stiffened. He turned and looked straight at me and deliberately tried to twist the doll's head off, then fell to the floor sobbing, his flailing arms and legs splayed out over the carpeting while he tried over and over to smash the doll. His cries, woeful, screaming sounds, like a storm trying to break through steel walls, tore at my insides.

I started to go to him, to comfort him, but Dr. Randell motioned me back and put his finger to his lips. I felt his words, although he hadn't made a sound. *Be quiet now. Just watch.*

Timmy raised his head and turned toward me with his mouth open, although it wasn't moving. The room grew dim and I heard my father's voice.

"Cookie!"

He pulled himself up, walked over to me and dropped the doll into my lap. *"Cookie! Cookie!"* His face twisted into a horrible, confused grimace and his eyes implored me. *Please understand me, please!*

"Darling," I whispered, "what are you trying to tell me?" I glanced at Dr. Randell. He frowned, trying to warn me off, but I couldn't stop.

"Are you hungry, honey?" I looked at the doctor again. "He just said 'cookie' again. You did hear it this time, didn't you?"

Dr. Randell scratched the side of his neck, clearly perplexed. "I saw him put the doll in your lap, but he didn't say anything."

I felt my face flushing. He didn't hear anything. Again.

He stared at me for a long moment, then seemed to make up his mind about something. "Just let me check something here." He turned to my son. "Did you just tell your mother you want a cookie?"

My son looked down at the floor and shook his head.

I picked up the doll and turned it over. "This is the same one he put upstairs with the male doll, isn't it?"

The doctor nodded.

"Is it supposed to represent me? If it is, what could he be trying to tell us?"

I turned to Timmy. "Sweetheart, what is it you want?"

He shook his head and pulled away.

"Maybe he's trying to tell us who it really represents," the doctor murmured, writing as he spoke.

"Is that it, Timmy?" I put my hand under his chin and lifted it so his eyes had to look into mine. "Are you trying to tell us the doll's name?"

He gave me a tentative nod.

Dr. Randell's head shot up. "The doll's name is Cookie?" Clearly he was as baffled as I was.

Timmy wouldn't look at him.

"Are you saying you want a cookie? Is that it?"

Timmy reached into my lap, snatched the doll and threw it into the doctor's wastebasket as hard as he could.

"CookieCookieCookieCookieCookie!" he screamed in his own anguished voice, then fell to the floor again, sobbing uncontrollably.

"Well," said Dr. Randell, "I heard him that time."

I bent to gather my son into my arms. I could feel his heart pounding too fast and held him close, stroking his neck, willing him to stop crying, to be okay again. I looked up.

I guess you did, Doctor. This time it was in his own voice and language.

THIRTY THREE

Mac showed up at the station early the next morning even though they'd gone over files until almost two a.m.

She handed Jack a plastic container of coffee and perched on the corner of his desk. "Anything from up north yet?"

He glanced toward the fax machine in the corner at some sheets coming through. She jumped off his desk and snatched them, reading as she headed toward him.

"My oh my," she murmured, almost under her breath, "will you just take a look at this!" She handed him the papers one at a time.

He hunched over his desk reading. The more he read, the more his insides churned at the thought of Raven finding out about all this, if she didn't already know.

At seventeen, Red had run away from a foster home in Florida, where he'd been ever since he was twelve and his parents had disappeared. He'd helped himself to a goodly amount of money at the foster home before he ran and wound up working for a place called Jim's Carnival in Florida that traveled around the South. The foster home warrant had expired long ago.

He'd worked as a general roustabout at the carnival, along with handling pitch booths from time to time and left after five years.

The next entry was at age twenty-nine, when he did three years in Joliet Prison for molesting several inhabitants of a home for sexually abused teenage girls in Chicago, where he'd somehow wrangled a job as custodian.

There was nothing after that. Jack figured it was right about then he'd headed for Valdez and landed a job at the high school.

"He shouldn't have been anywhere near a school, but there you go," said Mac. "He probably used fake I.D.'s and background, and then to make matters worse, he started the Boy Scout troop here. Mr.

Outstanding Citizen himself."

"Jeezus," Jack muttered. "It's beginning to look like nobody in this town is who they say they are."

"A lot of them probably aren't," she said, "and if the person's a particularly shady con-man type like this guy seems to be, it can take years to figure it out, if anyone ever does."

Mac hunched over, scribbling on a yellow office pad. He tried to take a peek, but she had her arm over the pad and he could only see a few words.

She raised her head. "I'm making notes. I think better when I do it in longhand, then I convert it later on my laptop."

"For?"

"I'm compiling your UNSUB's profile." She flashed a quick grin his way, then ducked her head again.

He fumbled around in his desk, looking for some aspirin, didn't find any so he leaned back and shut his eyes.

"What is it?" Her voice seemed to float around the room, bouncing off the walls like his thoughts.

He kept his eyes closed. "I'm wondering how Raven's going to take this."

"Raven?"

"Red's wife. They have three kids. Hell of a nice woman,"

She snorted. "Forgive my cynical outlook, but Jack, you can't let yourself get sidetracked just because you like someone, I'm surprised I even have to tell you that."

His eyes snapped open. "You didn't and she is nice, she's a real decent woman. I almost can't do this to her, it's going to make everything worse. She's got enough problems as it is."

"You didn't do anything to her, her husband did if he kept all this from her." She put her pen down and leaned back. "What problems are you talking about?"

He told her everything he knew, including the fact Raven had insisted she'd seen Kit at least an hour after he knew for sure Kit was dead.

"Hmm," she said, ducking her head and scribbling again. "Has she always been like this?"

"Not that I know of. She's always been the most stable person in the world, at least I thought so. Do you want to talk to her?"

"Nope, my job's strictly composing this profile, which I'm going to type up for you in a bit."

He took another look at the pad. She'd already filled several pages.

The fax machine started its usual click-buzz sound again. He beat Mac to it this time and grabbed the papers, reading Carolyn's background check as the sheets slid out. The hairs on the back of his neck stood at full attention by the time he'd read a couple of paragraphs.

"I'll be double-dip damned!"

She looked up from her notebook. "What?"

"Carolyn Crumbe—my God—" His eyes raced, trying to read the whole thing at once. He slowed down and backtracked so he could digest it all.

She held out her hand. "Give."

He gave. She started to read, then looked up at him.

"Well, at least you've got your connection to one of your suspects. We have here an outwardly sedate English teacher who once worked as a tattooed belly dancer and part-time hooker in a carnival down south, which I'm betting is the same carnival Red worked at all those years ago." She looked up at him and grinned. "Love her stage name. Cookie Crumb."

THIRTY FOUR

Timmy slumped in the large overstuffed chair, exhausted, and didn't say another word for the rest of his session.

Dr. Randell finally pushed the buzzer for his nurse and asked her to take Timmy to the outer office. After they left, he turned back to me.

"Mrs. Morressey—"

"Why don't you just call me Raven," I said.

He nodded. "Raven, then. Well, Raven, I think we've had a small but important breakthrough today when he finally spoke."

I sat with my hands clasped on my lap, listening.

"But he didn't say enough to tell us what brought on such hysteria. I'd like to try something fairly new with him. It's called RET, Rapid Eye Technology. It's becoming a very popular method among psychologists for treating PTSD."

He picked up a pen, scribbled something on his yellow pad, then looked up. "Raven, here's what's bothering me the most. For Timmy to have such a strong reaction to seeing that body in your back yard when he wasn't in any real danger himself, and given that he appears to have been a normal child otherwise up to that point, I feel there's got to be a lot we don't know or at least haven't considered." He paused. "Would you mind answering a few questions for me before we go any further?"

I was wary but determined to help Timmy get past whatever was causing his silence. "I don't mind. At least I think I don't."

He settled back in his chair, eyeing me. "Tell me about your marriage, Raven. Is it a happy one?"

I looked away. "I suppose it's as happy as most."

"As happy as most?" His still gaze pierced me, reminding me of the way I'd always thought a fly must feel when it sees a swatter coming fast and knows it's too late to escape.

"Doesn't everyone have disagreements?"

He allowed himself a faint smile. "Of course. Does your husband know you've been hearing things nobody else hears?"

His abrupt switch shocked me into silence.

"Didn't you tell him, Raven?"

I didn't want to look at him. "I haven't told anybody everything."

"What did you tell him?"

"He knows I think I saw Kit—the second murder victim—about an hour after Kit was murdered."

"You think you saw?"

"I saw him standing in my front yard looking at me, reaching out to me."

"Did he say anything?"

"Not a word."

"Are you sure of the time?"

"Yes."

"Are the authorities sure of the time he was murdered?"

"They are."

"So you told your husband—"

"I didn't mean to tell him," I interrupted. "It was right after they found Kit's body and I was confused because I knew I saw him when I said I did."

"Did your husband believe you?"

I raised my eyebrows. "Do you believe me?"

"Why haven't you told him about the voices?"

I turned to look out the window. A tanker moved over the horizon far in the distance, sunlight bounced off the superstructure, a few dark-edged cumulus clouds hovered overhead, small boats close to the docks moved slowly, ever so slowly…

"I don't know. Maybe because I'm pretty sure he wouldn't understand."

"Is he abusive to you or the children, Raven?"

"If you mean physically, no. Dr. Randell, what's this all about?"

"If he's not physically abusive, then what about mentally?"

"Most of the time, no," I said, still dodging. "We live a fairly uncomplicated life. Whatever is, just is, and I deal with it."

"Yes, but do you feel free to confide in him?"

The answer to that is no, Doctor. "Sometimes, I guess. Usually I just take care of whatever has to be taken care of."

"Are you saying there's no real communication between the two of you?" He leaned closer now, forcing me to look into dark eyes that seemed to fill his face.

The answer to that, Doctor, is yes. "We talk, if that's what you're asking. But I try to spare him."

"Why?"

The question hung in the air between us.

"What about Timmy?"

"I talk to Timmy a lot."

He shook his head impatiently. "No, no, I mean what about Timmy's relationship with his father. Are they close?"

Another long silence. "Not really," I finally admitted. "Timmy came along when we weren't expecting any more children and..."

"And?"

"Red was angry that I was pregnant again. For some reason, he's never been close to Timmy." *Or the other two.*

"What about your other children? Are they close to their father? Do they communicate well?"

I fought the tears threatening to spill over. "He's never been that kind of father. He goes through the paces, but as for real closeness or intimacy, he's not like that. He's actually pretty remote most of the time." She forced a shrug. "It's just the way he is."

"How does he treat Timmy?"

I reached for a tissue on his desk and dabbed at tears I couldn't hold back any longer. "If you want the truth," I blurted, "most of the time he treats him like he's not there."

Dr. Randell stopped taking notes and gave me a long, searching look.

"It's not that he doesn't love us—them," I said, "I think he does, in his own way. He just seems almost, well, unable to show it most of the time."

He nodded. "And you try to compensate for that?"

"He says I do. I suppose he's right. As I said, I try to spare him."

"Or are you sparing them?" he asked in a soft voice.

His question stunned me. He had hit on the truth without ever having met Red or my other two children.

He glanced at his watch. "Our time's over for today. When we meet next time I'm going to start RET with Timmy. I think I may be able to help him now."

"What exactly is this RET?"

"You'll see. I will tell you that it may be hard on him and possibly you also, but we need to do this if we're going to help him."

I frowned. "It won't hurt him, will it?"

He gave me the first genuinely friendly smile he'd ever given me. "Not physically, but he has to face a few things before he can overcome the traumas he's had."

"Traumas? But he only saw one body," I protested.

"Maybe," he said. "But we don't know that and we've got to find out what exactly is behind all this anger.

"One more thing, then I'll let you go." His eyes seemed to peer into my soul. "Have you given any thought to seeing the counselor I recommended?"

"I'm thinking about it, Dr. Randell."

He nodded. "I think you should, Raven, for all your sakes. It's not going to do much good to get Timmy straightened out if you—" He stopped abruptly and stood, offering his hand for the first time. "I think you definitely need to talk to someone, if only for Timmy's sake."

All the way home the same thought kept running through my mind, nauseating me beyond belief.

If I'm going insane they'll take my children away.

THIRTY FIVE

After Jack located the number of Jim's Carnival in Florida and dialed, the phone rang fifteen times. Might be a long shot, but it was worth a try.

"This is Jack O'Banion, Chief of Police in Valdez, Alaska," Jack said when the receiver was lifted. "I need to speak to somebody in charge who can answer a few questions."

"That would be me. I'm Jim. What's your problem?"

"Jim, I'm calling in regard to something that may have happened in your carnival around twenty years ago. I need some information."

He heard a disgusted snort. "Twenty years ago? Do I carry a calendar around in my head? What kind of information are you talking about?"

"Do you recall a man named Red and a woman named Cookie who worked at your carnival around that time?"

There was a long pause, then, "Who did you say you are?"

Jack repeated his name and title.

"How do I know that's who you really are?"

"You could call me back," Jack said, winking at Mac.

"The hell I will. I don't talk to anybody over the phone, not about something like this. You want to talk to me about that pair, show me a badge and maybe we'll talk." He hung up before Jack could say goodbye.

Jack gave Mac a rueful look. "I should have been a preacher like my grandma wanted. At least people feed you and talk nice to you once in a while." He picked up the phone and dialed 411 again.

"Who are you calling now?" she asked.

"I'm going to get the police down there to drop in on Jim. I want answers and I want them now."

A few minutes later Mac looked up from her typing as he hung up after he finished talking to the chief of police in Florida.

"Your profile is as ready as I can get it without more to go on. I'll print it out, then it's time for me to head back to Anchorage. I'm catching the afternoon flight, my cab should be here any minute."

She hooked up her laptop to a small portable printer and punched a few keys, glancing at him from time to time while the pages began to slide out.

He reached for a few.

First page was a short list of known clues. One green thread. Yeah, good luck with that. Two Alaska Native masks painted on rocks. Candy and gum wrappers sent for DNA. A boot print and part of a palm print in Carolyn's apartment, also sent up north. No answers yet.

He looked up to find her watching him. "Not a lot here," he said.

She shrugged. "Sometimes there isn't. Sometimes there's nothing. At least you have something."

The next six pages were all currently known information on the three victims. Addresses, ages, locations, times of death as close as they could determine, family members and neighbors, friends interviewed. Almost nothing on Vera.

"You're pretty thorough with victim information, I have to give you that," he said.

"That's my job. I'll add to it when I get more."

He grabbed the rest of the pages.

Page seven began the actual profile. He glanced at her as he read, suddenly wondering why the hell he'd asked for a profiler.

The first page of this section was general theory on serial killers. Different types, individual methods. Like he didn't know all that. Like any cop wouldn't.

Then and only then, the actual profile of his UNSUB.

First, there had to be a common denominator among the three victims which they didn't yet know and which could be anything.

"This is about as clear as swamp water," he muttered under his breath.

The masks painted on the rocks might have some sort of

Raven Talks Back

significance. For instance, it could point to an Alaska Native as the UNSUB, but that wasn't conclusive and none had yet been found connected to Vera's death.

"No kidding," he said, looking up. "What is?"

"What is what?" she asked.

"Conclusive. About the rocks or anything else."

"Read on. Maybe something will hit you."

He read on. The UNSUB had to be somebody who knew their way well around Valdez.

"How hard can that be?" he asked.

"What?"

"Well, hell, Mac, anybody who's been here more than a half hour knows their way around town. You can drive all the way through from one end to the other in ten minutes."

"True, maybe."

"Maybe what?"

"Just maybe," she said. "Your main street's not the only street in town, and you said yourself, most Alaska Natives around here live out of town in their own villages."

He had to give her that. Next item: The UNSUB would be somebody with enough strength to quickly and quietly decapitate a human being and lift the body in order to move it to another location.

"Mac," he said, trying not to sound like he was complaining, "damn it all, this could be just about any man in town."

She just smiled.

The UNSUB would most likely be—what the hell was this? Of undetermined race. Male. Age, mid thirties or more.

"Okay, where did this come from?" he asked. "Most serial killers start at around nineteen or so, and most of them are white males. Why are you placing this one around 35, maybe older?"

"Jack. It could be something in my subconscious when I looked through the crime scene photos last night, or maybe it was something I felt but can't yet identify. I just have the strong feeling this is not a young man, although I think it is probably a man and I have the feeling he's probably done this before."

"Probably?"

"Everything in a criminal profile is 'probably', Jack. A lot of profiling is based on instinct and experience, you should know that."

He read on.

The UNSUB was organized and somebody who knew exactly how to use a knife to make a swift, clean kill.

"Jeezus," he said, "just about every man in town knows how to use a knife, how to make a fast, clean cut. That's what they do here. They hunt. They fish. They clean 'em and cut 'em up. Give me something I don't know."

She smiled. "I have to put what I think fits in the profile."

"There's something else," he said. "This killer may be organized, he probably is, to have committed three murders without being seen or heard, but in my opinion he's messy as hell too. You should have seen Carolyn's apartment. I don't see anything organized about whoever did that."

"You're entitled to your opinion, but it's my profile. I think whoever did this planned it all ahead of time and did a right fine job of it." She smiled again, not as much this time.

Next point: The UNSUB, if he was, for instance, a revenge killer, would be somebody in a big hurry to see his version of justice done and took care of it himself with three kills in a very short span of time.

He looked up. "At least we agree that this could be some kind of a revenge killing. I was thinking the same thing early on, right after the first murder."

He stopped short, thinking back. A lot of men in town disliked Red, although not one would tell him why. He was back to thinking maybe somebody had planted the first body in Red's yard to point the finger at him. But then why not just kill him?

Red was nearby when the first two occurred. Jack couldn't say for sure where Red was around the time of Vera's murder, and Doc couldn't pinpoint the exact time on that.

"You've got a definite serial killer down here, Jack, and there's never a logical reason why they kill, except maybe to themselves. You'd better find out who it is fast or you're going to have more than just a profiler down here."

"Right." He was distracted by this garbled bunch of crap, although he didn't want to say so.

Next to last point: The UNSUB had something important to him in his past which triggered these kills.

Two days with a profiler and here he was with another murder and still back where he started. No clear indication who the UNSUB might be and no way to find out, unless the killer felt like stopping him on the street and saying, "Yo, Chief, guess what. I'm your killer."

He read the last point.

The UNSUB, if they were revenge kills, would have a good reason known only to himself to methodically plan and commit all three murders and feel fully justified in doing so.

That stopped him again and he looked up. "Hell, Mac, most all killers feel justified and there's never any justification for murder. My question is, why would anybody in Valdez think they had to kill Vera when she didn't even live here?"

"I don't know." She was beginning to pack papers back into her attaché case but she stopped and looked up at him. "That's the main thing that makes me think it's possibly a psychopath, someone who likes to kill. Maybe he killed before he came here. If that's the case, unless these were revenge kills, he'll kill again. You definitely need to investigate everyone who recently moved here."

She reached for her jacket. "Look, Jack, it seems to me your focus right now is mainly on Vera's murder. You'd better get your head out of your ass. You can ask why he killed her after you catch him, but in the meantime, find the commonality between all three murders and don't just concentrate on why someone would kill Vera. It doesn't matter why. The only thing that matters is getting him off the streets before he does it again."

"Or her," he said.

She shrugged. "Or her, maybe. You got any females in town who lift weights?"

"How the hell do I know?"

She shrugged again. "Go find out."

THIRTY SIX

After dinner Timmy went straight to bed and fell asleep. Alice and Charlie had gone off to their friends' houses, and Red was at the mechanic's getting his truck's air conditioner fixed. I walked around the living room idly touching things, trying to reassure myself I was really in my own home, doing normal things.

I knelt by our old CD player, looking through the various titles we'd collected through the years, wondering where the CD's I brought home from college had gone.

My Eighties music. I smiled, remembering those lazy nights when my roommates and I did nothing but sit around dreaming about our futures, discussing men we barely knew, judging them all on a scale of one to ten as future husbands and giggling as we discarded them all.

Where was my Beatles music, REM's *The One I Love*, all of the old Michael Jacksons? Songs Alice and Charlie had both sneered at when they saw the covers. Ancient history to them, but a time of uncomplicated peace to me. Where were they? I'd had them out, looking at them only a couple of years ago.

My head snapped up. *Oh!*

It wasn't only a couple of years ago. I hadn't seen them for quite a few years.

How many years?

I had stopped playing them when I married Red.

Why?

I didn't know, but I wanted them now.

I rushed out to the garage, pulled out boxes, scrabbled through old clothes, tossed them on the floor, tore open another box, nothing but old blankets in there and why had I kept so many ratty, worn old blankets?

Where were my CD's?

Box after box, everything on the concrete floor now, shoes, pans, an old broiler, half a coffee set, underwear too small when I was pregnant with Timmy but they were expensive and I couldn't bear to throw them away and then I forgot about them.

By this time I was sobbing, tears running down my face, into my blouse, onto the floor. I reached for another box, ripped it open, nothing in here. Another box, nothing there.

Where were they? Breath coming short, sobbing, gasping for air, I had to find them, had to hear them again, had to know I was okay. They couldn't take Timmy. I wanted my music!

God, let me dance again, please, just let me dance one more time...

I found them in a small black plastic box behind Red's tool chest and picked them up as though they were the Holy Grail. To me at that moment, they were. I wiped my eyes and headed into the house with my music, my young years, my everything at the time.

I pulled them all out one by one and smiled when I saw Michael Jackson's Thriller. I was the only woman in my dorm who could do the Electric Slide. My friends blamed it on my Athabascan blood and they liked to see me do it. My claim to fame. My fifteen minutes.

I put the CD on, closed my eyes, listening to the music, and began to move slowly, a little faster, everywhere at once, sliding backward past the furniture, over the slick hardwood floor and once again I was eighteen years old with nothing but fun on my mind. One foot forward, slide back, forward, back. I threw back my head and laughed out loud.

I can still do it. I'm still me!

Behind me, I heard a giggle and a familiar snort.

Alice. And Timmy. I hadn't heard him giggle since...

I wheeled around. "Alice, what are you doing here?"

"Mom, I live here, remember?"

The music was still playing but I had stopped. "How did you get home?"

"Shelly's mom brought me. Why are you doing that stupid dance? Nobody does it anymore."

Timmy stood behind Alice, grinning. He walked toward me and held his arms out and I almost lost my breath. I took his hand. "Would you like to dance with me?"

He nodded.

"You want me to teach you how to do the Electric Slide?"

He threw back his head as I had just done and laughed out loud, a joyous sound that echoed throughout the darkness that had invaded our home.

I took his hand and step by step began to teach him how to move his feet and body backward at the same time. Sweating with excitement he caught on fairly quickly and slid around the living room with me, laughing.

So much love for this child…God, how I love him.

I had never loved him more.

I might never again do this in my lifetime, but I could at least, for now, pass a little of my young years on to my small son, who hadn't heard me laugh in a very long time, and had never seen me dance.

THIRTY SEVEN

Jack sent his men back out to double-check everything with the victims' friends and neighbors, and fielded irritating questions from reporters and town people the rest of the day.

That evening, when he got home after he ate a solitary dinner over at the wharf, he had a couple of beers and then switched on his computer to see what was going on there.

At first he saw nothing more than the usual on the kids' main chat line. Both Charlie and Jason were there, schmoozing the girls. Then Jason typed "Let's talk," and both boys disappeared. He hooked into their private room fast, thankful again that he could do it without being seen, and sat back to watch.

Cyberdarth666: "You really think we should do it even after what happened to Kit?"

Shoesize13: "Why not? That didn't have anything to do with us doing this. Besides, I have two I.D.'s now and they'll still be good July 4th."

Cyberdarth666: "You sure?"

Shoesize13: "Checked one of them out myself today while I was in Anchorage with my mom. She was getting her hair done and I beat it over to the main office. Slid in the ID and walked in slick as cow pies after a rainstorm. Nobody stopped me. Nobody even noticed me. Hell, I could've walked away with half the building."

Cyberdarth666: "Yeah, but that's a lot different than actually walking into the terminal."

Shoesize13: "I don't see why. Two I.D.'s, both males. They're not photo I.D.'s. What more can you ask?"

Cyberdarth666: "Are you sure your aunt won't miss them?"

Shoesize13: "Hell no, she just tosses them in her desk drawer if people turn them in when they leave, and most don't. She's got dozens in there, but most of 'em are expired by now. I don't want to take any chances with anything older than a couple of weeks, that's too risky."

He stopped reading long enough to try and figure out what they were talking about. Then it hit him. Jason's aunt worked at one of the separate oil personnel offices for contract hires.

Uh oh.

Apparently nobody was canceling electronic I.D. cards when they were turned in. The boys were going to use the I.D.'s of recent oil company contract employees to get into the terminal.

Jeezus! Kids that age with minds like that.

He wondered how long it'd taken them to dream up this caper, not to mention that it entailed several felonies, which they didn't seem to realize.

Shoesize13: "Charlie, you with me or not?"

Cyberdarth666: "I guess, but it doesn't sound like as much fun as it did when we first thought about it. What if somebody gets hurt?"

Shoesize13: "Nobody's going to get hurt. The damn lid'll blow or else it'll blow a hole in the side, there's nothing in there but fumes anyhow so it's not like they're going to lose any oil. They'll just raise hell and everybody'll get a big show on the Fourth for a change. They'll never know who did it. We'll be gone before it blows."

Cyberdarth666: "You got the timer and the explosives?"

Shoesize13: "Yep. Picked up instructions off the Internet and they mailed everything, no questions asked. We'll walk out of there after we drop it and when we're about halfway back across the bridge I'll set off the signal with my cell. I found out how to do that on the Internet too."

Cyberdarth666: "What if we get caught?"

Shoesize13: "Who's gonna catch us? They won't know what we're doing. We stick the I.D.'s in the security system, no problem, just like at the head office. We'll walk around a little bit, up the hill behind the containers like we're tourists, drop the pack next to the empty one and we're out of there. The whole thing won't take more than ten or fifteen minutes."

Cyberdarth666: "I don't know. It sounded like more fun when Kit was here."

Shoesize13: "Kit was crazy, you know that. We're better off without him. Two's better than three anyhow, less visible."

Cyberdarth666: "What if somebody recognizes us?"

Shoesize13: "At dusk? Everybody we know will be home eating dinner. We'll be fine, we're just raising a little hell. The kids'll be talking about it for the next five years, wondering who did it. It won't even cost the oil company anything, they'll just collect insurance and fix the hole. They've got money they don't even know what to do with, my aunt told me that."

Jack was tempted to go pick them both up right then but he looked up at the ceiling, grinning. Nah. He liked his original plan better.

The next morning at nine sharp he called the oil company's main office in Anchorage and told them he'd been given information by a reliable source that their employee I.D. cards weren't being retrieved when employees left, and weren't being deleted from their system immediately and then destroyed, which created a security breach that could affect the oil terminal.

They didn't seem to comprehend what he was getting at until he told them they could be used to get into both the main office in Anchorage and the oil terminal in Valdez. The clerk, clearly bored, said they'd look into it. Jack hung up, called the AST and gave them the same information. He got even less response there. The clerk he spoke to said someone would look into it. He hung up sorely frustrated, wishing he was Brian Williams and had his own evening news show.

Beth Anderson

THIRTY EIGHT

Early the next morning I picked up the small box of brownies I'd made for Hopscotch, jumped in my car and headed for the police station.

Jack was at his desk, looking disgusted as he hung up his phone but his eyes lit up when he saw me, surprising me, and he smiled, waving me in. I went around the front desk and stood at the door, waiting.

He pointed to a chair. "Come on in and sit a spell, Raven. How are you? What's in the box? Goodies, I hope."

I stayed where I was. "I'm fine. I don't have time to sit and chat, though. I just brought some brownies for Hopscotch. Is he still here?"

A voice called from down the hallway. "I'm still here, Raven. You brought brownies? Really? You're a lifesaver, mate!"

Jack scowled. "As you just heard, he's still here."

"May I see him?"

He looked at the box, at me, at the box. "This is pretty unusual, Raven. Sit down and we'll talk about it."

"Jack, I'm in a hurry, I have to get to work. You have a friend of mine here and I brought him some brownies. Do you want to inspect them first?"

Jack closed his eyes and shook his head, opened his eyes again. "Raven. Of course I'm going to take a look. People don't just blast in here bringing treats for prisoners. You're the first one to try it since I've been in Valdez."

I could feel my temper starting to rise. "You don't trust me with a box of brownies?"

He jerked his head back and a shock of rumpled hair fell down over his eye. He swiped it away. "I trust you, Raven, but it's standard procedure." He held out his hand. "Give me the box, please."

I stared at him, incredulous.

He sighed. "Will you bring it here, or do I have to come get it?"

I sighed louder than he did, walked to his desk and handed him the box. He opened it and poked around, lifted the top layer, looked under the second layer, then closed the lid. "I'll make sure he gets it," he said without looking at me.

I felt anger coming from him in waves, or was it my own, heading his way? "Would you mind telling me what crime I've committed by coming to see a friend? It's not like I've got a hacksaw hidden in there."

"I can see that." He looked up at me, still holding the box, obviously trying to control his expression, but his stiffness was getting to me.

"What is your problem, Jack?"

"Raven, why are you sounding so hostile all of a sudden?"

"I'm hostile? You should see yourself, you look like you're ready to tear the whole building apart!"

He set the box down. "Sorry about that. This is just my natural expression when I have three unsolved murders to worry about."

"Now you're getting sarcastic, Jack. Why have you arrested Hopscotch? What are the charges?"

He sighed again. "Raven, I can't discuss that with you."

I wanted to slap the obstinate look off his face. "Does he at least have a lawyer?"

"I can't discuss that with you either."

"Jack, what's happening here? Why are you giving me such a hard time? All I did was make—"

"Yes, I know. You made brownies for your friend." Nobody could have missed his derogatory tone of voice.

"Well, can I see him for just a minute?"

"Visiting hours are between seven and eight tonight. If he's still here, you can see him then."

I almost stomped my foot in frustration. "You know what, Jack, you're just nasty! Eat the brownies yourself, maybe they'll sweeten you up. I don't care what you do with them!"

Jack looked straight at me. "Well, they do look good."

I wheeled around and headed for the door, turning back to glare at him one more time. He had the box open, half a brownie in his hand, and he was chewing very slowly, thoughtfully, still staring at me. He stopped chewing.

"Thank you, Raven. They are delicious."

I stomped out of the station, slammed the door behind me, switched on my car ignition, gunned the motor, and then looked back at the door. Jack was leaning against it, still chewing, still watching me.

THIRTY NINE

The Edgewater chief of police called back early in the afternoon while Jack was sitting at his desk making a new list of questions he wanted answered and double-checking to see if there was anything he hadn't previously thought of.

"Chief Braxton here. I just finished talking to Jim out at the carnival home. He wasn't happy about talking to me, but I think I got some pretty good information out of him."

"Good. Let's have it." Jack grabbed a pen and a clean piece of paper.

"Carolyn Crumbe—he called her Cookie—was hired first. She started out as a shill outside of a pitch booth. Jim moved her to a spot in the sideshow after he saw her dancing with most of her clothes off one night in a local bar. He says the way she danced was really erotic and her scarification was a huge draw because nobody had seen it before."

"Keep going," Jack said, writing as fast as he could.

"Well, Jim says he tried to get into her pants and she put him off, kept him dangling, so to speak."

Jack rolled his eyes at the ceiling. "Okay, what then?"

"Red showed up. Your friend Jim says Red took one look at her and the next thing Jim knew, Red and Cookie were carrying on pretty much all over the place. Really hot stuff. Big battles all the time, then they'd disappear off somewhere to have make-up sex. He said this went on for about six months or so."

"And?" Jack prodded, thinking this was like trying to move a whole herd of cattle uphill with a Q Tip.

"Everyone at the carnival knew about it, but that in itself wasn't so unusual. Young guy, young female, both good looking, according to Jim. Anyhow, Jim gave up and looked the other way. Had to, his wife was around all the time and he didn't think it was worth all the trouble he'd be in if she got wind of what he was trying to pull off himself with Cookie. Then he found out what Red and Cookie were really doing."

"What was that?"

"Well, apparently Red had set himself up as Cookie's pimp and Cookie wound up with a new part-time job taking care of customers looking for something more than pitching balls for teddy bears. Red collected the money first and arranged her meets with the johns."

"What happened then?"

"According to Jim, Red made the mistake of helping himself to the contents of some guy's wallet while the guy was availing himself of Cookie's services. Our guys went looking for Red the next morning because the john told them he figured Red lifted it while he was undressed. That was the first Jim knew of their sideline business.

"Evidently Red got wind of the bust before our guys could locate him. According to Jim, Red and Cookie slipped into the office through the back way, tied Jim up and helped themselves to the safe combination, which Cookie knew Jim kept in his wallet. They took five thousand bucks out of the safe and left town.

"Apparently Jim was too embarrassed to tell our guys about the money they stole from him. He says he just wanted it all to go away so he never pressed charges and never saw either one of them again."

"Do you have a record of all that?"

"I'd only have the part about the initial call, it's probably somewhere buried in the basement, I'll look it up and fax it to you if you need it. I can fax you a write-up of my trip out there while ago, though. Do you need me to search the old records, or is this enough?"

"I think your write-up will do it for now. Thanks much for the information."

"Hope it helps. Call me back if you need more."

Jack hung up, reached for a pen and moved Red's name back up to the top of his suspect list, then picked up the phone to see if he was home. He wanted to talk to Red face-to-face.

FORTY

That afternoon I took Timmy shopping for the first time since the day of the first murder. After I stopped at the Eagle for some canned goods, we headed over to the No Name Pizza, his favorite place.

He was very quiet, but pleased when I ordered pizza with extra cheese so he could pull long strings of it from his plate to his mouth. I smiled inside as he ate. At least he still loved pizza.

After we finished we headed over to The Prospector on Galena so I could pick up a few things. I normally did my shopping by mail order, just about everyone in town did, but I was mainly looking to have a stress-free outing for Timmy. We were walking between racks, trying to find a pair of sneakers, when his knees buckled and he fell face down to the floor, gasping for breath.

"Timmy?" I knelt and touched his forehead to see if he had a fever. "Honey, what's wrong?"

He opened his eyes, now dark and troubled again as they had been in Dr. Randell's office the day before, pointed toward the back wall, shivered and closed his eyes again, his small chest heaving with his effort to breathe normally.

My eyes followed the direction he had pointed to and I found myself staring at a replica of an Alaska Native ceremonial mask hanging on the wall, along with several others. I'd forgotten almost every store in town carried them during tourist season.

I held him close, rubbing his back, "Honey, it's just a mask, a pretend face. It can't hurt you."

Timmy's mouth opened and I heard it softly at first, then it grew louder. *"Cookie! Cookie!"* The words echoed, filling the store.

My father's voice. Cookie.

Again.

When I pulled into the driveway I saw Jack's car at the curbside. I took Timmy in through the back door and straight to his room, sitting beside his bed for about ten minutes and stroking his forehead while he fell asleep. Then I went back into the kitchen, picked up my packages, and was getting ready to take them into the living room to show Red when I heard his voice.

I stopped behind the swinging door, listening.

"I don't know what you're talking about," Red said.

"I'm talking about you and Carolyn Crumbe and Jim's Rides twenty years ago. I think you know exactly what I'm getting at."

"I never worked at a carnival. Where was this supposed to be?"

"Florida. Stop horsing around, Red. You know where it was."

"Look, do I need a lawyer? Am I being arrested for something?"

"Why? Have you done something wrong?"

"Not that I know of." I heard Red's recliner being pushed back.

"Let's start again, Red. I know you were there. Tell me about it."

"I wasn't there."

"Red, quit the crap. I have your whole background. I know about the money you stole from the foster home. I know you did hard time for rape in Chicago. I know you worked at the carnival in Florida when Carolyn did, and I know you were never prosecuted for the things the owner says you did there. I'm just trying to hear your side of the story."

Red was in prison? For rape?

I focused on my kitchen walls. How different they looked, so much darker than they'd been only minutes ago. My mouth felt full of cotton batting. I wanted to run out the door screaming.

I couldn't move.

I heard the recliner squeak and bump as it shot upward. "Jack, I swear to you, I haven't done anything wrong since I moved here."

"Red. I know you and Carolyn Crumbe were having a very hot affair when you were both in Florida. I know she was working one of the booths before Jim changed her name to Cookie and put her in one of his shows. I know you were rolling her johns when you were pimping for her and I know you robbed Jim of five thousand dollars when you and Carolyn left. Let's get serious. I want to hear your side of all this."

"No, you've got it wrong, Jack. There must be someone else with the same name as me. Look, Raven will be home soon. I don't want her to hear this."

I heard the recliner inching backward again.

"I have more questions, Red."

Red didn't respond. I heard the sound of his newspaper rustling, then a sharp, crackling sound that could only have been the paper being knocked out of his hand.

"Why did you do that? I told you you've got the wrong man!"

Jack's voice was lower now but I could still hear every word. "Answer my question, Red. Did you continue your affair with Carolyn Crumbe after she moved up here?"

"I didn't know she was anywhere near here."

"You knew she was here, you both worked at the high school. Did you help her get that job?"

A long silence, then, "No."

Cookie.

I shivered, my teeth chattered, I couldn't control them, I was terrified they might hear me.

"You're refusing to answer questions that could lead to an obstruction of justice charge, Red. I'm going to give you one more chance."

"And then what?"

"Then all bets are off."

"Just for the record, Jack, although you didn't ask me, I didn't have anything to do with any of those murders. Please go find your killer and leave me alone."

Another long silence. "If that's the way you want it, Red, but I'll be back."

I heard footsteps and the front door open and close. Papers rustled and the chair squeaked again as Red pushed it back. I inched silently toward the counter, laid my packages back on the counter without making a sound, then opened the side screen door.

Jack stood on the sidewalk by his car, looking back at the house. I walked toward him, still irritated because of his attitude that morning, but at the same time I had to feel sorry for him because of the anguished expression that swept over his face when he saw me. I bumped into my porch chair, looked down and sank into it, trying not to cry.

Cookie.

Red had been having an affair with Carolyn Crumbe and I'd never suspected a thing.

Jack walked quickly toward me. "Raven..." I could barely see him through my tears.

He cupped his hands around my face and wiped the tears away with his thumbs. Such a gentle, reassuring touch, but at the same time I felt a shock all the way down to my toes. He must have felt it too, because he yanked his hands away as though he'd just touched an open flame.

"Ah, God, Raven." He shook his head. "You heard everything, didn't you?"

Heard everything.

I looked around, frantic. The flowers in my hanging baskets needed trimming, there were brown edges everywhere. The reds were okay, so were the yellows, but I'd have to clip the oranges and wasn't that the way life always seemed to turn out, something so beautiful always turned up with brown edges just when you least expected it.

"I'm so, so sorry," he almost whispered. "I wouldn't have hurt you like that for anything in the world, you have to know I wouldn't do that, Raven. I'm sorry about this morning, it was just—" He shook his head. "Dammit. Never mind. I thought you were out for the afternoon, Red said you were. I don't know what else to say."

I looked up at him. "Is it true, all those things you were saying in there?"

He gave a heavy sigh. "According to my reports it is, unless he's telling the truth and they've got him mixed up with somebody else, but I don't—Raven, he never told you anything about his past, did he." His last words, spoken so quickly, were a statement not a question.

I shook my head. "He never talked about it. I guess I know why, if all those things are true."

Deep sadness darkened his eyes and his fingers flexed as he moved toward me again but he stopped and pulled back.

"Raven, you understand I'd never do anything to hurt you, don't you?" His words seemed to float toward me. "This morning I was just being stupid. I did give Hopscotch the brownies as soon as you left and I'm terribly sorry about everything you heard, but I still have to do my job. I'm so sorry."

He turned away and headed for his car, glancing back at me over my shoulder. I could only watch him walk away.

Yes, I understood all right, but unimaginable pain was pushing everything else aside.

He got into his car, switched on the ignition, still looking at me, and pulled away from the curb.

I watched his car turn the corner, then my head sank down onto my arms and this time I didn't even try to hold back the tears.

I don't know how long I sat there until I felt a soft hand on my back. I raised my head.

A tiny lady with white hair, wearing a housedress and tennis shoes, stood patting my shoulder, making soothing sounds.

"Who are you?" I whispered.

She smiled and gave my shoulder another gentle pat. "Child, I'm your brand new next door neighbor. My name's Kimberley, Kimberley Clarke. I saw you sitting here so troubled and I came over to see if I could do anything to help." She shook her finger, reminding me of one of the teachers in elementary school. "But don't you go telling my son or his wife you saw me walking out here."

I glanced at the wheelchair parked at the back of her house. "Why not?"

Kimberley pulled out a chair and lowered herself into it. "Those idiots think I can't walk. I just let them think it. Some days I actually can't, very well anyhow, but they're gone, and today I can, so here I am. Now, what's got all those tears messing up that pretty face of yours?"

"How did you know I was crying?"

Kimberley chuckled. "I have my window up there." She pointed at the small window I'd noticed but never given much thought to. "I see things from up there nobody else sees. Keeps a body entertained most of the time, but I could see you were crying." She fished a tissue out of her pocket and handed it to me. "Here. This'll take care of it for now. I always keep one with me. You never know when one'll come in handy. What's your name, by the way?"

I took the tissue and wiped my eyes. "I'm Raven," I said, sniffling. "Thank you for the tissue."

"You're welcome. So now, what's bothering you, Raven? I'm just an old lady, but I've seen plenty of troubles in my time. Maybe I can help."

"Nobody can help. I just heard something terrible but I'll have to deal with it."

"Was it something about the dead body they found in your yard?" Kimberley's blue eyes sparkled and narrowed at the same time.

"It has something to do with that, yes. Did you see the body?"

She nodded. "I saw them find it."

"You didn't see who put it there, did you?"

She smiled. "If I did I'd have to be crazier than I am to say so, wouldn't I? That'd put a body in danger pretty fast, I'd think."

I felt my face flush. "If you did see something you have to say so. They think my husband did it."

"Has he been arrested?"

"No, but I just heard the chief of police talking to him, and from what he said, I know that's what they think."

"And what do you think?"

I stared through the tabletop and down to the criss-cross shadowed pattern the sun made on the concrete porch. "I don't know what to think. I just found out he knew the first victim pretty well a long time ago, before he and I were married."

"So did my husband," said Kimberley, "but he's dead now."

I looked up. "I'm so sorry. When did he die?"

"Oh," she waved her hand and shrugged, "a while back."

"How well did your husband know her?" I felt my face flaming with embarrassment that I'd asked such a personal question. "Forgive me, that's really none of my business."

Kimberley's face twisted into a wry grimace that made the lines around her eyes and mouth deepen. "He knew her well enough to give her money down in the lower forty-eight so she could get a teaching degree. And well enough to leave her a ton of oil stocks when he died."

My jaw dropped. "You knew he was giving her money?"

"I knew about her in Houston. I didn't know she'd moved up here or anything about the oil stock until the day his will was read. I wondered why he wanted so badly to build a house here. He probably helped her get her job. He was the one who bought this property and set up the whole house deal."

"But why did you still move here after he was gone? You could have sold the property."

Kimberley smiled. "Well, I like the feel of the whole town. It's a nice little place most of the time and people here pretty much seem to mind their own business."

She rubbed her arms. I saw that and realized it was growing chilly with oncoming cloud shadows. "My son likes it here, too," she said. "He came here a few times with my husband, so he was all for the move. He has a good job waiting in the oil company where my husband was CEO as soon as he finishes one more engineering course. He's been such a lazy son of a—well, I guess I shouldn't say bitch, should I?"

She laughed. "Might give people the wrong idea about me. But the truth is, he's been living off me for a long time and it's time he got off his dead butt and did some real work for a change. His wife's not much better. I mostly just sit back and laugh at them. I manage to keep them somewhat off-balance."

"He didn't inherit money of his own from your husband?"

"No. My husband didn't have any use for him. The only two people mentioned in his will, aside from the phrase that specifically disinherited my son, were myself and Carolyn Crumbe."

"If your husband didn't have any use for him, how did he wind up with a job in the same company?"

"I pulled a few strings myself. I had to do something. My husband was pretty much justified in his opinion, but I want to give him one more chance. He's had a lot of problems. Drugs, drinking, gambling, you name it. I'm just waiting to see how he does with his new career before I completely give up on him."

I thought back over all the things she'd said. "Why didn't you contest the will when Carolyn got the stock?"

Kimberley smiled. "Oh, I thought about it, but it actually wasn't that much. Enough to keep her comfortable for a while, if she wanted to sell it, maybe. I don't know whether she did or not."

"You didn't hate her?"

"Lord no, child! She took care of what I didn't want to. Why should I hate her for that? Besides, think of the scandal if I did. I just let it go. He left me more than I'll ever need in my lifetime anyhow."

"But how could you just ignore something like that?"

"Oh, child, the crowd we ran with back in Houston, that sort of thing happens all the time. You either turn your head and put up with it or you raise a stink and find yourself out in the cold. I liked my lifestyle just the way it was, I wasn't about to change it over something that unimportant."

I wondered how she could seem so sophisticated and yet so uncomplicated at the same time. "So to you, adultery isn't important?"

Kimberley smiled. "Is that why you were crying?"

"Well, partly, yes. I do think it is."

Her eyes narrowed. "And you consider it adultery if he slept with Carolyn before he knew you? How long ago was that?"

"At least twenty years, maybe more, but the thing is, did he sleep with her after she moved up here."

She half-smiled. "Did he?"

"I don't know." Yes I did. *Cookie.*

"What would you do if you found out he did?"

"I don't know that either. In my family divorce is unheard of. It may sound silly in this day and age, but that's the way I was raised. Nobody in my family ever got a divorce."

"Well, child," Kimberley said, patting my hand as she rose, "you do have a lot to think about. I'll leave you to your thoughts since you seem to have calmed down, but I'll tell you this. There are other ways to get even with a cheating man."

"I don't want to get even, I just don't know if I can ever live in the same house with him again, but I don't know if I could divorce him either. I don't know what I'll do if that turns out to be true."

Of course it was true, and somehow my son knew it. *Or my father did.*

Kimberley turned away. "We'll talk again soon. Just keep your ears and eyes open." She turned back, her eyes flashing some sort of signal I didn't understand. "There's a very bad wind blowing through this town right now, Raven. Look out for your children."

I watched her struggle with her wheelchair as she pushed it toward the front of her house, wondering at the strangeness of this whole conversation and the look in her eyes when she'd said, "Look out for your children." Did she know more than she was saying? Were my children at risk? Was I?

I sat back, thinking for a few minutes, trying to work up enough nerve to go inside. Did I want to confront Red? Or did I want to just keep my mouth shut and my eyes open, as my father always used to tell me?

Don't ever lie, but don't tell everything you know either, daughter. Everything you need will come to you when it's time.

The sky had that peculiar late afternoon, almost muted pastel color, still light but changing slightly, just enough to cast faint forecasts of shadows on the surrounding mountaintops. I headed inside, glancing up at Kimberley's window.

She was already there, sitting perfectly still, looking down, an eerie reminder of Mother Bates in *Psycho*.

Kimberley knew a lot more about the first murder than she was letting on. I couldn't shake the feeling that something was very, very odd about her. She seemed nice enough, but on the other hand, Carolyn's body...and then seeing Kit...

Both had happened in this yard after Kimberley moved here.

FORTY ONE

The minute Jack had touched her face, he knew.
Dammit!
He drove two blocks, then pulled over because he couldn't drive any further and sat with his head against the steering wheel, holding onto the sides so hard his fingers ached.
Dammit, dammit, dammit!
After all the years spent sliding away from any commitment, after swearing he'd never fall so hard for any woman he couldn't live without her—after all that, one touch and he knew he was lost. Her cheeks were so sweet and warm, they reminded him of a soft brown Indian blanket he had on his bed when he was a boy. He wanted to grab her and bury his nose in her hair and inhale the scent of her like he'd never taken a true breath in his whole life before.
Dammit!
All the pros and cons ran past his eyes like a kinetoscope from the late 1800's, where the pictures flipped so fast when people looked through the peephole they looked as though they were moving.
Lord, she was beautiful. She was decent, everything he'd ever thought a woman should be and he wanted her more than he'd ever wanted anyone in his life, and he didn't just want her. He loved her enough to want to spend the rest of his days and nights with her. But she was the wife of a man he was beginning to seriously suspect of three murders.
How could I have let this happen?
He switched on the ignition and drove to one of his favorite thinking spots in front of the community college housing units, a twenty-foot tall, carved wooden Indianhead, colorful and old and beautiful. He liked to sit in the squad car and stare at it, pondering things from time to time. He pulled over for a few minutes.

Okay. First things first. He'd go back to Carolyn's apartment and talk to her manager, see if Red had been seen going in or out of Carolyn's apartment before she was killed. Then have his men check with her neighbors again, see who went in and out besides Hopscotch, see where that led him. If it was Hopscotch and he was guilty of Carolyn's murder, this charge would override the parole charge in Minnesota. In that case, he'd sit in this jail a long time. He switched on the ignition and had almost pulled out when a new question occurred to him.

Why the hell hadn't he stayed in Dallas, where he was one of many detectives? Here, he was it, along with a few local officers, all of whom had no heavy-duty experience except for Bill.

On the other hand, if he'd never come here he'd never have met Raven, the one bright spot in his life, although he knew she had no idea what he was thinking and feeling. With all he was doing to her family, she was going to detest the sight of him anyhow. He didn't know what to do about that, but he did know what to do about his job. He gave the Indianhead a quick salute, pulled away from the curb and headed, for the second time, to Carolyn's apartment house.

"I'm surprised to see you here again," said the manager when she answered the door.

He looked around for a chair, took out his recorder and clicked it on. "I need to ask you a few more questions about Carolyn Crumbe. Please state your name."

She blinked. "DeeDee McCoy. I thought you knew that."

"My recorder doesn't. You've been manager here for how long now?"

"Ever since these apartments were built, about ten years or so."

"I need you to think back and tell me if you remember anyone who may have visited Carolyn here from time to time."

"You mean a boyfriend?" She grinned.

"Any man."

Her eyes lit up. "Yes! There was an older gentleman who used to go in and out, he had his own key. That started about oh, eight years or so ago, right after she moved in. I haven't seen him for a couple of years now, though."

"Description?"

She scratched her head and for the first time he realized she was wearing a wig, because it had moved about a quarter of an inch when she scratched. She unconsciously adjusted it to its original location.

"I would guess he was about sixty-five, or seventy. Gray-white hair, heavy built, very well dressed. He always wore a suit and tie. I don't think he lived anywhere around here, I never saw him anywhere else but here. Does that help?"

"It might. Did you ever hear a name mentioned?"

"No."

"Did he come around often?"

"Maybe once a month. He'd stay overnight, leave early the next morning, then I wouldn't see him again for a while."

"Did he drive a vehicle?"

"He always came and left in a taxi."

Good, he could check that out.

"How about any of the men here in town? Did you see anyone else coming around frequently, or even infrequently?"

She shrugged. "I don't think so except for Hopscotch, but I already told your officers about that."

"You're sure there were no other men from around here at all?"

"I never saw any and I probably would have, I'm almost always here." She thought a minute. "Her classes were all in the morning. So she would come home, then disappear for an hour or so early in the afternoon. That happened a lot."

"She never said where she went?"

"No, Carolyn was very close-mouthed. I really didn't know much about her at all."

"Unfortunately, neither did anyone else." He stood and headed for the door. "Thanks, you've been a real big help."

He opened the door and left, climbed in his vehicle and looked back. She was standing at the door watching him. He took out his cell and called the cab company to ask them to check back a few years for someone who would have taken a cab to DeeDee's address about once a month. He heard papers shuffling, drawers opening and closing. No computer printout happening there.

The supervisor finally came back and told him the only information he had of fares to that address was from the oil company office or the airport, and the passenger always paid cash. No description, no name. His driver had moved somewhere down to the lower forty-eight a year or so ago, he didn't know where.

Another dead end, although Jack could track the driver down if he had to. He had just put his cell back in its holder when it rang.

"Chief, this is Bill. Look, have you ever met Kimi, John North's wife?"

Jack thought a minute. "Can't say I have. Why?"

"I stopped downtown at the tent the Alaska Natives set up, I just thought I'd take a look around, see what they have this year. My wife wants another Ulu, she gave hers away last fall when her aunt was here. Anyhow, Kimi's there, selling something I think you should take a look at."

"What is it?"

"She's got some masks, one of them's the spitting image of the one painted on the rock we found with Carolyn's body. Looks like it could even be the same paint, but for sure it's the same face. I asked her where she got them and she said John makes them on weekends when he leaves Klem's place and goes home."

"You know her pretty well?"

"Naw, not really, I saw them in town together once and he introduced her to me. I recognized her and went over to say hello. Chief, I really think you need to take a look at this mask."

"I want it, but I'll let you handle the buy, since you already looked at it. Got any money on you?"

"I have some but not enough to buy one of these masks, it's the real deal, not one of those replicas like they sell in the stores. Hell, all of this authentic stuff's expensive."

"Yeah, I know. Okay, look, don't say anything to John's wife, meet me at the station in five minutes, I'll give you the cash so you can go back and buy it. Just tell her it's a gift for your wife."

They hung up, leaving Jack to ponder this new development, if it was one. It was going to cost him some serious cash, but this might be the break they needed.

Once a while in the summertime, after the tourists arrived, Alaska Natives would come in from the bush with their authentic handmade wares and set up tents and sell them. Beautiful stuff, Jack had filled his house with them.

Wooden bear claw salad servers, authentic Alaska Native dolls that went for four, five hundred dollars and more. Wooden bowls that could never be replicated, they sold fast no matter what they cost, hundreds of dollars, some of them. Rounded knives, Ulus, originally made for cutting up whale blubber. Miniature fur-topped Mukluks, attached with strips of leather to hang on walls in the lower forty-eight for those lucky enough to find them.

This didn't happen often, these things were time and labor intensive, as the dolls were, and not many people knew how to make them anymore. Another dying art, along with their language. Smarter tourists knew these things were real and some came back to Valdez time and again just to buy more of them.

Jack hadn't understood at first why Valdez didn't have many Alaska Natives living within the city limits, because he'd found most of them to be good and decent people. Even so, Valdez had grown into a small town of around four thousand people.

Built in the late 1800's by shipping companies for men looking to grab a stake in the Klondike gold fields, Valdez had been expanded later to create housing for those who came to work on the pipeline. It was pretty much a Caucasian town, a fishing and vacation village except for those who worked for the oil companies. The Native villages themselves were far, far out of town, where not many vacationers ever ventured. Jack had visited a few, and then like everybody else, headed back to the world where he was most comfortable.

It was then he had realized why most Alaska Natives, at least the ones around Valdez, stayed out in the bush. They didn't have to straddle two different cultures out there.

A half hour later, Bill brought the mask and Jack was two hundred fifty dollars poorer. Sure enough, it was exactly the same face, painted in exactly the same way. It might not mean anything but then again, it might.

"Wrap it up good," Jack said, "and get it to the post office right away, send it special delivery. I want the paint compared to the paint on both of those rocks, and I want it fast."

FORTY TWO

After Kimberley left, I went back in through the kitchen to the living room where Red was reading the paper. He looked up and smiled. "Hi, honey. Need any help in the kitchen?"

He'd never offered to help in the kitchen, even when we brought our newborns home from the hospital.

"I think I can handle it."

He followed me into the kitchen anyhow, spotted the large bag of canned soup and vegetables I'd bought earlier and reached into it, pulling things out and setting them on the countertop. He looked up, obviously perplexed. "Where do these go?"

"Top left cabinet, right behind you."

He managed to empty the whole bag. When he was done he folded it and looked around. "Where do you keep these?"

"In the garage." I watched him fumble with the bag, then head out to the garage.

He came back smiling and rubbing his hands. "What's for dinner? Can I help? Peel some potatoes, cut up something for salad?"

I looked up. "Sure. Thanks. You can peel five potatoes."

He looked around, pulled open a couple of drawers, riffled through them. "Where's the peeler?"

"Far left drawer."

He found the old peeler, stared at it, and then looked up. "The potatoes?"

I pointed at the potato bin that had been standing in the same spot since we built our house. He reached in, took a few out, walked to the sink, turned back toward me. A slow flush moved up his neck and covered his face but he managed a half-embarrassed smile. "How do you work this thing?"

I sighed, took the peeler out of his hand and began to peel the potatoes myself.

He watched me for a couple of minutes, looking confused, and finally said, "Okay then, anything else I can do?"

I didn't answer. He came over behind me and put his arms around my waist, nuzzling my neck. I finished peeling, ran the water, rinsed them off, dropped them in the pot. He still had his arms around me. I felt his hands move up under my breasts, squeezing my nipples.

"I really do love you. You know that, don't you, baby?"

How long had it been since he'd said that? I didn't know. I only knew if I had any doubt about his betrayal before, it was set in granite now.

I didn't answer, just moved a little to free my breasts from his grip. I felt him hesitate, stiffen slightly behind me, then he patted my rear and kissed the back of my neck.

"I guess I'm not much good in the kitchen. I'll just go back in the living room and leave you alone."

You do that. "Dinner will be ready in about a half hour." I turned to him, keeping my face deliberately impassive.

He gave me a half-smile and walked out of the room.

I heard the chair squeak as he settled back into it. I knew he was wondering if I'd overheard any of his conversation with Jack.

I wasn't going to say one word.

Not yet.

FORTY THREE

When I went to the police station at seven o'clock I saw Jack, still in his office, reading some papers. He looked up when I tapped on his door.

"It's seven o'clock," I said, still simmering. "Is it okay if I see Hopscotch for a few minutes now?"

He looked dismayed but I wasn't about to back down. "Give me a minute," he said. "I'll fix you up in the interview room."

"The brownies were nice," said Hopscotch a couple of minutes later, settling into a chair across the table from me. "Thank you."

I fumbled with my purse. "I don't know what to say now that I'm here."

"I understand." He smiled. "You look good."

"I wish I felt good. This has been a horrible day."

"Why?" He leaned across the table and touched my hand.

I looked toward the doorway. Jack was sitting across the hall, openly watching us and scowling.

I pulled my hand away. "I guess my troubles aren't as bad as yours. Why are you here, Hopscotch?" I glanced at Jack again. It was obvious he could hear every word we were saying.

"The problem I told you about. I'll take care of it, it's nothing for you to worry about, Raven, so please don't."

"Will you come back to Valdez after you take care of it?"

He looked down, then across the hall, avoiding my eyes. "We'll have to see about that." He inched a little closer to the table. "I will if I can. I'll give it my best."

I moved my watch around on my wrist and looked back up at him. "You've lost your British accent all of a sudden. You're not really from England, are you?"

He chuckled softly. "No. I'm sorry I had to lie to you about that."

"Me, too." I nodded in Jack's direction and lowered my voice. "You know he's listening, don't you?"

"Of course. I understand, though. He has to."

"You haven't been accused of anything here, have you?"

"No, but I can tell you for sure I haven't done anything wrong here, as far as I know." He looked away. "Other than a few things I had to lie about."

"Do they think you had anything to do with the murders?"

"I don't know what they think. I'm just waiting for someone from Minnesota to come pick me up."

I nodded toward Jack. "I don't understand what's bothering him."

"I do," said Hopscotch, half-smiling.

"Well, explain it to me. He was horrible this morning."

"You really don't know?" He was still smiling.

"No, except..."

"Except what?"

"Did you know that Red used to know Carolyn?"

His smile vanished. "Yes," he admitted.

"Did you ever see them together?"

"She mentioned she'd known him for a long time."

I turned toward the door. Jack didn't appear to be listening, he was furiously scribbling something on a pad of paper. I leaned across the table and whispered, "What else did she tell you?"

He looked down, cracking his knuckles, then he looked back up. "Raven, why do you want to know things that might hurt you?"

"Because Jack thinks Red could have murdered Carolyn."

Hopscotch leaned back in his chair, silent for a minute. "Well, he could have," he finally said.

"So he was seeing her again here?"

"Raven, please—" His eyes were dark with sorrow. "I don't want to hurt you, but—"

"Okay, folks, time's up!" Jack stomped across the hall toward us.

"But it's not even seven thirty yet!" I protested.

"I said time's up. Come on, Hopscotch, let's go." He jerked Hopscotch's chair back.

"But I—" My mouth was wide open with disbelief.

Jack led Hopscotch down toward the end of the hall and ushered him into his cell. I heard the bars clank shut.

He came back into the interview room. "Raven, you need to go on home now. Please."

"Why did you do that?"

"Do what?"

"Interrupt us just as he was about to tell me something."

Jack sighed. "He doesn't have to tell you anything, Raven. He has to tell me if he knows anything about those murders."

"He didn't say he knew anything about that."

"Raven." Jack slid into the chair Hopscotch had vacated and leaned toward me. "There's something you don't understand about Hopscotch."

"What?"

He held up his hand. "People aren't always what you think, Raven. You can't take them at face value because they'll show you the face they want you to see. Do you understand what I'm saying?"

I shook my head, watching his eyes, suddenly realizing they weren't brown, as I'd always thought, but hazel, with tiny flecks of green. Easy to get lost in.

He sighed. "Let me put it this way. You don't know Hopscotch. You think you do, but you can't trust him to tell the truth about anything. He was in some serious trouble before he came here. He's in more serious trouble now. He can say anything that he thinks might benefit him and it may or may not be true."

He spread his hands open. "Look, I've seen this too many times in my career as a law enforcement officer. People lie. They lie for all kinds of reasons, but you have to understand, they do lie. Most people aren't like you, Raven. I doubt you even know how to lie, I know the code of your people. I make it my business to know these things. In his case, if he thinks he needs to lie for any reason, then no matter how he feels about you, he'll lie to you and anyone else. Don't for a minute think he won't."

"I don't believe you."

"No? Well, try this on for size, then this conversation is over. His name is not what you think it is and that's only for starters. You basically know nothing about this man, Raven. You just think you do."

He stood. "Look, I'd love to have you stay and talk to me, but I have a lot of work to do."

I raised my eyes. "If you know I don't lie, then you at least believe the things I've told you, right?"

"I believe you're not lying because you believe those things, Raven, and you may be right about everything, who knows? All I can do is work with what I can prove to be true."

"I understand," I said, pulling myself up and heading for the door. I stopped and turned back. "But I think you're wrong about Hopscotch."

FORTY FOUR

Jack left the station, heading for Kimberley's house. This was a long shot and he knew it, but if Carolyn Crumbe had been seeing Red again, if by chance she had ever come to his house when she disappeared in the afternoons as Dee Dee had said, maybe Kimberley might have seen something. Well, it was worth a try. When he pulled into her driveway he turned on his recorder and stuck it in his shirt pocket.

Her face brightened when she saw him. "Hey, hey! Look what the bird dog just drug in."

He climbed the steps to the front porch, where she was sitting alone. She set her book down and waved him over to the porch swing. "Sit," she ordered.

He sat, glad to see her looking like she might be lucid this evening. "Where's your family, Kimberley?"

"I don't know, out for a while. Why?"

"I want to ask you a couple of questions and I don't want anybody else around when I do."

"That sounds pretty serious." Her eyebrows formed the same sideways wavy question marks they always did.

"It could be," he allowed.

She tapped on her knees with her fingertips, watching him. "Well, let's have it."

He leaned forward. "Kimberley, I know you spend a lot of time up at that window when your family's gone."

"So far we're in agreement."

Good. She was lucid.

"I know you want to be a good neighbor."

"And now you're going to ask me not to, am I right?"

"Depends on whether it's more important for you to help me solve three murders or be a good neighbor."

She grinned. "I take excitement any way I can get it nowadays. Shoot."

"First, did you know Carolyn Crumbe?"

Her eyes grew wary, drooping slightly.

"You're talking about the corpse they took out of the back yard next door?"

He nodded.

"Why would I know her?"

"I was just asking if you did."

Her eyes narrowed. "But what made you ask? Did someone tell you I knew her?"

"No."

She sat silent for a minute. He could hear a couple of birds in the distance, probably getting on to their dinnertime. He turned away to look, then back at Kimberley.

She was studying him. "I might have seen her at one time or another," she said slowly, "or I might not have. What are you getting at?"

He drew a deep breath. "I know you haven't been here long, but I need to know if you ever saw her going into Red and Raven's house in the afternoon, or anytime, for that matter."

He sat back, watching. She was a cool one. She didn't move a muscle but her eyes began to glaze over.

"Hey," she said, now grinning, "you wanta go in the house and watch a couple of my movies?"

Damn. Gone again that fast. Or acting like it.

"Kimberley, please," he pleaded, putting on his best hopeful little boy look. "I need to know whether Carolyn was coming here at any time recently while Raven was at work."

"I did over five hundred of them movies," she said, plucking at her skirt.

"Kimberley, look at me."

She looked up. "You wanta see 'em?"

"Not right now. I want you to help me, okay? Just tell me the truth."

"I did tell you the truth. I have 'em upstairs in my room. In the closet. In a box under some blankets."

"No, Kimberley. The question was about Carolyn Crumbe. After you moved here, did you ever see her going into Red's house when Raven was at work, in the afternoon or any time? Did you ever see them together?"

She looked past him, focusing on something far in the distance. He turned to see what she was looking at.

"Them flowers up on the mountains," she said. "Ain't they pretty?"

"Yes they are. Kimberley?"

She was still totally focused on the mountainside, but a host of different emotions ran across her face, one after the other.

"I'm thinking," she said.

He smiled. "I can see that."

"About what I want to say."

"I understand, but you realize I have to find out who killed three innocent people in this town, don't you?"

She was quiet for a few more minutes.

He waited.

Finally she turned back to him. "Maybe they weren't all that innocent."

He nodded. "Go on."

"You know, sonny, Raven's a very nice woman."

"Yes, she is," he said.

She peered into his eyes. "You're in love with her, aren't you?"

He almost choked and for a minute couldn't answer, but he finally cleared his throat. "Kimberley, if you know anything, I'd surely appreciate it if you'd just tell me."

"I don't want to be part of anything that might hurt Raven. There's been enough of that already."

"I'll do everything I can to protect both her and you, but I can't do anything until you tell me what you saw."

"Well, the problem is, I didn't see all of it."

He frowned. "What does that mean?"

She pulled a tissue out of her pocket and blew her nose. "I don't know anything about the others."

"What others?"

"The boy and the other woman, the other victims."

"Ah, I understand. That's okay. Just tell me what you know about Carolyn. Please."

"I can tell you she was not a nice woman."

"How do you know that?"

"Because..." She hesitated.

"How, Kimberley?"

"Well, Carolyn had a long-time affair with my husband when we lived in Houston."

His jaw dropped open. "Your husband?"

"Yes. He gave her a lot of money during that time. When I found out about the money, I thought maybe she was blackmailing him because he had good standing in the community. Wealthy oil man, tons of influence, you know."

He nodded and gulped, still trying to hide his astonishment at this bizarre turn of events.

"I just looked the other way. That's the way we handled those things in Houston, I'm sure you know what I mean."

"Yes."

"Anyhow, as I said, I ignored the affair."

"Your husband's dead, is that correct?"

"Yes. Two years now."

Bingo!

"What color was his hair?"

"White by that time. Anyhow, another reason I ignored the affair was that even though I'd been a porno star, that was true, you know, I'd risen above all that long before I met him. I was the perfect society wife and he knew it. I knew he'd never divorce me for an out-and-out whore, which she was then, that's how he met her. When it all started with her I just never took it seriously. It went on for years, then I heard she was going to college and he was paying for it. After that she disappeared from Houston and I figured she was out of the picture, then I heard some time later he'd moved her someplace in the Northwest and helped her get a job teaching."

She grinned. "I actually thought it was funny that she was a teacher. Anyhow, after he died and the will was read, that's when I found out he'd left her a lot of stock." She shrugged. "Even that didn't bother me, I had plenty without it."

"When did you find out she was here?"

"Well, to my surprise, right after we moved here. I saw her going into the house next door in the afternoon every few days."

Bingo again! "Did she know you'd seen her?"

"No. I was in my chair and she never looked up."

"Was Red home at the time?"

"He was the only one home at the time. Because school was still in session. The children were at school, and Raven was working. He apparently had some afternoons off."

"How long did she stay?" *Thank you, Lord, for reminding me to turn on my recorder.*

"Long enough, I expect. She was a whore. Get it done, you know? Before the children come home? Only, once one of them did."

"Which one?"

She shook her head with disgust. "The little boy."

Timmy. "Can you tell me what happened?"

"I only saw the child slip into the house, then run back out again at top speed about four, five minutes later."

"Did Red come outside after him?"

"No. About twenty minutes or so later, Carolyn came out, got in her car and left. He left a few minutes later."

"How long was that before Carolyn's body was found in Red's yard?"

She looked up at the sky, thinking. "About two weeks or so. I saw y'all down there and when I saw the body lying on the ground I knew it was her. I got down from the window and off that chair fast because I didn't want to be involved."

"How were you so sure it was Carolyn, when her head was missing?"

"The tattoos."

"When did you see her tattoos?"

"In the photos I found after my husband died."

"Do you still have them?"

She shook her head. "Nope. I burned them the same day I found them."

"Did you see anything or anyone in the back yard before she was found there, maybe late at night?"

"No."

"Do you have any reason to believe Red murdered her?"

"I wouldn't at all put it past him. I hate to see him get away with what he's been doing to Raven. From what I can tell, she doesn't deserve that."

He had to silently agree. He said his goodbyes, left and headed back to the station to talk to Hopscotch. He'd had a couple of days now to think things over after he'd refused to say a word to Bill all the way back down to Valdez, but he hadn't been talking to anyone but Raven.

This was going to be tricky. He hadn't been charged with anything here or asked for a lawyer. He probably would soon, though.

Jack swung into the station, stopped to talk with the night dispatcher for a few minutes, then headed toward Hopscotch's cell.

"I already know all about it," Hopscotch said when he tapped on the bars.

"Know all about what?"

"The state of Minnesota's not in any big hurry to pick me up and drag me back there. I heard you talking to one of your men."

"You heard that all the way back here? Even though we were talking low?"

"Yep. Same way I heard you and Raven bickering over my brownies this morning. I have twenty-twenty hearing."

"Very funny, Hopscotch. Thanks for telling me."

"Think nothing of it. Can I offer you a drink or a sandwich? I think we have some ham left. We seem to be out of mayo, though. I'll have to speak to the chef."

"You're just a laugh a minute, aren't you."

"I try," said Hopscotch, stretching and yawning.

"Try some other time. I need to talk to you."

"At this hour? Isn't that cruel and unusual punishment?"

"Call the police and file a complaint." Jack unlocked the cell. "Follow me."

Hopscotch rolled out of the bunk, fished around for his shoes, took his time putting them on, stood and saluted.

"Seaman First Class Maloney reporting for duty, Sir!" He marched out of the cell, did a smart left turn, and halted.

"You let me know when you're finished with your routine, Hopscotch, but I can tell you it's already getting old. First door to your left."

They walked into the interview room.

"Looks familiar," remarked Hopscotch. "I think though, since I'll be staying for a while, I'd like to order new window coverings. Venetian blinds are so Seventies, don't you think?"

"Sit down, Hopscotch."

Hopscotch swept his hand toward the other chair. "After you. I insist."

Jack put his hand on Hopscotch's shoulder and pressed. "I've had a bad day, Hopscotch. Sit the hell down. Now."

Hopscotch sat down, sighing heavily. "Whatever happened to gentility?"

Jack pulled out the other chair and hunched over the table. "Put that in your complaint and let's cut the crap. I have some questions, I want answers."

"Excuse me, am I being charged with something?" Hopscotch leaned back, smiling.

"You're not being charged with anything. Since Minnesota isn't in any hurry for you, you're my guest for the time being. As a good guest, I'm sure you want to be helpful. You can thank a rash of murders in Minneapolis for your extended vacation, by the way. Where were you this past weekend, starting from when you got off the plane in Anchorage Friday afternoon?"

Hopscotch chuckled. "Well, I can assure you I definitely wasn't traveling between Anchorage and Minneapolis."

"I didn't ask where you weren't. Where were you?"

"Drinking in Anchorage."

"You're hell-bent on making this hard on yourself, aren't you?

Where, exactly, were you drinking, and who, exactly, were you drinking with?"

Hopscotch looked out the window. "That's a hard one to answer, mate. I usually do my drinking alone."

"Try anyway. Where did you start?"

"In my car."

"Your car?"

"My car. I keep a bottle there for emergencies."

"What do you consider an emergency?"

He shrugged. "When I get thirsty."

"Where did you buy your first drink?"

"That day? The Moose's Tooth, over on Seward."

"Can anyone verify that?"

"Maybe."

"How long were you there?"

"I don't remember."

"What the hell do you mean, you don't remember?"

"I get drunk quickly, mate. I got drunk. Quickly."

"Where'd you go next?"

"I couldn't tell you. I was drunk."

"What about Saturday?"

"I don't know."

"Sunday?"

"No idea."

"You're telling me that you don't know where you were, all weekend?"

Hopscotch sighed. "That's what I'm telling you."

"You stayed drunk all weekend?"

"I guess I did. I woke up in my car Sunday afternoon. I've never blacked out like that before. I did this weekend."

Jack stretched back, eyeing him. "So on top of everything else, besides depriving yourself of an alibi while two more murders were being committed here, you're saying that you have a serious drinking problem?"

"Looks like it, mate. I never really thought I did, I always stopped sometime Saturday to give myself plenty of time to sober up before I headed back to Valdez. This time I didn't."

Jack closed his eyes and rubbed his forehead. "You already know we can't verify your whereabouts the week before Carolyn's body was discovered."

"I do. I told you, I go to work and I come home."

"And sometimes you went to Carolyn's."

"Sometimes," he agreed. "But I wasn't seeing Carolyn by that time."

Jack's eyes snapped open. "You didn't tell us that before."

"Nobody asked me."

"Why weren't you seeing Carolyn by that time?"

"She told me she was also seeing Red. I'm not into double-dipping, so if you'll pardon the expression, I pulled out."

"When exactly did this happen?"

"About two, three weeks before she was murdered."

"Did you know Kit well?"

"Kit?"

"The kid who was murdered."

"I don't know one kid from the other."

"Was that a yes or a no?"

"A definite no."

"Did you know Vera?"

"I knew *of* Vera."

"You knew what about Vera?"

"I knew you were shagging her."

"Where'd you hear that?"

"I don't remember. A lot of people knew it."

"Did you ever see her?"

"Yeah, somebody pointed her out to me once."

"Who?"

"I'll have to think on that, mate. Offhand, I don't remember."

Jack stared up at the ceiling, then back. Hopscotch was looking straight at him. Either he was innocent as hell or he was a damn good liar. Scratch that. He already knew Hopscotch was more than a good liar, he was a regular Walter Mitty.

"You know it's possible you're in a lot of trouble here if we can't verify your whereabouts, don't you, Hopscotch?"

"If you want to count the way things look, I suppose I could be. But I had nothing to do with those murders. Never even thought of something like that."

"You did once," Jack reminded him.

Hopscotch flushed. "I had good reason then, and I didn't think about it at all, actually. It was over before I realized what I'd done."

"Were you drinking then, too?"

"Matter of fact, I was."

Jack sighed. "Okay, we're done for tonight. But I have the feeling we're not done for good."

"Am I dismissed then, Sir?"

"Let's go, Hopscotch. Your feather bed's waiting."

They reached the cell, Jack opened the door, Hopscotch walked in. Jack started to walk away then turned back. "You want a little piece of advice, Hopscotch?"

Hopscotch waved him away. "Don't bother, mate. I realize that you mean well, but I've heard it all before. Besides, where I'm headed now, they don't serve cocktails."

FORTY FIVE

The next day was supposed to have been Timmy's appointment with Dr. Randell but it was cancelled because of some sort of emergency the doctor's assistant didn't explain. We'd see him in two days at the regular time.

    I went through my early morning routine thinking about Red, trying to reconcile what I knew to be true. He was good at subterfuge, that was for sure, because I'd never noticed anything different about him. He'd always been highly sexed, eager to make love. He hadn't changed a bit there.

    Maybe it was because I was now starting to imagine things. In all fairness, I had to admit that even if Red had been seeing Carolyn again, it didn't necessarily mean he killed her. Did he really have it in him to kill anyone, much less three people? I didn't know. There was a lot I'd never known about him.

    Wasn't it true that rape was just one step short of murder, that men who raped often went on to kill, a compulsive stepping-stone of increasing horror that no one else saw? I was sure I'd read that somewhere. Still, there were three murders now, and why would he have killed Kit and then the woman from the cruise ship?

    Unless...no. He couldn't have been sleeping with *two* other women—could he? Even if he had been, why would he kill both of them? Why Kit? Unless Kit knew something.

    I was putting dishes away when I realized I needed to talk to Jack about Red, since I still couldn't bring myself to believe Red had actually murdered anyone. Jack would just have to find his killer and leave my family alone to work out its problems. I'd find some way to cope.

    It all seemed so simple, put that way.

    I thought about it a few more minutes, then went upstairs to

Alice's room.

She was sitting at her vanity, desperately trying to weave her hair into French braids. Normally I would have helped, but not this time. "I have to go out for a little while, Alice."

Alice looked at my reflection in the mirror. "So?"

"I need you to watch Timmy. I'll tell Charlie too. I want all three of you to stay in the house and not let anyone in. I won't be gone long, but it's important."

Alice's mouth twisted into a grimace of disgust. "Oh, Mom, are you still afraid the boogyman'll come in here and—"

I felt my blood pressure rising. "Alice, stop it. I need your help. Promise me you won't open the door to anyone while I'm gone, okay?"

Alice rolled her eyes, nodded and turned her attention back to her hair.

I told Charlie the same thing although I realizied I was talking to a sleeping boy. I scratched a note and propped it against his clock, that was the best I could do. They'd be okay for an hour or so while I was gone.

I dialed the police station, saying a silent prayer that I'd be able to convince Jack to leave my family alone.

He came to the phone after a couple of minutes. "Hello, Raven. What can I do for you?"

"I need to talk to you in private."

There was a pause for a few seconds. "You can't come to the station?"

"I just think it'd be better if we had some privacy, if you can arrange that."

"Give me a second." I heard breathing and a sound like he might be drumming his fingertips on the desktop.

He came back online. "Okay, how about the city dock. Twenty minutes. I'll bring coffee and—you drink tea, don't you. I'll bring some. We can talk there. Nobody'll think anything of it even if they do see us."

I knew he was right. The city dock was a tranquil spot at the end of Hazelet Street where townspeople dropped by to watch otters play in the water. A quiet place to sit and think, completely out in the open. No one would think anything of it if they saw us standing by our cars talking.

I said yes, I'd meet him there.

I walked around the house, picked up a cup I found in the living room, straightened sofa pillows on my way to the kitchen, washed the cup and wiped out the sink, everything I could think of to procrastinate while I thought about what I wanted to say. I left the house ten minutes later still without any real plan in mind.

Jack was waiting for me, sipping a container of coffee when I pulled into a spot next to his car. Other than the two of us, no one else was there this morning. His eyes lit up when he saw me and even though I was still miffed with him over Hopscotch, I couldn't help but think what a really good-looking man he was. His short sleeved shirt fit tight across his chest. Much too tight for my comfort, I thought, when a twinge I'd rather not have felt at that moment shot through me.

His hand touched mine when he handed me a foam cup with a tea label hanging out and I felt the same twinge again. I took a sip and looked out over the water, avoiding his eyes.

He indicated an open donut box on his front fender. "Want one?"

"Not right now, thanks."

We stood sipping our drinks for a couple of minutes without saying anything more. The otters were nowhere to be seen but I hadn't expected they would be. Evenings, when more people were around, was their time to play and show off. But fish jumped in the water, sunlight reflecting on their blue and silver fins, and a couple of charter fishing boats crawled by, far out in the Sound.

I loved the smell of the water. I'd been there with my father many times, and I could still feel his presence hovering nearby. I also felt Jack's eyes on me even though he was facing the water.

"You have something to tell me, Raven?"

I stared at my cup, watching steam swirl up out of the opening. "Yes, but I'm almost afraid to."

He was still looking out over the Sound. "Please don't ever be afraid to tell me anything." He turned to face me. "What is it?"

I drew in a long, deep breath. "Jack, do you remember at the campground, when Charlie told you I said I saw Kit an hour or so after Doc Martin said he was killed?" I gasped at my own words. I hadn't meant to start that way.

He crossed his legs and leaned back against his car. "As it turns out, Raven, it's closer to two hours."

I clutched my cup, watching to be sure I didn't crush it. "Jack, I don't know how to explain this, I know you think I'm crazy—"

He made a waving motion. "Just relax, Raven. I don't know what's going on, but I don't think you're crazy. Stressed maybe, that's only natural."

"But that's not all that's been happening, Jack, and all of this started the day they found Carolyn's body in my yard. These things never happened to me before." I felt my face flush as I groped to find the right words.

"Look, Jack, there have been many times I've watched the fog roll down the mountainsides and felt I could hear the voices of relatives who are gone now. I know this can be explained away as wishful thinking, but you know the fog and the way it moves. It really does seem to pull you into a different place."

"That it does."

"But Jack, this is different. This is real."

"Okay. Start at the beginning and tell me everything." He smiled, obviously trying to reassure me.

"Jack, I have been hearing my father's voice coming from Timmy. Sometimes it's soft, like a whisper, and sometimes it's loud and it echoes all around me."

His eyes flickered and he turned away toward the water. "What does this voice say?"

Sweat trickled under my armpits. "The first time, Timmy was waving at his bedroom window but no one was there. When I asked him who he was waving at, he said, 'My grandfather is singing to me.' But his words were my father's voice and in our native language."

"Did Timmy's mouth move?" He was watching me now.

"No, that's the puzzling thing. I have seen his mouth open right before it happens, but I've never actually seen it move. The voice just comes out and almost overpowers me. Once I heard it coming from his doctor's office, screaming out that he was frightened, but again it was my own father's voice and in our native language. This has happened several times and it's always my father's voice."

"Does Timmy speak Athabascan?"

"He only knows a couple of words. He's almost never been around anyone who speaks it and then for only a very short time. Jack, I don't understand what's happening, but there's always that voice."

"And always in the Athabascan language?"

"It was, until a couple of days ago."

"What happened then?"

"In the doctor's office was when I heard my father's voice saying 'Cookie.' After a few minutes Timmy himself said it several times in his own voice and in English. Dr. Randell heard him that time."

Jack's eyes grew dark. He set his coffee down abruptly onto his bumper, splashing what was left of it onto the windshield. I watched the coffee run down the fender and onto the ground.

"Has the doctor ever heard the other voice, the one that speaks only Athabascan?"

"Nobody but me has ever heard it, Jack, but he definitely heard Timmy saying 'Cookie' over and over while he was crying and kicking the floor."

Jack's jaw muscles worked, his eyes narrowing almost to slits. He turned away from me and crushed his cup, then wiped his hand on his jeans and looked up at me. "Okay. Anything else?"

"This is even crazier. I've been seeing things, too. The past couple of weeks I've had flashes of someone—a man. Just parts of a man. His hand. The back of his neck."

He struggled, trying to control his reaction. "Who is it?"

"I don't know."

He frowned. "Who do you think it might be?"

"Really, I don't know. I just know I'm seeing flashes of a man, and that's real too, the same as the night I saw Kit."

"But Raven, seeing Kit could have been your imagination if you were half asleep, couldn't it?"

"No." I looked straight at him. "Jack, I saw Kit. He was there, standing in the street reaching out to me. I know I saw him, I know he was real."

He frowned. "I don't see how you could."

"I don't either. I just know all of it must have something to do with what's been going on. I've never been psychic, or even thought I might be. None of these things ever happened to me before the first murder, but now they are happening and it keeps getting worse. It's scaring me half to death."

"You've been thinking about your father a lot lately, haven't you?"

I nodded.

"Couldn't it be a flashback to your childhood, when he was still alive?"

"I suppose it could be. They're only quick glimpses, then they disappear. They're just so vivid, always surrounded by bright light or total darkness. Look, I don't understand any of this, Jack, and there's something else."

"Let's have it." He tried to smile, but with great effort.

"When I heard you talking to Red yesterday it sounded like you've pretty much got him pegged as the killer. I guess that's really why I wanted to talk to you."

He looked down at the ground. "I never said I suspect him of murder, Raven."

I stared at him for a minute. "Then what about Cookie?"

His gaze rose to meet mine and I could see that there was something he was trying to hide. "What?"

"Cookie. I heard you say Carolyn was called 'Cookie' twenty years ago at that carnival."

"I did, yes. I'm sorry you heard that."

I turned away, lowering my voice although there was nobody else around. "Jack, what am I going to do? What should I do?"

"About what?"

"About my husband and Carolyn."

"Nothing you can do now, Raven. Carolyn's dead."

"That's not what I mean. Look at me, please."

He looked and I saw sadness in his eyes.

"Was Red seeing Carolyn again after she moved to Valdez?"

His voice was strained. "Raven, I can't talk about this case, surely you understand that."

"But this is affecting me and my children!"

"I know it is, but please understand, I'm an officer of the law. I can't discuss anything pertaining to this with you. I can only ask questions and listen to what you have to say. I don't like keeping things from you, but this is the way it has to be right now."

"So you won't tell me if it's true."

"Raven, I can't tell you anything. Not right now."

"Then it is true, Jack." I turned away from him so he couldn't see my tears. "If it wasn't, you could have told me."

FORTY SIX

Jack struggled, trying to think of something to say so she wouldn't be so unhappy, but she was right and he was stuck. He couldn't tell her because it was true. It was going to come out publicly sooner or later and it was going to hurt her, and there wasn't a damn thing he could do to stop it.

"Jack?"

She had turned back toward him. He tried not to look directly at her but he had to, and he knew that was a mistake the minute he did it because now he wanted to pull her close and make everything else go away.

He forced himself to speak normally. "I don't know what to say, Raven, except I'm so sorry about all this."

He saw her tears and watched her fumble in her pocket. He pulled a paper napkin out of the donut box and handed it to her. "Here, use this, it's a little sticky, but it's all I've got."

She wiped her eyes and tried to smile. "I seem to be doing this a lot lately."

"Well, you're entitled. I feel the same way myself from time to time." He didn't dare touch her. She wasn't his to touch.

"Jack, did you ever reach a point in your life where you really didn't know what to do next?"

He looked out over the water. "Yes."

He could see her watching him from the corner of his eyes while he stared at the water lapping toward them in soft, lazy waves.

"What happened, can you tell me?"

He scratched the side of his nose. "It's not something I usually talk about, Raven."

She touched his arm lightly. "You know you can talk to me about anything. Or you should know."

He drew a deep breath and turned to her. "If you really want to hear this—"

"I do."

"Well." He shook his head as if to clear it. "Back in Dallas, one of the last big cases I handled was a triple murder. A man kidnapped and killed his three kids. All of them were under five years old."

He had to pause for a minute while he controlled his anger, which, as always whenever he thought about it, began to build again.

"He didn't just kill them, Raven. He strangled all three of them and mailed them in boxes, one after the other from three different states, to his ex-wife." He heard her gasp.

"I thought, the day we went to her house to collect the first body, that nothing I would ever have to handle again could be as bad as that day. And then for the next two days the other two kids—well—anyhow, we were all pretty broken up about it."

"Did you catch him?"

"We did, yes. It took a while, though. The guy was a real horror show. We found out he'd committed several other unsolved murders. So, several cases were closed, but after that I felt I'd seen enough of humanity, or rather the lack of humanity in so many people, and those were the main types I was dealing with day after day. I took a leave of absence to think things over, mainly whether or not I wanted to remain a police officer. Rode up here on my Harley just to be alone for a while."

He looked down at his badge. "You know, it's one thing to help people, all cops love that and we're happy as hell when things turn out right. It's when they don't turn out right that being a cop begins to chip away at your soul, and sometimes your mind. It's easy to lose your perspective, no matter how hard you try to prevent it. The divorce rate among cops is very high, so is the suicide rate. So I had to make a decision, and then it was more or less made for me."

"Was that when you got the offer to come up here?"

"Yes. I had stopped in at the station here, talked to the chief at the time and the first thing I knew they contacted me. Until the day Carolyn's body was discovered, I always felt I'd made the right decision."

He looked across the Sound to the mountains, where glaciers in the distance were almost hidden in fog that hadn't quite gone away over there, although it was warm and sunny where they stood. A few seagulls flew over the water a mile or so away, a crumpled cigar band floated at the edge of the Sound.

"And now there are three open murder cases here. This is such a nice town," he said almost under his breath. "I always thought it was, anyway, until this happened."

"It's still a nice town, Jack, and you've done a good job here."

He swung around toward her. "But is it worth it, Raven, what this job does to the personal life of every law enforcement officer? I'd like to have one myself some day, a family, kids maybe. I'm just not sure I want to drag anyone else into this life because murder happens everywhere and every time it happens it beats a little more hell into the cop who works the case. How long will it be until there's nothing left of me?"

She was standing too close to him now, he could smell her hair, feel her hand resting on his shoulder. He took a quick look around.

Still nobody else in the parking lot. Good.

She dropped her hand and stepped back. "I can't imagine you doing anything else other than exactly what you're doing. I thought, just the other day, someone's going to be very lucky to have you. I still feel that way. Maybe even more so now."

But would she ever really want to be married to a cop? Never knowing if there would be another night together, or another morning sitting in the kitchen over breakfast, talking about the coming day. He didn't know. He might never know.

She stood with her back to him now.

"Jack?"

"What?"

"Should I divorce Red?"

Every nerve in his body tingled but he struggled to be cautious with his answer. "I can't say, Raven. I don't know anything about your marriage. That's something you'll have to work out."

She nodded.

"I'm a bad one to ask anyway. I've never been married."

She smiled. "Well, I guess I know why, now."

"There's one more thing I didn't tell you. My mom left me and my dad when I was just eight. My dad was never the same after that. I swore that was never going to happen to me."

And he'd never let it really work its way into his mind again until this minute, standing at this dock with this woman, the one person he knew could heal the scars inside his head.

She eyed him. "I used to say I'd never marry, myself, but the minute I met Red that was all it took. Then, and I never gave this much of a thought before all this happened, I started seeing flashes of something bad in his eyes from time to time. My family didn't want me to marry him. In fact, they never came around because of him. Timmy hasn't even met my aunt, she's the only one I have left."

"Are things between the two of you any different now than they were before all this happened, though?"

"Everything's different now, Jack. I honestly don't know what I should do."

He cleared his throat. "Well, like I said, Raven, I'm not the right one to advise you, since I've never been involved in a marital situation myself."

She raised her head and the doubt in her eyes was evident. "I know you think I'm crazy. I guess I can't blame you. Timmy's doctor has been advising me to see a psychologist and he only knows about the voices. What do you think? Should I?"

"It might be a good idea, Raven. You might get a different perspective on things."

Raven touched his shirt again. "Jack, please believe me. All those things I told you did happen, they really did."

He looked down at her hand. Such a light touch, but it burned a hole straight through to his gut. "I believe you, Raven, but maybe you ought to find out why they're happening."

She looked back out over the water again. "Timmy has an appointment day after tomorrow. I'll talk to Dr. Randell again and ask him to give me the name of the doctor he gave me a couple of weeks ago. I have no idea what I did with it."

Come with me, Raven. Let me take care of you. The thought, so loud and clear, rattled him.

He opened her car door. She climbed in and switched on the ignition, looking back at him.

He climbed into his vehicle, watching as she drove off, then punched Mark's code into his cell phone.

"You look like you just did something to start World War Three," Mark said when Jack walked into his home office. "What's up? Want a beer?"

"Can't, I'm on duty." Jack pulled a halfway comfortable looking chair over to the side of Mark's desk. Like every place else he went, the damn chair was green. "Were you able to find the Flashbangs?"

"Sure, I found two, ready to go. What's up?"

Jack shrugged. "I might need one or two. You mentioned you had a couple one time, I just happened to think about it this morning. Appreciate it."

"Anytime, buddy." Mark reached under his desk and pulled out a box and handed it to him. "You know how to use these, right?"

"Pop it, toss it, and cover your ears." Jack grinned. "How'd you manage to sneak these out when you left the Seals?"

Mark laughed. "Oh, they expect us to keep a few souvenirs. They must, nobody ever said anything. How's everything else going? Any hot leads yet?"

Jack shrugged. "Not really. I am worried about Raven, though."

"Raven? Why?"

"Oh, she's got some weird-ass mental thing going on. She's seeing and hearing things and she thinks it has something to do with the murders."

Mark frowned. "Hearing and seeing what things?"

"For one thing, she swears she saw Kit standing in her yard a couple hours after Doc says he was dead. Then, she says, he disappeared."

"What the hell was she doing up that time of night?"

"She said because she heard noises outside. The problem is, she described exactly what Kit was wearing when I saw his body after he was killed. Now she says she's seeing parts of some man, just flashes of him. Says she has no idea who it is."

Mark grinned. "Which parts?"

"Nothing like what you're thinking. Back of a neck, a hand, that's all."

Mark shuffled some papers, picked up a pen, put it back down. Finally he looked up. "You know, Jack, I hate to say this, but it sounds to me like you need to be taking a closer look at both her and Red."

"I am looking at Red for sure. He's at the top of my list, and Hopscotch has almost dropped down to second place."

Mark laughed. "Hopscotch? You think that wuss might have done three murders?"

"He may talk and act like a wuss around here, but he's got a hell of a rap sheet behind him and he was dating Carolyn, you knew that, didn't you?"

"I saw him go into her apartment house once or twice. I wasn't sure if it was her or the landlady."

Jack shrugged. "Well, you never know. Thanks for the stuff, Mark. Say hi to Susan for me."

"Will do, buddy. We're having the usual party on the Fourth. Stop by."

"I'll be there, probably late though. Save me a steak." He left and headed back to the station.

"I want to run some things past you, see what you think," Jack said to Bill a few minutes later.

"Okay, shoot." Bill closed a file two inches thick and leaned back.

Jack eyed the file. "Charlie and Jason. You remember what I thought they might be up to, right? Along with Kit?"

Bill nodded.

"I was on the Internet last night. They're planning to pull their caper Fourth of July night."

Bill swore under his breath.

"What's wrong now?"

"Aw, Jack, me and the wife were planning a long weekend in Anchorage. I was going to ask you for the time off today."

"Can't do it. I definitely need you here." Jack filled him in on the details.

"So they're actually going to try it, even with Kit dead."

"Yep. Looks like it's just the two of them. I picked up some Flashbangs a little while ago at Mark's."

Bill nodded.

Jack draped his leg over the chair arm. "We'll probably only need one. It shouldn't take long. We'll get them before they ever make it to the container yard."

"How do you want to handle it?"

"Set up a roadblock on the outer road and as soon as we see them coming, if Jason doesn't slow down we'll toss a Flashbang at them. Maybe both Flashbangs, they'll stop for sure then. We'll separate them, get them to talk. After they do, we'll cuff them and take them in."

Bill stared at him in disbelief. "We're going to arrest them? Can we do that, the way you got your information?"

"I don't want to do it officially, just scare 'em a little. The AST could always search their computers and get everything if it comes to that, but I'd rather not involve them. I want to stop them at the git-go and keep them from going to prison. They're just stupid, otherwise they're good kids."

Bill nodded.

"But we can, like I said, put a good scare into them. Neither one of those assholes realizes they're committing felonies all over the place. Jason's story is, the oil companies have more money than they know what to do with anyhow so it's not really hurting anything, they can always fix the container."

Bill laughed and Jack shrugged. "That's what he said, swear to God. Charlie has no idea what kind of trouble he's getting into. They both think it's a big joke."

"They *are* stupid."

"I think I just said that. One of the things they said was, it'd just blow a hole in the container. They don't know much about explosives and oil fumes, that's for damn sure. What I'm thinking is, at this point in time we have a pretty good chance to not only stop them, but turn them around."

His eyes darkened. "Bill, I saw kids in Dallas who were so street-wise by the time they were ten you couldn't do anything but arrest them and put them in Juvie. But these two—so far, except for this idiotic scheme, they've both been good kids. Annoying as hell but so were we at that age. I know I was."

"I probably was," said Bill, grinning. He stared out the window for a minute. "Yeah, I was. So okay, we do the bust, scare 'em, then show 'em the error of their ways, right?"

"Right," said Jack. "Then we call their parents. I hate like hell to do it, Raven's having serious problems at home, she doesn't need this. One thing I just found out myself a little while ago, Red was definitely playing around with Carolyn again here, had been for some time. Raven guessed it but she doesn't know for sure, at least I didn't come out and say so. Right now, she just thinks he was."

He got up and poured himself a cup of coffee. "And that's not all," he said, still stirring the coffee when he sat down.

"Kimberley Clark told me she saw the youngest kid, Timmy, go in the house one day when Red and his girlfriend were there, probably going at it. Anyway, they were alone. She said Timmy ran right back out, fast. You saw what happened when Carolyn's body surfaced. Timmy stopped talking."

Bill grimaced. "Yep. He saw something he shouldn't have."

"Looks like it. That's probably at the bottom of all his problems. When Raven finds that out, all hell's really going to break loose. She asked me while ago if I thought she should divorce Red."

Bill grinned. "What'd you tell her?"

Jack shrugged, trying for a casual look. "I told her I didn't know anything about that, she had to decide for herself. I also told her maybe she should make an appointment with the shrink Timmy's doctor recommended. I'm thinking either she's going wonky out of stress, or else something else is going on I'd rather not have to worry about."

"Like what?"

"Well, I know it sounds crazy, but some Alaska Natives say they see and hear things. I don't know much about that stuff, I just know a lot of them really believe they're psychic."

Bill eyed Jack's coffee. "Do you believe she is?"

"I don't know. I want to believe she is. I halfway do, but there's something else."

Bill got up and poured himself a cup. "There always is." He took a gulp.

"She's been hearing Timmy say things in Athabascan, only she says it's her father's voice she's hearing. Nobody else hears it, from what she tells me. She also tells me she's heard Timmy saying "Cookie", but in her father's voice."

"Some imagination," said Bill.

"I'd agree with you, except for one thing."

Bill cocked an eyebrow, waiting.

"Okay, hear me out. Timmy's a wreck over all this. He hasn't spoken at all, except to finally say "Cookie" in the doctor's office the other day when he was hysterical. That time he said it in his own voice."

Bill frowned. "I'm not following you."

"Bill—" Jack leaned toward him. "Why would Raven start hearing a nickname she never knew her husband's girlfriend had? Especially if she just now found out Carolyn was her husband's girlfriend?"

Bill looked away, out the window. "Did you ever stop to think maybe she did know he had a girlfriend and maybe she did know her nickname?"

Jack knew what was coming.

"It seems to me we'd better be taking a good hard look at Raven in connection with these murders."

Jack's eyes narrowed. "God, I hate to think that."

"So do I, but Carolyn's body was found in Raven's yard. She gets up in the middle of the night, she told you that. She knew where Kit would be that night and she says she saw him and she knew what he was wearing. What if she's got some kind of split identity thing or something like that going on?"

Jack studied the floor. "Or maybe she saw something the night Carolyn's body was buried in her back yard. Maybe she was walking in her sleep that night, something like that. Maybe that's why she's seeing flashes of a man she doesn't know. She says she doesn't take sleeping pills, but who knows?" He looked up. "You really think she could have killed somebody by herself the way Carolyn was killed?"

Bill shrugged. "I don't know, maybe she could if she was mad enough."

"Could be, but why hide the body in her own yard when she'd have to know it was going to be dug up? Also, why would she want to kill Kit, and why Vera?"

"I don't know. Maybe Kit knew something. I don't know about Vera. Hell, you're the chief with all the detective experience, I'm just a street cop. We gotta find out why, that's all I know. Has any more information come in from Anchorage yet? I haven't seen anything since I checked in this morning."

"No ID on the palm print in Carolyn's apartment yet. Not much on the boot print. They pinpointed the brand, but hell, everybody in town wears those." He looked down at his feet. "I do myself. The only thing they're sure of is the make and that they're size eleven and a half."

"Anything in on Vera yet?"

Jack shook his head. "Nope."

He was getting ready to leave when his rookie called from the front desk. "Chief, Kit's blood test results just came back."

"What'd they find?"

"Cocaine. He was full of it the night he was killed."

"Jeezus!" Bill shot up, his eyes bulging with surprise.

Jack could feel the slow burn starting. *Cocaine.*

Bill frowned. "I didn't think we had that going on here. This is bad in more ways than one."

Jack's face hardened. "If it's true, it's not only bad, this is war. I won't have that going on in my town."

"I couldn't agree more, chief."

"Okay then. We're on Fourth of July night, right?"

"Sure. I'll call the wife and tell her."

"Tell her you get an extra couple of days after all this is over. That ought to sweeten her up some."

Jack picked up Kit's blood report after Bill left and stood at the front desk, drinking coffee and reading, then took the report into his office, put his feet up on his desk and leaned back, thinking.

There was no way this could have been going on without anyone else in town knowing about it. Charlie and Jason had to know and they'd both lied by not telling him, which gave him even more reason to be pissed than he already was over all the lies and omissions he'd put up with in the past few weeks. He was getting angrier by the minute and now Hopscotch was pounding on the bars. Still simmering, he slammed his feet down and headed down the hall toward the cell.

Beth Anderson

FORTY SEVEN

A light fog surrounded Valdez when Timmy and I boarded the plane Friday morning and it took a while for the plane to break through the clouds. By the time it did we'd almost reached Anchorage.

We took a taxi to the doctor's office. Timmy was deep in thought and never looked up except when we passed by a small store that served ice cream.

"We'll stop and have some when we're finished today," I said. The wounded look in his eyes when he looked away made me wonder once again what he was thinking.

"I definitely want to try Rapid Eye Technology, the R.E.T. I told you about the other day," Dr. Randell said when we sat in his office a few minutes later. "I've seen for myself how much it can help children with deep depression, although it's mainly used on adults. We're going to make his sessions a little shorter because he's so young, but I think there's a good chance it'll help." He twirled his pen, studying my face. "I'll have to ask you to wait outside though."

"I will," I said, "but please explain the treatment to me first."

He smiled. "Basically, it's a method of helping the patient release whatever trauma is causing the problem. It's a natural process of emotional discharge that simulates REM in the patient's brain, even though the patient is awake and fully conscious of what both patient and doctor are saying. It will help him tremendously, I think, because it addresses all levels of the mind and body."

"How does it work?"

"The simple explanation is, through rapid movement of the patient's eyes. It seems to re-calibrate something in the brain's wiring because it's done by flashing a lighted wand back and forth, which causes the patient to blink. He follows the light with his eyes and I talk to him, telling him to release the memory of whatever is troubling him, to let it go."

"Something as simple as that actually works?"

"Most of the time, yes. My patients almost always feel some relief after the first session. I would have tried it with him before, but he's very young. However, nothing else seems to be working, so I think we need to try. It may take several sessions if whatever is troubling him is buried deeply enough." He turned to Timmy. "How about it, are you ready?"

Timmy shook his head.

"Just for a few minutes, son. It won't take long and your mother will be right outside, okay?"

Timmy sighed and looked out the window.

Dr. Randell motioned for me to leave. I bent to give Timmy a kiss and whispered, "I'll sit and talk to the nice nurse who gives you stickers, okay?"

He looked down at the floor as I left the room.

This time I didn't hear anything while I sat in the waiting room, but my mind spun with a thousand thoughts and images. My back yard, still untouched. The body, scarred with many colors. Kit. Light and fog and shimmering mist. A man's head. A hand. Dark eyes. Kit's funeral, sad and small. Red's temper, always on edge. Timmy's eyes, lost and unhappy. Racing dreams and wind and things howling in the night, filling my house, my mind, my life—

I felt a tap on my shoulder and jumped. I hadn't heard Dr. Randell come out of his office. I glanced at my watch and saw thirty minutes had passed in what seemed only seconds.

"I think our little guy is going to be all right," he said, "but I need you to come into my office. My nurse will take care of him while we talk."

"Did he say anything?"

"Yes."

"What did he say?"

Dr. Randell's eyes were lowered, almost hidden. When I saw that, everything in my body began to tighten. He was going to tell me something horrible. I didn't want to hear it.

I have to hear it.

I didn't want to.

I have to.

"We'll talk about it inside," he said, guiding me toward the door.

When we entered his office, Timmy was gone.

"My nurse took him out the side door." He indicated the chair in front of his desk. "Please have a seat."

I sank into it, half afraid to look at him. If I didn't look he couldn't tell me—

I have to look. He has to tell me.

He sat rubbing his forehead, obviously troubled.

My skin crawled.

I waited.

Finally he looked up. "I don't know whether he'll talk to you or not once you leave the office, but he did while we were going through the session. I think the flashing light made him temporarily forget his fear of speaking.

"I'm very disturbed by what he told me, Raven. The last thing I want to do is tell you. Normally I wouldn't, but this is very serious and it has affected him badly."

He looked down at a piece of paper then looked back up.

"Do you know you're the only one he feels safe with? He told me that." He tried to smile, but to me it looked like a tortured grimace.

"We could wait and see if he tells you anything on his own, but R.E.T. is supposed to help him let go of the trauma, not dwell on it. We want him to let it go once and for all, and realize it will never happen again.

"In other words, we try, and normally succeed in convincing the patient that the trauma is no longer important, he's safe, it can't hurt him any longer and he should be able to completely let it go. But in this case it's hard to tell him that and expect him to believe me. Right now, I'm not sure he can."

My stomach started cramping. "What did he tell you?"

His eyes flickered and he gave a little sigh. "He's afraid his father will cut his head off if he tells anybody what he saw."

My breath left my body.

"That's why he can't speak. It's not that he won't, he hasn't been able to because he's so afraid of his father."

"But what on earth would make him think such a thing? Red has always been very strict with him, I'll grant you that, but I can't imagine—"

"It's not just that he saw the body in your yard, Raven. It's because of what he saw a few weeks before, and then after that, saw the body." His voice was soft, compassionate.

Saw?

I didn't want to hear this. I already knew, but I had to hear it.

I forced myself to speak. "What did he see?"

He looked past my shoulder. "Apparently Timmy's school is very close to your house, is this correct?"

"Yes, it's just a few doors up and across the street."

"From what he told me, he snuck out of school one afternoon after lunch because he felt sick to his stomach and he knew his father would be home—"

"Go on." I couldn't breathe, couldn't hear this—

"He went upstairs and opened your bedroom door and—I'm sorry, Raven, really sorry—he told me he saw his father in bed with a woman who was covered with tattoos. The way he described it to me was, he heard his father calling her 'Cookie' and he thought his father was choking her because she was moaning, so he turned around and ran back to school and threw up when he got there. The school nurse called your husband and he came and got Timmy."

Dear God! "I remember the day that happened." I couldn't believe my voice was so calm.

"When the body was unearthed in your front yard he knew it was the same woman. He thought his father had choked her and then cut off her head and buried her body out back. He still thinks this."

He stopped for a minute to let me digest what he'd said.

"You've told me Red has always been very strict with him and didn't want another child when Timmy was born. Timmy has probably always felt this, and now he very much believes his father will kill him if he says anything."

He let out a long, heavy sigh. "I'm going to have to notify the authorities in your town, I want you to know this ahead of time. They should know what Timmy said to me whether it has any bearing on the resolution of the case or not. It might be evidence of some sort, it might not, but I can't conceal even uncertain evidence in a murder case."

I was frozen. As cold as it gets in Valdez in the winter, I had never, even on hunting trips with my father when it was well below zero, been this cold. *Or this calm.*

"Go ahead and call them."

The pity in his eyes was evident. "Good enough, then. I'll see you both Monday morning, same time?"

I lifted my chin. "We'll be here."

FORTY EIGHT

Jack stood in the hallway outside of Hopscotch's cell, glaring. "What the hell do you want now?"

"I say, no need to get your knickers in such a twist, is there?" Hopscotch grinned. "I wanted to compliment you on today's luncheon. It's not often one is privy to a taco and a bologna sandwich in the same meal. The mustard was a nice touch also. It went admirably with the taco sauce."

Jack grabbed the bars. "Cut the crap, Hopscotch, I'm not in the mood for this."

Hopscotch flopped down on his cot. "I'd think not, with all the problems I hear you're having."

Jack shot him a nasty look. "And you're one of them."

Hopscotch leaned back against his pillow. "I like to listen, mate. I know it's annoying, but I learn a lot that way. I have to say there's one thing I know for sure." He looked up at the ceiling, pursing his lips.

Jack had to force himself not to unlock the cell and reach for his throat. "What?"

"Well, mate, think about it. Raven's not your killer, I heard Bill hinting at that, but no, she's not."

"And you're basing that on what, your vast experience?"

Hopscotch frowned. "That's so beneath you."

"The hell it is. Stop calling me back here, I've got work to do." He turned to leave.

"That work, my friend, is my real reason for this discourse."

Jack gritted his teeth and swiveled back around. "Okay. Talk to me."

Hopscotch pulled himself to a standing position and brushed a bread crumb off his shirt. "Mate, it appears to me that you're not thinking things through enough. For instance, who in this town has the capability to sneak into wherever they please and murder his victims before they've even made a sound, and then get away without being seen? Think about it."

Jack felt his blood pressure rising. "I have been thinking about it."

"So, mate, can you tell me who your suspects are?" He coughed delicately. "Besides me, of course."

"You're right at the top of the list."

Hopscotch shook his head. "No, no, mate. You've got it all wrong. I had no reason to kill those people."

Jack gave him a sour grin. "If you did, we'll find out what it was."

Hopscotch shook his head again. "I can see you're still determined to make me look bad, but let's try this another way. Who in this town gets around *enough*, is seen everywhere *enough* as to be almost invisible? So much so that people might not even notice him? In addition to that, who in this town has the background to have done exactly what your killer has done not once, but three times in less than a month?"

Jack stared at him. "What the hell are you getting at? If you know anything about this you'd better come out with it now."

"I don't *know* anything, mate, but I will tell you that on three different occasions when I was still seeing Carolyn, I saw Mark Taylor parked up the street, watching her apartment building. It never even registered until I started thinking about it a few minutes ago. See what I mean?"

Jack turned to leave. "Thanks for the tip."

Hopscotch nodded in agreement. "And of course, we can't forget that Red has the same attributes and talents, from what I've heard here and there." He grinned. "Mostly here."

"I suppose you saw him parked up the street too?"

"No, but think about it." Hopscotch spread his hands. "You already know he was involved with Carolyn, apparently a lot more than I thought I was. You don't need me to tell you that. To bury her in his own yard would be a master stroke, in my opinion. Nobody would think anything of it if they saw him back there at night. And he was in the vicinity when Kit was killed. As for Vera, I don't know. Maybe he was shagging her too."

"Shut the hell up, Hopscotch. Don't call me back here again." Jack stomped down the hallway, trying to ignore the infuriating sound of Hopscotch's laughter following him all the way to the door.

Beth Anderson

FORTY NINE

Timmy hadn't made a sound so far when the taxi dropped us off at the ice cream shop but he was noticeably brighter. I ordered his usual three-scoop banana split along with hot tea for myself because I was still having chills, still horrified at what he'd seen and heard.

I didn't care what this had done to my marriage. I was ice-cold with rage over the traumas my son had endured, and probably always would in some way because of it.

Eight years old and his own father did this to him.

I sat across from him, trying not to look as though I were watching while he dug into the ice cream. About halfway through, he looked up at me and grinned. "Good ice cream, Mom."

I almost dropped my cup but I forced myself to answer naturally, fighting back tears. "It does look good. I should have ordered some myself."

He offered me a spoonful but I shook my head. "No, you go ahead, honey. You earned it."

He picked at his ice cream then looked up again, his eyes dark and serious. "Mom, do we have to go home now?"

I'd been thinking about that ever since we left the doctor's office and had already made my decision. I would not take him home until I finished what I had to do there.

"How about after we get off the plane we drive out and see your Great Aunt Lucy?" I watched to see his reaction.

He frowned, puzzled, and his eyes seemed to have grown larger than I'd ever seen them. "Did I ever see her before?"

I had to smile. "She saw you when you were very small, but I don't think you'd remember her. She lives in our village and she doesn't usually come into town, but I know she'd love to see you again. I was thinking maybe you might like to spend a day or so with her while I straighten out some things at home. How about it?"

He scooped up a cherry and chewed it thoughtfully for a minute. "I don't know. It might be okay. Does she have any kids?"

"No, she never had any of her own, but there are kids all over the place, they run in and out of her cabin all the time. You'll have plenty to play with."

He grinned. "I'll think about it." He didn't seem to recall he hadn't been talking for a while.

"Finish your ice cream then, and we'll head for the airport. We've got a big afternoon ahead of us."

His face lit up and I made a silent promise to him as I sipped the last of my tea.

Whatever else might happen, you'll smile a lot from now on if I can help it. And I can.

Aunt Lucy's cabin was exactly an hour's drive out of Valdez on Richardson Highway, and then another half-hour through a narrow, winding dirt road.

I turned up the path I'd traveled so many times as a child and Timmy turned to me, wide-eyed. "Mom, is this a real street? I never even saw it before you turned in here!"

"I know you didn't, honey. Others never see this road as they pass by. That's the way our people want it."

"Why?"

"Because those who still live this far out in the bush want as little outside interference with their lives as possible. They hunt and fish and manage to grow whatever they need right here. They call that subsistance."

"What does that mean?"

"It means they try to take care of themselves with whatever the land and the water and the Spirit gives them."

"So they have all the food and everything they want, all the time?"

She shook her head. "Not always. This land doesn't give up its subsistance easily. It's a hard life, and many of our people leave to make their way in the larger cities, as I did. But our hearts always remain in our villages."

I glanced at him. He was studying my face. "Really? Always?"

I smiled. "It is always so, yes, but then, when we have children, our hearts grow so they can hold all the love we have for them too." I ruffled his hair and he squirmed, turning his head to look out the side window, but I could tell he was smiling.

Aunt Lucy's one-room log cabin stood at the end of a winding muddy dirt road haphazardly lined with similar cabins. There were no electricity or phone lines, in fact nothing visible of the outside world. Her cabin sat on the edge of a small lake formed from melting glaciers created thousands of years ago high in the Chugach Mountains.

Clotheslines drooped with drying clothes and chicken wire dog kennels surrounded the cabins. Smoke sifted lazily out of small, round chimneys, telling the children running around everywhere that it was almost time to eat. The air smelled like my childhood and my mouth watered, although I was far from hungry.

Aunt Lucy stood by the road, shielding her eyes from the late afternoon sun as she watched our car approach. I knew she'd be waiting. It was the way of my people to know, and they were seldom wrong.

Aunt Lucy, a large woman with black curly hair that framed her face like a halo and short, fat arms perfect for cuddling small children, waved when she saw us. Her *kuspuk*, a light summer jacket, lifted and rippled over her skirt along with her gentle arm movements.

I pulled to a stop and Aunt Lucy gave us a beautiful big smile, holding out her arms in welcome.

"A white dove flew over my house today," she called. "He told me you were coming! And this little man, is this Timmy? Come here, you little man, come give your Aunt Lucy a big hug."

Timmy looked at me, then climbed slowly out of the car. Aunt Lucy immediately, as I had known she would, swooped him into her arms, laughing raucously out loud, swinging him around in big circles and making him laugh when she said, "You're not so little any more, you know that?"

Her glance connected with mine as she put him down but

neither of us said anything. There was no need to. Together we watched Timmy throw a stick far across the yard for the dogs to chase, then streak around the corner of the house after them.

"So. You got troubles," my aunt said under her breath as soon as we were alone. She pulled me to her bosom and hugged me tight while I nodded.

God, it felt so good to be in her arms again, just like when I was a little kid and had skinned my knee.

My aunt drew back and looked into my eyes. "*Cheechako gussak?*", asking, in our language, if the trouble was because of the newcomer white man. *Cheechako* was the way our people referred to anyone who wasn't born in Alaska, and *gussak* was a huge insult.

I didn't have to answer. Aunt Lucy looked around and spotted Timmy, still tossing the stick, shrieking with laughter at the dogs, and now followed by several laughing children.

"Timmy," she called, "you come here a minute, okay?"

Timmy ran back to us with three dogs swarming around his legs, barking for another stick toss.

"You came on the best day, little man, you know that?"

He shook his head, puzzled.

"Just in time for *potlatch*! It's tonight! I bet you didn't know that, did you?"

He shook his head. "What is it?"

"Ha! It's a party! Lots of people, lots of food, I got it cookin' right now, we all do, see the smoke?" Aunt Lucy pointed toward the chimneys. "Hey, we got sourdough and gum boots and cabbage, we got lots of stuff! You stay here with me tonight, okay?"

Timmy looked up at me. "Should I, Mom?"

"Hey, you gotta stay!" Aunt Lucy almost sang the words. "We got fun coming up! We're gonna have a blanket toss and the knuckle hop and the ear pull, oh man, we're gonna have a big time! Eat, play, laugh! You stay tonight, maybe tomorrow?"

She eyed me. "You're gonna let this little man stay here with me, right?"

"If he wants to." I looked at Timmy. "Would you like to stay? I'll come back and get you tomorrow afternoon if you want to stay for the party."

He looked down at the ground, then back up, his eyes troubled. "You promise you'll come back tomorrow and get me?"

I knelt and pulled him close. "Of course I promise! I'll be here by tomorrow afternoon. You'll be safe with Aunt Lucy. Nobody will know you're here."

He still looked doubtful. "Not even dad?"

"He doesn't know where this is. He's never been here."

He thought a minute more, then smiled up at Aunt Lucy. "I guess I could stay till tomorrow. I like parties."

"Good!" She turned toward me. "You eat before you go? Come on in, I got plenty."

I shook my head. "I need to get back, I have some things I have to do and it's getting late."

She eyed me for a moment, then nodded. "Okay, you go on home now. Timmy will be fine. I'll teach him some of our ways."

She took me by the arm and led me to my car, out of Timmy's earshot.

"Remember our law, daughter," she said in a low voice, "if the husband mistreats you, the father will take you back, even though none of us have ever done it. He's gone now, your mama too, so I'm all you got now and I'm takin' over."

She swept her hand in a large circle, indicating the water, the air, the mountains. "I got all I need here. There's plenty for you and your kids so don't you worry about nothing, you hear me?"

I held her close and nodded, unable to speak. Maybe this wonderful woman had nothing in the eyes of the outer world, but I knew differently. Inside, Aunt Lucy had everything.

I climbed into my car and sat watching Timmy for a couple of minutes until Aunt Lucy tapped on the window. "Go on now, you go home, take care of what needs to be done and don't you worry none. Your little man will be safe here with me."

"I know he will. And don't you worry about me. I'll be fine."

Aunt Lucy snorted. "Give the *gussak* *a blue ticket home*. We knew he'd do you bad sooner or later."

I drove back through the long dirt road toward the highway.

A blue ticket home.
A one-way ticket to anywhere but here.

It was dusk when I arrived home. I got out of the car and looked around at my flowers, now subdued in the waning light. My grass, thick and lush, was growing dark where clouds drifting overhead cast their shadows.

I went in through the kitchen door, lay my purse on the counter and walked into the living room.

Red was sitting in his chair watching television. He switched it off and turned to me. "Where's Timmy?"

I was ice-cold calm. "Don't worry about where Timmy is. Come out to the garage. I want to talk to you and the children don't need to hear this."

His eyebrows shot up, then lowered as his eyes narrowed, but he followed me out to the garage. He left the door open. I walked back past him and closed it, then turned to face him.

"I'm going to make this quick. Pack your clothes and get out of my house. I just spoke to a lawyer this afternoon."

He laughed. "You what?"

"I'm divorcing you."

He reared back. "What the hell's going on here? A divorce? On what grounds?"

"I shouldn't even have to answer that, Red. Just think about it. Why would I divorce you after all this time? What would make me do such a thing, when divorce has always been one of the last things I'd ever dream of doing?"

His forehead turned pink. "I don't know what you're talking about unless you're talking about my job. Is that it? You're divorcing me because I'm out of a job?" He snapped his fingers. "I can find another one just like that, so get off your high horse."

"What about your job?"

"Oh, you didn't know?" He shrugged. "Well, the school board has decided to replace me. That's what I was told this afternoon when they called. They didn't give me a reason."

"Why do you think they decided to do that, Red?"

He looked away. "I don't know and it doesn't matter. I'll get another job, don't worry about it."

"I'm not worried about it. Your job is of no concern to me. I'm sorry you lost it, but I'm sure you know why as well as I do. They don't want you and neither do I, because you're morally bankrupt."

His mouth twisted into a disbelieving half-smile. "What the hell is this all of a sudden? I'm the breadwinner in this family. You think you can do all this by yourself?" He swept his arms around, indicating the house, the garage. "You don't make that kind of money, you know you don't."

"Maybe not, Red, but I will not live in the same house with you any longer. You brought another woman into my home while I was working and our children were in school. You took her into my bed and violated every vow you took with me. Is that enough or do you want more?"

His eyes were wide open by that time, changing from blue to gray, as they always had done whenever he was trying to hide something.

"I don't know what you're talking about. Where are you getting all of this? Who told you that?" His voice had lowered and there was a dangerous edge to it I'd never heard before, even when he was angry.

I stood my ground. "I don't have to tell you, Red, but I will because I want to see your face when you hear it.

"Timmy saw you in bed with her. He heard you saying her name. Cookie, Red, don't deny it. He saw her tattoos and he knew who it was the minute they dug up her body."

He took a step backward, his mouth open.

"And he thought you'd cut his head off, too, if he told anyone. Isn't that pitiful? Your own son, an eight-year-old child, thought his own father would kill him if he told anyone he'd seen the tattooed woman in *my* bed with his father. He had no idea what you were doing. He thought you were choking her and then cut her head off."

I stepped toward him. "Why do you think he couldn't speak or walk? Eight years old, Red. You took that woman into my bed and Timmy saw it. You've almost destroyed him. You *have* destroyed his childhood."

"Bullshit, you can't prove that. No court would believe a kid that age."

"He's never going to court, Red. He doesn't have to and I won't allow it. You're going to pack your clothes and leave and never come back. You're going to sign the divorce papers, and you had better never try to contact any of my children."

He threw his head back and laughed. "You're going to divorce me over a little thing like that? Forget it. You're not divorcing me and I'm not going anywhere."

"Oh, yes I am, Red, and you are going. Our marriage was over the minute you started your affair again here with Carolyn, but it's not that. Believe me, who you sleep with now doesn't matter to me at all. It's what you did to Timmy, what you've done to this family. I want a divorce, I'm going to get it, and you're going to get out of our lives and stay out."

He stared at me for a minute, then his expression changed to a smirk. "Oh, I get it. You did hear Jack yesterday. I wondered if you did. Well, too bad, because nobody can prove I killed anybody."

I shrugged. "If you did, they'll eventually convict you. If you didn't, you're free to go wherever you want as long as it's not here. I don't see how you could possibly think I'd stay married to you after what you've done to my son."

He arched his hands, wiggling his fingers and shaking his head, mocking my words. "I didn't do anything to him. He did it himself when he came in my bedroom without knocking. He knows better than to ever do that."

"Our bedroom, Red. *Our* bedroom. He went in there to get you because he was sick. Remember the day they called you from school to come pick him up? He'd already been home, that's when this happened. Red, how *could* you?"

His mouth opened, then shut again. He shrugged. "Okay, I've been a bad boy. I'm sorry. But I think you're doing this because you think I'm a killer."

"It doesn't matter but just so you know, I can't totally bring myself to believe even you could do that."

"Well, thank you very much, I guess." He thought for a minute and his lips curled into a thin smirk. "I suppose you think you'll be fine financially, but you won't."

"As a matter of fact, Red, I will be fine. I transferred all but a thousand dollars out of our account into a new account in my name this afternoon. I left the thousand for you, so pack your clothes and whatever else you want and go get your money and get out of my life. I don't want to see you or hear from you. My lawyer will contact you. If he can't find you, the divorce will go through anyway."

He took a step toward me. The muscles and sinews on his arms and neck stood out in purple against his sunburned skin. I could almost count every hair on his arms. He pulled back as if he were going to swing at me. I shook inside but I would not let him see it.

"Just go, Red. If your children want to look you up when they're grown, that's up to them. I'll take care of them and this house will be a happy one, not a house full of anger the way it has been for a long, long time."

He stepped back. "Raven, look. I really am sorry about Carolyn. That was...well...I don't know, it was..."

"It was in my house and my eight year old son saw you in bed with her. Don't expect me to ever forgive you for that. I could forgive you almost anything else, but not when you've shocked Timmy to the point where he's deathly afraid to be in his own home with you."

I slammed my hand on the fender. "I will not subject my son any longer to the kind of life he's had with you here. Get your things and get out. Now!"

He stared at me for a couple of minutes, beyond angry, I knew. I fought to keep him from seeing how frightened I was.

His voice was low, controlled, but I could feel the anger coming toward me in waves. "I'll leave for now, Raven." He walked toward the door, and then turned back. "But you are going to be very sorry you did this."

He yanked the door open and stomped back into the house, slamming the door behind him.

I stayed in the garage. I didn't want to see him. I didn't want him to see me. Fifteen minutes later I heard his truck roar out of the driveway.

    I went upstairs. When I entered the bedroom, it was as if he'd never been there. Every sign of him was gone except for one.

    I took our wedding picture down from the wall and put it in my closet behind my winter clothes, facing the wall. Then for the first time in a long time, I stood in my bedroom and looked around, breathing deeply.

    I could finally, in this room, feel the sweet sensation of fresh air filling my lungs.

FIFTY

Jack sat at his desk trying to decide whether to go home and eat or stop somewhere for dinner when the phone rang. He picked it up.

"Jack, it's Raven. I thought I should let you know I just made Red pack his clothes and leave. He's gone."

His jaw dropped. "Gone? Where's he headed?"

"I don't know. He took everything he wanted and got in his truck and drove off a few minutes ago."

"Okay. Thanks for letting me know, Raven. I'll get back to you." He hung up, picked up the phone again and called the airport.

"Is Red Morressey anywhere around there?"

"I haven't seen him."

"Watch for him. One of my men is on his way out there. If Red shows up before he gets there, don't let him leave, we need to speak to him."

"Will do."

He ran into the outer office. "Riley, set up a roadblock for Red Morressey on both ends of town, do it fast. Emerson, check all the motels, do the airport first, I've already called them but get out there and look around. I want a twenty-four hour tail on him as soon as you find him. If you can't find him, call me right away so I can put out an APB. We need to set up a three-shift schedule so we know where he is every minute if he's still here. If he starts to leave town, whoever's on duty should call me immediately. We can't let him out of our sight."

Dammit! Of all the days for Raven to throw Red out. Now, in addition to everything else, he had to worry about where Red was. On the other hand, at least he wouldn't have to arrest him at home in front of the kids.

The phone rang again. Emerson. "I found Red, he just checked in at the Keystone. He's in his room. Should I bring him in?"

"Negative. Stay where you are. Somebody'll be there to spell you at eleven."

"Aw, Chief, I was supposed to be home at six!"

"You're going to be there till eleven, got that?"

"Yes, sir, I guess so."

"Fine, good job, stay right on him. If he looks like he's going anywhere call me but don't let him out of your sight."

"Okay, Chief." He sounded as though Jack had just let the air out of all four of his tires.

Jack dialed Mac in Anchorage. It took him almost fifteen minutes to track her down.

"Mac, did you see that report on Kit?"

"I certainly did, I was the one who faxed it to you. I finally got your girlfriend's DNA and background too, if you want to hear them."

She paused for a couple of seconds, long enough to make him nervous. "Unless you already know all about her. Do you?"

"Do I know what about her?"

"First, her hair, which was not natural platinum blonde in case you didn't know, showed small traces of cocaine. That doesn't mean she used, she could have been just handling, which is what we believe.

"Her DNA and description, except for hair and eye color, are a perfect match to that of a woman named Luciana Puerta, who we found out has been missing from the FBI radar for a few years. I just put a call in to the cruise line to find out if they found any kind of drugs in her cabin. They'll stonewall us, they always do with anything like that, but we'll find out sooner or later."

"Wait a minute! You think that's the connection? Cocaine?"

"Hell yes, I do. It makes as much sense as anything else. We know Vera was trafficking. We know Kit was using. We don't know what Carolyn had to do with it yet but my guess is, she was the connection between Kit and Vera.

"By the way, speaking of connections, just look who Vera was playing house with every time she hit Valdez. Doesn't look very damn good for the chief of police down there, now does it?"

There was a long silence while he tried to take in what she'd just said.

"I'm having a hard time believing this," he said, knowing how naïve he sounded.

She snorted. "You were looking at her tits, that's all you saw."

"I'm serious, there was never any indication of this."

"I hear you, Jack, but you're not looking at the report I'm looking at right now."

He glanced around for his coffee, picked up the cup and peered into it. Empty. Figured.

"Okay, what else have you got?"

"First, she had counterfeit I.D.'s back on the ship in her luggage, they did give that to us. Good ID's, too, you almost can't tell the difference from real thing. She's been using the Social Security number and name of a woman who's been dead for five years. Cute, huh?"

He still couldn't believe it.

"She was originally from a small town in Argentina, with a rap sheet in Argentina and here in the U.S. Minor prostitution and street dealing charges to start with, then she moved up to serious drug trafficking. We're looking into a possible connection with another case we're working for one of the airlines she used.

"Anyhow, the last we have on the Puerta name was five years ago, before she started using Vera Cruz. I'm pretty sure this is the connection to the dead kid unless you know any other drug dealers down there."

He ignored the last crack. "What about prison?"

"Nope. Good lawyer, got her off every time. Apparently she had some heavy connections here in the States, too. Anyhow, she never did hard time. Minor gigs, no prison time."

"But Mac, wait a minute. We never found traces of cocaine in Carolyn's apartment. I headed up that search myself."

"You weren't looking for it, were you?"

She had him. Dammit! "No."

"Go back and look again. Tear up the carpeting. Take the whole apartment apart, walls, cabinets, everything in the place if you have to. I'll fax you a search warrant. Jack, you know Carolyn's background, it's seedy as hell. She could have been working with Vera. There's got to be some past connection, it's there somewhere, I know it is, and Carolyn had access to the kids at school. Talk to the superintendent, see if there's been even a hint of drugs there, although he should have already told you if there was."

"A lot of people should have told me a lot of things," he muttered.

"Are you ready to give up and let AST come down and take over?"

"Tell 'em I said give me a few more days, I have some new leads to look at. I'll call you as soon as I get anything."

"Better move fast, Jack." She hung up.

FIFTY ONE

After Red left and I spoke to Jack, I called Charlie and Alice downstairs. They flopped into their seats in the living room, their eyes wary and questioning.

I spoke first. "I don't know any other way to tell you this other than just come right out and tell you. Your father and I are getting a divorce. He's moved out. I don't know where he's going, but I want to reassure you both that we'll be fine."

I couldn't let their shocked faces keep me from finishing what I had to say. "This has nothing to do with either of you, please don't think anything like that. Someday you'll be able to see him again, but not right now."

Alice was the first to speak and as usual went straight to the point.

"Mom, what'll we do for money? What happened?"

"What happened isn't something I can talk about, Alice, but we'll have enough to get by. I'll have to go to work full time, which will mean I'll need a little extra help from both of you as far as taking care of Timmy."

They glanced at each other.

"But I don't understand, Mom! When did all this happen? I didn't even know anything was going on!"

Charlie still hadn't made a sound.

I cleared my throat. "I don't want to make a big deal out of the reasons because they don't concern you. This is between your father and me."

"Well, then fix it! Why can't you like talk to a stupid counselor or something? Cheryl's mom and dad did and they're okay now. You could at least try!"

Charlie, hunched over staring at his feet, looked up. "Yeah, can't you talk to somebody? You're going to a shrink all the time anyhow. Talk to him about it!"

I reached over to touch his knee but he jerked away.

"This isn't something a counselor can fix, Charlie. I hate that this is happening, but sometimes things do happen between adults that can't be repaired no matter how much they both love their children."

Charlie jumped up and stood towering over me. "You don't even want to try? Then you don't love us and don't say you do. When I find out where Dad is I'm going to go live with him!" He ran upstairs. I heard his door slam.

Alice sat perfectly still, her glance roaming from one wall to the other, finally coming back to Raven. "Mom?"

"Yes, honey?"

"Do you have a...a...boyfriend or something? Is that what it is?"

I shook my head. "No, hon, it's nothing like that."

"Does Dad have a girlfriend?"

"Not that I know of, Alice."

I moved over next to Alice, then pulled her close and stroked her hair. "Sometimes this just happens, honey, and there's nothing you can do about it."

"But what did dad do?"

I pulled away and looked into Alice's eyes. "Someday I'll talk to you about it. Right now, please try to understand, I can't."

Alice began to sob desperately, as she'd done so many times when she was a little girl.

But this time I was the cause of the tears. This time I couldn't do anything other than hold her close and let them fall.

This time our lives were forever changed, and nothing would ever be the same again.

FIFTY TWO

As soon as Jack got into the office Saturday morning, his phone rang.

"This is Anna Mathias from the personnel agency out here on Richardson Highway."

He swore silently under his breath. "Yes ma'am, what can I do for you?"

"I understand you called the head office in Anchorage with a complaint about the way we're handling things here?"

"Not a complaint, ma'am. Just passing on information."

"You couldn't have called me first?"

"Ma'am, I have to call whoever's in charge when something like that comes to my attention."

"I'm in charge. You didn't call me."

"Yes, ma'am. I know you're in charge there, but this is a matter of national security. The head office needed to know."

"You're *so* overreacting. I keep all returned I.D.'s in my desk and turn them in every few months. That's the way we've always done it."

"Ma'am, do former employees always turn in their cards to you right away?"

"Absolutely!"

He shook his head in disgust. "Don't you realize what can happen if even one of those cards falls into the wrong hands?"

"That can't happen. Nobody ever goes into my desk drawer!"

"Do you keep it locked, ma'am?"

"Of course I do, when I go home at night!"

"I see. When you go home at night."

"And I keep the key in my purse."

"Yes, ma'am, and is your purse secure at all times?"

"What do you mean?"

"Is it kept in a safe when you're not carrying it on your person?"

"What kind of a question is that?"

"It's a very important question, ma'am."

She snorted. "Well, one of the head auditors is on his way down here right now to go over my records and collect the cards. As if I didn't have enough to do, now I have to go looking up all those—"

"All those missing cards, ma'am?"

Dead silence.

Dial tone.

Yes, ma'am. You look up all those cards right away now, and you're going to find at least three missing.

He called the high school principal and asked if there had been any signs of illegal drug use in school. The principal sounded annoyed that he'd even ask such a question but said no, absolutely not. Nothing like that had ever come up.

He looked at his watch. It was late in the morning, he was hungry and he'd irritated several citizens in the last thirty minutes, a record for him in Valdez up to now. He left, heading for the dock, where he might be able to sit and have a decent quiet lunch.

Early in the afternoon, armed with Mac's search warrant, Jack took Riley with him to search Carolyn's apartment again.

When the landlady answered he had to glance at his notes to remind himself of her name. *DeeDee McCoy. Right.*

"Miss McCoy, I hate to interrupt your Saturday like this, but I have a warrant to perform a more thorough inspection of Carolyn Crumbe's apartment." He handed her the warrant.

She read it and looked up at him. "This won't do you any good now, you cleared the apartment. I just finished painting the walls and installing brand new carpeting. There's nothing in there."

"Ma'am, we still have to go in. If we damage anything the department will reimburse you."

Her jaw dropped. "What kind of *damage* are you talking about? Are you insane? I installed that carpeting myself just three days ago!"

He abruptly held up his hand. "Ma'am, please unlock the apartment. We'll try and do as little damage as possible but there's no way around it. We'll let you know when we're done."

She stood still, obviously considering what he'd just told her, then nodded. "Follow me, I'll get the damn key."

The entire apartment was pristine this time, no visible sign anywhere that a brutal murder had been committed there less than a month ago.

"Smells a lot better now than it did last time, doesn't it," Riley said. "Where do we start?"

"Behind the cabinets," said Jack.

Riley's green eyes flashed with quiet humor. "Take 'em down? All of 'em?"

He nodded. "Pull the bottoms away from the walls, we'll do that first, look where the sink is, anyplace there's a hole or anything that looks like a hole has been patched. Let's hit it."

They pulled all the cabinets out and shoved them aside.

DeeDee chose that minute to enter the apartment. He didn't see her but he heard her. "What are you doing!"

He looked up. "Ma'am, wait outside, please. We'll put it all back when we're finished." Then he thought of something he hadn't asked before. "Did you have any patching done on any of these walls?"

She stood with her hands on her hips. "Only the one in the living room, but you looked at that last time. I suppose you're going to open it back up now?"

"Yes ma'am, we are."

She swung around without another word and stomped out of the apartment. Jack and Riley glanced at each other, waiting for her front door to slam.

Her front door slammed. Jack crawled under the sink and reached behind the trap but it was too small. He held out his hand. "Give me the claw hammer."

Riley slapped it into his hand. Jack made the hole a little bigger and felt around without finding anything. Nothing about this case had been easy so far, why would this?

He flicked on his flashlight and peered into the hole again. Yep.

Nothing for sure. They felt all the walls where the cabinets had been. No marks anywhere indicated anything had been patched.

"Guess we have to re-hang the cabinets, huh chief?"

"We'll do that last." Jack checked his watch. "I don't want to be here all day. Let's look at the other walls."

They found no patched holes in the walls other than the one in the living room.

"Start ripping the carpeting away from the molding."

Riley gave him a bemused look. "We're really going to tear her new carpeting out?"

"No choice, it's either us or the AST."

They both took claw hammers and started prying molding off, lifted the carpeting off of the nails and pulled it back. They were three fourths done rolling it to the south side of the room when Riley grunted. "Chief, look at this!"

Jack looked past him to a tiny square in the floor, neatly cut and fitted with a thin piece of rubber tubing to pull it up. He pulled on the tubing and aimed his flashlight into the hole. "Go get my kit out of the trunk."

Riley headed out the door. Five minutes later Jack had pulled several cotton swabs and swiped the inside of the hole in several places, bagged and marked them and put everything back, finally hauling himself up off the floor. They finished around two o'clock, left the apartment and tapped on the manager's door. She opened it. Jack noticed a distinct smell of bourbon in the air.

"Well?" she demanded.

"We had to tear up the carpeting," he said, watching her eyes flicker. "You did say, didn't you, that you put the carpeting down yourself?"

She shook her head.

"You did, ma'am, we both heard you. Now, we put crime scene tape over that door again. Nobody goes in or out of it, understand?"

"Why?"

"Because I said so. The new warrant is open and we may need to go back in. Nobody is to cross that tape, including you. And by the way, don't try to leave town for the time being."

She nodded.

She wasn't looking all that friendly right now. He had just swabbed several grains of cocaine out of the hole she'd covered with her new carpeting. She had to know the hole was there if she installed the carpeting herself. If she did, she most likely knew what had been in it.

They went outside to their vehicle where they sat for a minute. DeeDee was watching them exactly as she'd done the last time. Now he knew why.

He switched on the ignition, more than a little unhappy because now he had what looked to be another possible suspect.

If she was strong enough to paint all those walls and install an apartment full of carpeting by herself, she was strong enough to have murdered Carolyn in that apartment. If she didn't, she probably knew who did.

Another case of lies by omission.

FIFTY THREE

The next day, Saturday morning, I drove out to Aunt Lucy's to bring Timmy home. When I drove into the settlement I saw him playing with a half dozen or so boys and several dogs, screaming and laughing. I was so happy to see him like that for a change, I sat in the car for a few minutes watching them.

He spotted me and stopped short, staring at me, then walked toward me with his head down, kicking at small rocks in the pathway.

"Did you have a good time?"

He looked up. "Yeah. Mom, can't I just stay here and live with Aunt Lucy? It's fun here."

I was shocked. "Timmy, I came to take you home."

He didn't move, just looked down at the ground. "I don't want to go back there. I'll just stay here. You can come see me, okay?"

He looked so woebegone my heart went out to him. I climbed out of the car and drew him into my arms.

"I have something to tell you."

His voice was muffled. "What?"

I pulled away from him and lifted his chin so that he had to look at me. "Timmy, your father is not going to live with us any longer. He's already gone."

The changes in his expression were astonishing. First sorrow, then hope, then realization and a full-blown delighted smile that both melted my heart and made me weep inside.

"Really? Are you sure?"

I nodded and hugged him again. "I'm sure. You don't have to be afraid. It's going to be just you and me and Alice and Charlie now."

"Did he want to go?"

I shook my head. "One day when you're grown, if you want to, you can go see him."

He took a step back, looked around the settlement, then back at me. All the strain and worry I'd seen in the past seemed to have disappeared. "I think I probably won't. I'll go tell Aunt Lucy it's time for me to go home now."

FIFTY FOUR

The next morning Jack knocked on Klem's door three times, annoyed because nothing had come in yet on the paint comparison but he still needed to talk to both men.

Klem opened the door and gave a heavy sigh. "Come on in."

Jack did and looked into the living room. John was leaning over the edge of the sofa pulling his shoes on and didn't look happy to see him.

"Glad I caught you both here," Jack said.

"Yeah, us too," said John. "What's up now?"

Jack made himself comfortable in the same chair as before. "I want to re-hash a couple of things we talked about last time. This won't take long."

"Good," said John, "my wife's expecting me, we got *potlatch* going on out at the settlement I don't want to miss all of it. Bad enough I had to miss everything last night."

Jack glanced at Klem. "Mind sitting down, Klem? I just have a few questions. One main one, actually."

Klem ambled across the room, plopped down on the sofa by John and scratched his beard. "How about moving right to the main one?"

Jack nodded. "I can do that. Last time I was here you both indicated you thought maybe Red had something to do with Carolyn Crumbe's murder. I'd like to go over that again, maybe you can give me a little more information this time."

"I don't know nothin' about it," said John. "It's just a gut feeling I have is all. We was all talking about it at work and Mark said the same thing. We all think Red did it."

Klem nodded in agreement.

"Why would you have such a strong gut feeling about Red?"

Jack asked. "What did he do to you?"

"He never did nothin' to me," John said. He looked out the window.

"Did he ever do anything to anybody else you know of?"

"Well, that's a good question, ain't it."

"And I just asked it. Look, fellas, this case is going to go to AST pretty quick if we don't get some answers here, and they're not going to be nice about it if they find out you've been withholding evidence."

He looked at Klem. "Matter of fact, that could land you both in prison if you have any information concerning any of the murders and aren't forthcoming with it, so let's have it now."

They glanced at each other, then back at him. "This is your house," he said to Klem. "You go first."

Klem looked down at his shoes.

"The answer's not in your shoes, Klem."

Klem looked up. "We're all pretty disgusted because Red was screwing that teacher that got killed."

Jack fought to keep any expression off his face. "How do you know this?"

"We see things going on around town," said John.

"It's been goin' on for a long time," said Klem. "We all just felt real sorry for Raven. She's a nice little woman."

"How long?"

"Couple of years," said John. "We'd see Carolyn heading for his house off and on and that sweet woman of his never knew a thing about it."

"How do you know she didn't?"

John shrugged. "If she did, she'd of thrown him out, wouldn't she, at least we figured she would of. She never did so we figured she never knew."

"Unless she did and decided to take care of it herself," said Klem. "We were talking about that, too, earlier. Mark even said it, but nobody really thinks that. It's just a theory, is all. I think it was Red. We all do."

"That's the only reason you have for thinking Red committed

the first murder?"

They both nodded.

"Then what about the other ones?"

Their eyebrows raised in unison and they both shrugged. "Your guess is as good as mine," said Klem.

"Okay, let's take this one thing at a time. Did either one of you ever see Carolyn anywhere with Kit?"

Klem looked down at the floor again.

"Klem?"

"Once or twice, talking down by the docks."

"John?"

"I never saw 'em together."

"Any idea what they were discussing, Klem?"

Klem shook his head. "I wasn't that close."

"What about Vera? Either one of you ever see her with anyone in town?"

John's face grew red and he looked out the window again.

"John?"

He hesitated, then mumbled, "All due respect, chief, we all knew who she was screwing."

Jack had to fight hard to keep his face from turning red. He could still hear his grandma saying, "When you find yourself in a hole, first thing you got to do is stop diggin'." He couldn't stop digging, not this time.

"Did you ever see her with either of the other victims."

They both shook their heads.

"Anyone else?"

Klem looked away. "Just you."

They weren't going to let him off easy.

"Okay, here's another question for you. Do either one of you know anything about any drugs circulating here in town?"

Klem shrugged. "You mean like pot? Sure, everybody smokes it."

Jack's eyebrows shot up. "Everybody?"

Klem flushed. "Well, not everybody, I guess. Maybe not that many people. But I have seen it once or twice. Smelled it, too, in a couple of places, or I thought I did. Maybe the ones I thought I smelled were just regular homemade cigarettes, I don't know. I don't smoke it."

"Anything harder, either one of you?"

They both shook their heads.

"Is there anything else anyone wants to tell me?"

"Nope," they both said in unison.

"Okay then. Thanks for your help, both of you. And John, enjoy your party. They sure keep you busy out there, don't they?"

John shrugged. "Not really, my wife is the one who takes care of most everything."

"No hobbies? No honey-do list?"

"Nope," said John, "I got her trained right. When I go home I just hit the couch and don't do much of anything."

"I heard through the grapevine you paint those masks she sells in town sometimes, is that true?"

John looked around the room then back. "Yeah, sometimes," he admitted.

"They're pretty colorful, I hear. What kind of paint do you use on 'em?"

John looked down at the floor. "Just paint."

Jack leaned back a little, narrowing his eyes. "Where do you get it?"

John sat perfectly still. "I buy it."

"Where?"

"Oh, here and there. Why?"

"I'm wondering where you got the red paint you used on the mask she was selling that exactly matched the face on the rock we found with Carolyn."

Dead silence, then John mumbled something under his breath.

"Mind repeating that?" asked Jack.

"I said, you're gonna make me lose my job."

"Why?"

Klem laughed. "Oh, go ahead and tell him, John, we all do it."

John's face was deep crimson. "I took it off of Mark's truck, the red paint anyhow. He had a lot of it, I only took one little can."

Jack sat there for a minute, digesting this information.

"How'd you happen to exactly replicate the face on that rock?"

John shrugged. "I dunno, I didn't know that I did. I just make up faces. Are you gonna tell Mark I swiped his paint? The can wasn't even full."

Jack stared at him for a minute, thinking. "Don't worry yourself about it," he finally said. "I'm not going to tell him anything."

He left, heading for Oliver Jackson's place.

Oliver's wife and kids were out somewhere and he caught Oliver trying to take a nap. Oliver wasn't pleased to see him. "What now?" he asked, rubbing his eyes.

"Just a few questions, Oliver." Jack sat down across from him at his kitchen table and watched Oliver pour a cup of coffee for himself after Jack had said no, he didn't want any.

"I'm just wondering if you've had a change of heart about telling me why you were so pissed at Red last time I was here."

He took a sip of coffee. "Not really."

"Let me put it to you this way. AST is involved now. They want to come down here and take over. Do you want to talk to them or will you talk to me?"

He stared at Jack for a couple of minutes before he set down his cup. "Have you asked the other guys who work for Mark? We were talking about this earlier and we all say the same thing. Red was cheating on Raven with Carolyn. We all like Raven. End of story."

"Why didn't you tell me about that before, when I first asked you?"

"I figured it was none of my business what went on in that family."

Jack nodded. "I can understand that, but what about the two other victims. Why would Red kill them?"

Oliver shrugged. "That's your job, ain't it, to figure that out? The only thing I know is, Red's got a bad temper, I think I told you that before. Maybe one of 'em saw something they shouldn't have."

"But both of them?"

"I dunno." He took another long swig.

"Have you ever seen Carolyn and Kit together anywhere?"

Oliver eyed him with disgust. "You're gonna drag me into this whether I want to be or not, ain't you?"

"If you have any part in it you can be sure I will. Just tell me what you know and everything'll go a lot smoother."

"I seen 'em both sitting in Carolyn's car one afternoon after school was out a couple months ago. Not doing anything, just sitting there talking."

"Were they arguing?"

He thought back a minute. "Well, they didn't look happy, I can tell you that. But I was driving past, I didn't see much and I didn't think much of it till they both got killed."

Jack leaned forward. "Did you ever see either Carolyn or Kit with Vera at any time?"

"No, but I seen Red with Vera once."

"When? Where?"

Oliver looked out the window for a minute, then forced himself to look back. Jack could hardly miss the smile in the back of his eyes, although it seemed he was trying hard to hide it.

"About a day or so before her head turned up in the Sound. Anyhow, it was right after Kit got killed when everybody in town was running around like they were crazy."

"Was that Sunday or Monday when you saw them?"

"Sunday night, about seven, eight o'clock, I think. Could be wrong about that. They were sitting down at the docks, just talking."

"Arguing?"

"Naw, they were laughing, having a good time, looked like to me. I just figured Red was on the lookout for a new sweetie now that his other one was gone."

"How long were you there?"

"About thirty seconds, once I saw that. I just turned my truck around and backed up the road and left."

"Why didn't you tell me this before?"

"I just told you, I don't want to be involved in no murder cases. It don't have nothing to do with me."

"It does now. Anything else you can think of? Any connection at all between Carolyn and Vera and Kit that you know about?" He leaned forward, forcing Oliver to look his way.

"Look, Oliver, whoever did this is more than capable of doing it again. If there's anything else you know, tell me. Too much time has already gone by."

Oliver looked down at the floor. "I can't think of anything else."

"Okay." Jack got up to leave. Just as he was about to go out the door he turned back. "You're sure this was the Sunday evening right after Kit was killed, right?"

"Yeah, pretty sure. I had to go up to the store and pick up some milk for the kids and I missed half of a movie I wanted to see because of it."

"What were you doing over at the docks if all you had to do was run up to the Eagle? They're almost on opposite sides of the town."

He grinned. "Well, I was already missing the movie anyhow so I figured I'd just sit and have a cold beer all by myself. The kids were driving me crazy all afternoon and Maybelle won't let 'em out of the house unless one of us is out there with them. Pain in the ass. Don't tell Maybelle I said that."

Jack suppressed a grin. "I won't if I can help it."

He said his goodbyes and drove home thinking about small towns, where everybody knows what everybody else is doing but nobody ever wants to admit it.

Come to think of it, things weren't all that different in Valdez now than they'd been back in Dallas. The only difference was, in Valdez there were just more viable suspects per mile.

Beth Anderson

FIFTY FIVE

Monday morning Timmy and I headed back to Dr. Randell's office.

"I need to speak to the doctor alone before Timmy goes in," I told the receptionist. A few minutes later she told me to go on in and gave Timmy a color book and crayons.

Dr. Randell motioned for me to sit. "How has Timmy been over the weekend?"

"He's a totally different child. I took him to his aunt's out in the bush and left him there overnight. He had a great time playing with the kids."

"Any problem speaking?"

I shook my head. "None that I saw. My aunt said he was fine while he was there. He seems to have forgotten everything, but I have something I need to tell you before he comes in."

His smile turned into a frown. "Yes?"

"I made Red pack his clothes and leave Friday night. I'm divorcing him."

Dr. Randell's jaw dropped. "That was quick."

"I know, but I had to do it. I can't let Timmy suffer any longer, and he has been, much longer than I realized. He's so different now, it's incredible."

"Well, then…" He quickly looked down, and began shuffling papers around. "I called your chief of police Friday evening and told him what Timmy said."

I nodded. "That's okay. I spoke to him myself after Red left."

"Where is your husband, do you know?"

"I don't, and I really don't care. He's not in my home any longer. I'm sure the police are watching him, wherever he is. My two older children are very upset, but this had to happen. I hope it doesn't cause any more problems for Timmy."

"Well, we'll find out. Do you want to stay this time, or wait outside?"

"I'll wait outside. I need to know for sure he's really okay and not just hiding his feelings from me."

He nodded. "Before you go, have you heard any more strange sounds coming from him?"

"No, not a single one."

He frowned. "Odd. Very odd, that all this would have affected you in such a way. If you have any more episodes, please call me right away and I'll make you an appointment with another doctor so we can get you straightened out."

"I'll do that, but I'm sure I'm okay. Maybe it was stress over a longer period of time than I was aware of that caused it, I don't know. I can only tell you it seems to be gone now."

He smiled. "Good. You wait outside then, and tell Timmy to come on in. We'll do another R.E.T. session. We may be able to discontinue them after this if he's really alright and stays that way, but let's take it a step at a time."

I left his office and sat on the bench in the hallway, picked up a magazine, idly thumbing through, looking at recipes.

Thunder rolled through the room and I found myself surrounded by thick, strangling fog. I couldn't move. My aunts, my uncles, my mother and father were all in the room, whispering. I couldn't see them for the fog, I could barely hear them, but I knew they were talking about me.

"Someone must have whistled when qiuryaq came out."

"But I told her, daughter, never do that!"

"She didn't believe you after she got older. She told her friends and they all laughed."

"But I told her, I told her, it has always been so! My father told me many times and I said, daughter, if you whistle when qiuryaq is out, the spirits will swoop down and cut off your head! She has always known whistling is disrespectful when qiuryaq lights the sky, she knows the colors we see are light from their torches so they can enter the heavens! White man calls them Northern Lights, but we know they are spirit lamps! We know it is so!"

"Yes, but—"

"It is so. Three people have lost their heads. Three times someone whistled while qiuryaq was out, it is just like our fathers and their fathers before them told us."

"I remember now."

"Always remember. It is always so."

It was true, my father had told me and I had laughed about it when I told my college roommates about some of the old Athabascan legends.

A flash of light almost blinded me and a black-eyed mask and a man's hand and a ring swam before my eyes. I knew that ring, where had I seen it before, a thick gold man's ring with a round ruby in the center—whose hand was that?

The voices began to fade and I heard my father's voice from a distance now, as if it were somewhere outside all the other voices.

You know whose hand it is, daughter. It's right there in front of you. Soon, very soon you'll see...

His voice disappeared and I struggled to open my eyes.

It wasn't storming outside. The room lighting hadn't changed. Something was pushing at the back of my mind at the speed of light, trying to force itself out.

The ring...where had I seen that ring?

I looked at my watch. Thirty five minutes had passed.

Where had I been all that time?

Hearing voices again. Seeing things. Again.

This time I wasn't about to tell anybody. I had to have the answer and I knew I'd have it soon. My father, who had never lied to me, had just told me so.

We arrived home around three-thirty. Mark's men were in the back yard, evidently taking up where they'd left off—how long ago? I couldn't remember. My mind was still back in Dr. Randell's office where I'd left the voices.

Timmy stood in the driveway, indecision in his eyes when he saw the men were out back. He went into the house ahead of me and straight to his room.

I went to the kitchen to pull some meat from the freezer, put it in the microwave to thaw and emptied the dishwasher. Everything was so very heavy, as though I were sleepwalking. Cups, glasses, plates, silverware seemed blurred and unfamiliar. I put them away and headed upstairs to gather my laundry and take it downstairs. It took an eternity just to get up the steps.

I was standing in the upstairs hallway with the laundry basket in my arms, looking out the window at the driveway, when Mark's truck pulled to a stop almost directly below the window. I could see clearly into the front passenger seat and the breath left my body because the seat was covered with blood, hair, pieces of flesh...white matter, red blood everywhere, on the dashboard, on the floor, running down the outside, covering the passenger side window.

Blood.

I blinked, looked down again and saw Mark staring up at me through the window and I saw his hand on the steering wheel and he was wearing the ring. I almost screamed but I stopped myself just in time and closed my eyes. When I opened them again and looked at the passenger seat nothing was there, only a simple dark gray passenger seat. No blood anywhere, no sign of the horror I'd seen just seconds ago.

Mark stared up at me and I saw terrible pain in those dark eyes, deep sorrow, misery. The look of a distant hell was in them and I knew then he was the killer. His eyes said it all.

And he knew that I knew.

I turned away, dropped the basket and headed into my bedroom to call Jack. I had no idea what to say to him that would convince him, but I had to tell him Mark had killed Carolyn. And Kit. And Vera. There was no way he'd ever believe me, Mark had been his best friend for years, but I knew I was right.

I had seen their blood.

Jack picked up the phone. "Raven, what can I do for you?"

The words poured out and I couldn't stop them. "Jack, listen to me, I know you won't believe me but you have to, you have to because I saw him, I know he killed them. I know it's him because I heard the voices again this afternoon and I saw the ring and when I got home I saw him and I saw the blood and brains all over his truck and he had the ring on and he saw me and he knows I know he did it. Jack, please believe me, you have to believe me!"

I heard a sound like a chair scraping and falling. "Whoa Raven, hold on, wait a minute, what the hell are you saying? Whose blood did you see? Where?"

"I saw the ring, Jack, his ruby ring, he's the one I saw before, I saw the back of his head, his hand, his neck, his eyes, but I didn't know who it was then. I saw the ring today while Timmy was in the doctor's office and I still didn't know who it was until he pulled up into my driveway and then I saw the ring on his hand and it was the same one I saw earlier and the blood, Jack, it was horrible, it was all over his car and then the blood disappeared and he looked up at me and he knows, Jack. He knows I know he killed them."

"Raven. Who knows? Who are you talking about?"

"Mark. It's Mark. It is! I know it's Mark!"

"Wait a minute. Mark Taylor? The same guy who's building your greenhouse?"

"Yes!" I watched the door, afraid Mark would burst in on me.

"Raven?"

"Mark's truck is outside, he came to check on his men. I guess they started working again this afternoon and Timmy and I just got home and I saw all the blood and then it disappeared, and Jack, I know it's him. I saw the ring. I saw his hair. I saw his eyes. I saw his ring, Jack. I know it's him!"

"You're saying you think Mark Taylor is the killer because you had a vision?"

"Yes! It has to be him, he's the one I've been seeing all along! My father told me I'd know soon and not fifteen minutes after we got home I saw Mark and he looked up and I saw all that blood. Jack, the look in his eyes made me sick and he knows I saw it and I know you don't believe me but Jack, you have to!"

Another silence.

"Raven, first you have to calm down."

I didn't say anything.

"Look, Raven, Mark is my best friend. I've known him for years, he wouldn't kill anyone. He has no reason to do so. Whoever killed those three people did have a reason, we know that even if we don't know what it was yet."

I heard my own breath coming in quick, agonizing spurts.

"Raven, are you there?"

I struggled, trying to breathe and talk at the same time. "I'm here and he's outside."

I heard him sigh. "I'll be there right away. Stay where you are."

"No, you can't come here, he'll know I called you!"

"Raven, listen to me, how would he know if he's outside?"

"Jack, he will, I know he will. He knows I know and if he sees you he'll know I called you."

"I'll be there in a minute." He hung up.

I sat on the edge of my bed.

Five minutes later I heard a car pull up. I waited, thinking he'd come inside right away but when he didn't I looked outside and saw him talking and laughing with Mark. I couldn't believe my eyes, not after what I'd just told him.

How could he talk and laugh like that with a killer?

He didn't believe me. I hated him. *Hated him!*

Another few minutes passed and I heard footsteps, then a knock on my bedroom door. "Raven?"

I would not look up. Would not look at him.

"Come in."

I sat with my head down. I could see his boots in front of me.

"Raven."

"What?"

"Look at me."

"I don't want to look at you."

"Raven, please listen to me. I sent Mark's fingerprints and his handprint and all the info I had on him, when I sent everything else to the lab weeks ago. Nothing came back on him. Mark's not a killer, he's a very nice guy."

"If you say so."

He took another step and stopped directly in front of me, close enough to reach out and touch me and my heart was breaking because I remembered his soft and gentle touch on my face the other day and I thought...had thought...maybe someday...

"Raven, what happened today? When did you see all these things and hear voices again? You said you heard voices. Whose voices, exactly, did you hear?"

He sounded as though he were talking to a three-year-old child. I was so furious I almost couldn't answer but I did look up. His eyes were dark underneath. I hadn't noticed those deep shadows before. He looked like he'd lost weight too, but then I saw something else in his eyes that he was trying to hide. Compassion and concern.

My God. He thought I was insane.

I was *not* insane!

"I heard the voices I sometimes hear." My tongue felt thick but I was careful to enunciate every syllable so he wouldn't misunderstand anything. "I told you I hear my dead relatives sometimes, usually soft sounds, but not today."

"How did they sound today?"

"Upset, and my father sounded as though his voice was coming from somewhere else. He said I'd understand soon, he said I already knew. It was very clear, Jack."

He sat beside me on the bed and took my hand. I jerked it away. He reached over and took it again.

"Raven, you know voices and visions aren't evidence, don't you?"

"I can't help it. I know what I saw and I know what I heard."

"But none of that is evidence, Raven. I have to have solid evidence to make an arrest and take it to court."

"That's your job. Find some and do it."

Out of the corner of my eyes I saw him shake his head.

"I'm doing my job, Raven, as best I can. I sent everything I had to the lab up north. I had an AST profiler come down here. Nothing has come back on either you or Mark and they have on everyone else."

I turned to him. "You had them investigate me?"

"I sent your statement. I had to have you checked out. You were there. It was your yard where Carolyn was found."

"But—me?"

"I've had everybody I could think of investigated, Raven. I'm up against a vicious killer. I have to stop whoever it is from killing again, and he might."

"Yes, now that he feels threatened," I said, almost to myself.

His head jerked back. "What did you just say?"

"Mark knows that I know he's the killer. He saw it in my eyes."

He still held my hand. He dropped his head into his other hand and closed his eyes, then opened them and turned to me.

"Raven, isn't it possible your mind is telling you these things because you can't face that it might be Red?"

"It's not Red," I insisted. "It's Mark. And now he's going to kill me because I know."

Jack gave a heavy sigh. "Okay, look, I'll put a watch on your house so you'll at least feel safe here. Mark and his men are leaving in a minute and they won't be back till next week. I'll have someone watching the house all the time. Red's still in town but he's being watched around the clock, just so you know."

I nodded.

"But I want you to promise me something."

"What?"

He gave me that pitying look again. "I know it's too late today, but as soon as his office is open, I want you to call Timmy's doctor in Anchorage and have him make an appointment for you."

I stared at him. "So you really don't believe me."

"I believe you're hearing and seeing something, Raven, but I think your mind's playing tricks on you."

I turned away. "Okay, Jack. Just go on and do whatever you have to." I turned back. "Oh, and one more thing."

He stood and looked down at me. "Yes?"

"Don't ever speak to me again."

His hands fell to his sides and he opened his mouth as if he wanted to say something but he just shook his head again, swore under his breath and left the room.

I waited till I heard him go out the back door, then went downstairs and locked all the doors and windows and turned on the air conditioner. I wasn't going to let anyone out of the house until the killer was caught. It wouldn't be long now. Jack knew who it was, even if he didn't want to believe me.

He still knew.

FIFTY SIX

Mark's truck was gone when Jack went outside. He climbed into his vehicle, feeling as though he'd lost twenty pounds since he walked into Raven's house.

The air was still hot even though it was late in the afternoon. His backside stuck to the leather seat. He was hungry and sweaty and growing more frustrated by the minute.

Raven's scenario couldn't be possible. It couldn't. He'd thought he knew Raven pretty well but apparently he didn't. He was heartsick.

Voices. Visions. Three murdered citizens, a hysterical woman, two asshole kids on the verge of home-grown terrorism, a sadistic killer running around loose, everybody including out-of-town media driving him crazy twenty-four hours a day, and she wanted him to arrest his best friend because she thought her husband was about to be arrested for three murders and she just couldn't face it.

Did she still love Red even though she was divorcing him? He didn't know, but the look in her eyes when she told him never to speak to her again had spoken volumes.

He pulled out his cell and called the station. "Send someone over to the Morressey house right away, we need to set up a twenty four hour watch." He listened for a minute while his dispatcher bitched.

"Dammit, I *know* that we don't have enough men to watch everybody in town but this can't be helped. Raven thinks the killer is after her now. We'll have to work out a schedule and hope to hell nothing else happens."

He hung up and waited. Five minutes later Ryan, one of his second shift men, pulled up behind him. Jack got out and walked back to Ryan's vehicle.

"Stay here and watch the house. Make sure nobody goes in there, and I mean nobody."

"Affirmative, chief. Does Raven know we're here?"

"I told her. I'll have somebody spell you at eleven. You can see both entrances from here so don't move or look away."

Ryan pulled his hat down over his forehead to shield his eyes from the sun and settled in to stare at Raven's house.

Jack glanced at the dashboard clock when he climbed back into his vehicle. Almost dinnertime and his stomach was giving him fits, probably his old ulcer coming back. He drove toward Halibut House, then changed his mind and headed for the Eagle. He passed Pioneer Drive, made a u-turn, then pulled alongside the Indianhead and sat looking up at it.

Was it possible Raven really was psychic?

No. That was nuts. All that had to be her imagination.

On the other hand, according to John, the paint he used on that mask was Mark's and Mark had more. That could mean something.

It still wasn't evidence. Anybody could buy paint.

He switched his ignition back on.

Switched it off.

Ah, screw this, Mark wouldn't kill anyone. No way. He was too easygoing.

Switched it back on again.

Switched it off. Stared at the Indianhead, at all the carved nooks and crannies and colors embedded over time into the weathered wood.

Could he have known if it was Mark?

Sure. There'd have been something...

Switched his ignition on again.

Switched it off.

What? Nothing he'd seen had pointed anywhere near Mark.

But Hopscotch had described him and it fit, it made perfect sense in a weird way that it could be Mark. The paint on that mask had come straight from Mark's truck if John was telling the truth, and he seemed to be, since Klem had corroborated the paint source.

Not enough evidence there to convict, but still, if it turned out to be Mark, that could have been part of it.

For that matter, it could have been John himself, but John had a good alibi, at least for the days leading up to Carolyn's murder.

If his alibi was true. He and Klem had been each others' alibi. *Dammit!*

He pulled out his cell and found Mac's number, thinking she'd probably be gone. It rang a few times.

"Special Agent O'Toole." Good, she wasn't gone.

"Mac, have you got anything back on Mark Taylor and Raven Morressey?"

"Raven's clear from this end. I faxed her background a little while ago, didn't you get it?"

"I'm not in the office. What about Mark? Anything on him?"

"Not yet, we're checking him out, but you know how things dribble in, especially around a holiday. Soon as I get something I'll fax it over. Something going down?"

"I don't know yet but I need that information. Any way you can put a rush on it?"

"Over a holiday? Are you crazy?"

"Probably, but see what you can do. And Mac."

"Yes?"

"Don't just fax it. I want you to call me on my cell as soon as you get anything."

"Will do. Enjoy your holiday." He heard the grin in her voice.

"Yeah, right, Mac. You, too." They hung up and his mind suddenly shot back to something he'd read in high school.

The Kali Death Squads in Afghanistan. Trained assassins. Revenge killings, performed without a second thought.

Mac's profile had said these could be revenge kills.

Mark used to be a Navy Seal.

Trained to do it quick, do it quiet and get out.

It was possible.

He didn't want it to be, but it was possible.

No, dammit, it wasn't. Not Mark. Why would he murder three people? He had a good business, friends, nice home, a beautiful wife.

Nah. No way.

He wanted Mark's background information fast. He wanted Raven to be wrong even if it did mean something was messed up inside her head.

That could be fixed. Murder couldn't.

After Jack nuked a TV dinner he sat in front of his computer hoping the boys would be there. He was about to fall asleep in his chair when Charlie finally came on. A few minutes later Jason showed up. Jack quickly switched to their private room and hunched forward, wide awake.

Cyberdarth666: "I might not make it tomorrow night. My mom says we can't leave the house."

Shoesize13: "For crap's sake, what's wrong with her now?"

Cyberdarth666: "No clue. She's got the whole house shut down and there's a cop car out front. I asked her why but she won't tell me. She's mad as hell about something though."

Shoesize13: "Can't you sneak out?"

Cyberdarth666: "I'd have to go out the back window, the cop's been sitting where he can see both doors all afternoon and there's another one out there talking to him now."

Shoesize13: "Climb out the back window, it's not like you never did it before."

Cyberdarth666: "LOL! True!"

Shoesize13: "Look, we'll never have another chance like this to shake up the town. Everything's just right for it. I got the I.D.'s, it's foolproof and we might not get this lucky again, in fact I'm pretty sure we won't."

Cyberdarth666: "Why not?"

Shoesize13: "All the I.D.'s my aunt had in her desk drawer are gone, I looked this morning. I don't know what happened, they were always there before. Look, I have the explosives all ready and they're small enough nobody'll notice it, we can stick them under our shirts and just walk in with nothing but I.D.'s in our hands. The regular night guards probably won't be there anyhow because of the holiday so hell, man, it's perfect!"

Cyberdarth666: "Yeah, but I keep thinking if somebody gets hurt and we get caught…"

Shoesize13: "Nobody'll get hurt, man, the roof probably won't go up anyhow, it'll probably just blast a little hole in the side and we'll be gone when it does. Who's gonna catch us? Nobody in town's smart enough."

Cyberdarth666: "Yeah, I guess you're right."

Shoesize13: "Damn straight I am. Meet me on the street behind your house at nine tomorrow night. If you're not there I'm going anyhow. Don't miss out on the fun."

Cyberdarth666: "LOL, I can hear the sirens now."

Shoesize13: "Yeah, the cops'll probably run all over each other trying to get there first."

Cyberdarth666: "And nobody'll ever know who did it."

Shoesize13: "Right. Look, I gotta go, I got a girl waiting in the other room, if you know what I mean."

Cyberdarth666: "LOL! Okay, see you tomorrow night!"

They both disappeared and Jack turned his computer off.

Tomorrow was going to be a busy day.

He picked up Bill at eight the following night. July Fourth. Almost no traffic. For once he was glad nobody was doing fireworks. Some in town might, but they usually didn't and it was early yet.

"Ready for the big J D bust?"

"Yeah, I'm looking forward to it," said Bill. "My wife's still pissed about missing our trip, though."

"We'll make it up to her."

"Okay by me, I didn't want to go anyway. Heard any more from Jason and Charlie?"

He told Bill about the conversation the night before.

Bill laughed. "God, were we ever that dumb?"

They turned off Richardson Highway onto Dayville Road. "I was, almost, at times, but not as dumb as these kids."

Bill stretched. "Ah, they just have bigger ambitions than we did. When I was that age my biggest ambition was the blonde with the best T&A in school. Plus, I was pretty much of a sports jock."

Jack slowed for a bump in the road. "Football or basketball?"

"Hockey. I thought about turning pro but I went to college

instead, that's where I got interested in police work and switched my major from girls and sports to law enforcement."

They crossed Solomon Gulch, passed the hydroelectric plant, kept going till they crossed Allison Creek. Jack finally pulled his vehicle back from the oil terminal where they couldn't be seen from the road but they could still see the kids coming, and pull out fast.

They sat and talked while they waited. About nine Jack turned to him. "I'll pull out and block the road when we see them coming, then you toss both Flashbangs out the window so they land close to their car. Just stand back and let me talk when we get them out of the car, then we'll separate and question them individually."

Bill was watching the road. "You got it."

At nine twenty-five Jack saw them coming. He hit the lights and siren and pulled out, Bill tossed the Flashbangs and they exploded. Jason's car screeched to a halt and both boys ducked beneath the dashboard.

Jack climbed out of his vehicle with his gun drawn. "Come out with your hands up, both of you!"

Jason was the first to get out, rubbing his eyes. "Hey, we weren't speeding, we're just riding around. What'd we do?"

"I said get your hands up, now!"

"But we weren't doing anything!"

"The hell you weren't, get 'em up! Come on, get out of the damn car, Charlie."

Charlie climbed out and they both stumbled toward him with their hands in the air.

Jack motioned for them to stop. "Where are the explosives?"

"What explosives?" Jason blustered.

"One more time, where are they?"

Bill walked over to their car and aimed his flashlight inside. "They're in the back seat, right out in the open." He looked at the boys. "You could've at least hidden 'em and made us work for 'em." He reached into the back seat and pulled them out. Jack took a quick look. Amateur stuff but it could have done some damage.

"Walk over this way," Jack ordered. "Keep your hands up."

"But wait, Jack, we can explain," said Charlie.

"Chief to you. Bill, take Jason over there. I'll keep Charlie here."

"But let me tell you—" Charlie protested.

"Let me tell *you*," Jack said, "and you both better listen." Jason stopped and turned back.

"You're both under arrest for Conspiracy, a felony offense per Alaska Statute 11.31.120. 'If, with intent to promote or facilitate a serious felony offense, the offender agrees with one or more persons to engage in or cause the performance of that activity and the offender or one of the persons does an overt act in furtherance of the conspiracy, he's committing a felony'.

"See what I'm getting at? You think this is a game you're playing? Think again. You've both committed a felony just by planning this, and guess what that means. Prison, gentlemen."

Charlie opened his mouth to say something. Jack held up his hand to stop him. "You're both also charged with Alaska Statute 11.31.100. Attempt. 'A person is guilty of an attempt to commit a crime if, with intent to commit a crime, the person engages in conduct which constitutes a substantial step toward the commission of that crime'.

"Now look at the two of you doing exactly that, riding out here with explosives in your car. Felony number two. Not too swift, but we'll let a jury handle it.

"That's two felonies each, to be exact, gentlemen. That's gonna look real damn good on your college apps, isn't it?"

Charlie had inched over by the police car. "Hands over the top, Charlie, lean into the car." He proceeded to frisk Charlie and glanced at Bill. He was doing the same to Jason. Good.

"Okay," he said, "now turn around and talk to me. What were you doing with those explosives?"

Charlie looked everywhere but at him. "I didn't know they were there."

"Don't give me that. I know what you were doing."

Bill had finished patting Jason down and turned his way with cards in his hand, grinning. "Look at this, Jack. These here boys were going to use fake I.D.'s to get into the terminal, I bet. Isn't that something!"

"We were not!" Charlie protested. "I don't know anything about any fake I.D.'s."

Jack raised his eyebrows. "Stuff it, Charlie. I know what you were doing and I know how you were going to do it. Now answer me this. How long was Kit using cocaine?"

Charlie's eyes shot open. "I—I—I—what?"

"The truth, Charlie, make it fast. How long?"

He looked down at the ground. "I guess about six months."

"Was he the only one using?"

"The only one I know of. I never did."

"Where was he getting it?"

"Jack— "

"Chief to you," Jack reminded him. "Where?"

Charlie's eyes darted around, past his shoulder, across the road.

"I said where, Charlie."

"Miss Crumbe," he mumbled, half under his breath. "I couldn't tell anybody, not after what happened to her, and then Kit. I don't want whoever it is coming after me."

"They're not coming after you. Where'd she get the coke?"

"Honest to God, Jack—Chief, I don't know."

"Did you know Kit was using the night he was killed?"

"Well, he usually was."

"And you were hanging out with him. Your mother's going to be happy to hear all this, on top of everything else that's been going on at your house. Proud of yourself, asshole?"

Charlie looked down at his feet. "I know you're not gonna believe this, but I was trying to get him to quit. We both were."

"You and Jason?"

"Yeah."

"Do you know anything about any drug trafficking at school or anywhere else in town?"

"No and I don't want to. I think he was the first, I knew he was messing with Miss Crumbe, and the next thing I knew, he was hooked on coke."

"Messing with Miss Crumbe how?"

Charlie flushed. "They were having sex."

Jack fought to show no expression. "Okay. Now. Why were you and Jason out here with explosives in your car? I want to hear the whole thing and it better be the truth because believe me when I tell you this, I already know what the truth is. Lie to me once and you'll have a third felony against you and God help your ass when the AST gets hold of you."

Charlie opened his mouth but before he could get a word out, Jack's cell phone rang.

He pulled it out and looked at the name. AST. He flipped it open. "O'Banion."

"Jack, three things."

"Shoot."

"Notify whoever's watching Red Morressey that two of our agents are on their way down there to pick him up. They should be there soon, they left here heading down there almost three hours ago."

"What's the charge?"

"One count of first degree murder in Maryland."

"How'd that happen?"

"Cold case, 1982 murder, recently re-opened. I just found out about it, I got the duty at the last minute today, dammit. Red's fingerprints, all the prints you sent, were sent to IAFIS. A couple of retired detectives in Maryland were looking for a match yesterday and Red's fingerprints popped out.

"Seems he killed the victim, put the corpse in his own car, set it on fire and it went up so big the body was almost completely destroyed. The authorities down there thought the body was Red's because it was around his size and it was his car so they closed the case. The dead guy's DNA, which they just now ran for the first time, says he was a known criminal. Looks like he was Red's associate in some extortion scam they were pulling."

Jeezus! "Okay, good enough."

"Second thing. Your paint samples are a match, this just came in a few minutes ago. What's that all about?"

Jack paused.

"Jack?"

He looked over at the boys and Bill. "I'll tell you later, just an idea that might have something to do with the murders."

"Okay, get back to me on that. Now for the big news."

His skin crawled. "Okay."

"The palm print on the wall at the Crumbe murder scene."

"Yes?"

"Mark Taylor's. We got it from his service records and the hospital he was in after he got out. We won't have any problem, we got a 12-point match, it can't get any better than that. A confession will help if we're lucky enough to get one."

Jack's mind went blank for about thirty seconds.

"Jack? Are you there?"

"I'm here." They were all watching him. Bill had stopped talking to Jason. He lowered his voice. "I'm in the middle of a bust here. A couple of JD's thought they were going to raise more than a little hell for the holiday."

"Get rid of them, you need to pick up this guy fast. While he was in the Seals his first wife and his eleven-year-old twin boys were murdered, massive crossfire in an L.A. cocaine war they stumbled into by accident. They got the guys who did it but Taylor went off the deep end and they had to muster him out with a medical discharge. He wound up in a psych ward for a while, then he seemed okay to go home, but he had no family and his house had been repo'd while he was in the hospital. That's about the time he met his current wife and you know the rest. Looks like he found out about the coke coming in down there and that's probably what triggered these kills."

"Okay."

"Sorry it took so long, but we had a lot of background work to do on this and some of these agencies fight giving out info like that, even to us."

"It's okay."

"Jack."

"Yeah?"

"Be careful. He's very dangerous."

"Always am. Thanks." He closed his cell.

It rang again.

"Jack, I've been trying to reach you," Raven whispered. "I think he's here, in the house."

"Mark?"

"Yes. I'm sure I heard something downstairs. It was faint, but I heard something."

"How could he get in there? I have someone watching your house, both entrances."

"I don't know. I just heard something. It's him, I know it's him."

"Where's Timmy?"

"Here, with me, in my room."

"Keep him in there, lock the door."

"It's already locked."

"Where's Alice?"

"At a friend's house two blocks away. Charlie's in his room asleep, I guess."

He turned to Charlie. "How'd you get out of the house?"

Charlie's eyes were wide open. "I climbed out the kitchen window."

"Did you close it?"

"Yeah, I think so."

"Did you lock it?"

"How could I, from the outside?"

"Raven?"

Her voice was faint. "Yes."

"Charlie's with me, he's fine. I'll be right there."

Charlie spoke. "What's going on with my mom?"

Jack ignored him and turned to Bill. "Let's go."

"But—" from Charlie

"Go straight to Jason's house, both of you. Stay there till I call you. Go."

"But—"

"I said go!" Jack was already heading for his vehicle, motioning for Bill to hurry.

"But—"

Jack opened the door and slid in, started his vehicle, pulled up beside Jason's car. "Get the hell out of here, now! Don't interfere with me, I'm warning you. Go to Jason's house and stay there or you *will* do hard time."

The boys scrambled into the car. Jason ground the gears. His car stalled. He tried again. It started and they roared off without looking back.

Good. Gone.

Jack and Bill took off. Jack tried to call Ryan while he drove. No answer.

"Mind telling me what the hell's going on?" shouted Bill, holding on to the door while they flew out over the road heading for the highway.

"Mark Taylor's our guy. AST just confirmed it. Raven thinks he's in her house. Ryan's not answering."

"Ah, Jeezus. Drive faster."

Jack kept his eyes on the road. "Call the station. Red's being picked up by the Feds shortly. I want two cars over at Mark's house right now, pick him up if he's there. The rest, meet us at Raven's, we'll be there almost as soon as they will. No lights, no sirens. Tell 'em to surround the house quietly. We're going to have to sneak up on Mark if he's in there. Dammit!"

He floored it again and switched on his lights and siren while Bill made the call.

They flew past Jason's car, back past the hydro plant, back down Dayville Road, skidded out onto Richardson Highway. When they hit the city limits, Jack reached over and switched off the lights and siren. "I hope you're in good shooting form tonight."

"Not a problem."

"Okay."

Two police vehicles were just pulling in front of Raven's house when they turned the corner. One officer got out and leaned over Ryan's window. Only Ryan's hand was visible, slowly reaching out over the side.

Jack swore softly. "Go check on him then follow me in and be damn quiet. I'm going in the same way Charlie came out."

"Be right behind you."

Jack ran across the back yard, unsnapping his holster as he headed for the back window.

Beth Anderson

FIFTY SEVEN

My blood raced. Every nerve tingled.

He was down there.

I felt it. I knew it.

I was alone with Timmy, Alice could walk in the house and Mark was down there.

"Timmy," I whispered. He huddled on the bed, wide-eyed. "Did you hear something downstairs?"

He nodded.

"Get in the closet."

He shook his head no.

"You have to. Get in the closet and pull the door shut."

He was breathing heavily. He couldn't seem to move.

I tiptoed to the bed and picked him up, carried him to the closet, opened it with my free hand and laid him on the floor. I was about to close the door when I remembered my father's old seal hunting gun, a single shot Stevens 12 gauge with an old canvas web shotgun shell belt, hidden high on the shelf behind some garment bags. I hadn't thought about it since I'd hidden it there years ago.

I pulled it and the half empty belt down and fumbled with one of the massive three inch magnum shells, finally freeing it from the belt. "You stay in here," I whispered, struggling to hold it to my side so he wouldn't see it, but he had and I saw him cringe. He turned away, curling up with his back to the closet door, whimpering.

I shut the door looked down at the gun.

No longer for food. Not now.

A killing machine now.

But too heavy for me to lift and aim.

I couldn't do it.

I listened for sounds downstairs as I thumbed the shotgun's top lever, opening the action, slid the long red shell deep into the chamber. I snapped the action shut again, and felt it lock solidly in place.

Loaded. Had I really just loaded my father's seal gun?

Yes, I had.

One shell.

One chance.

Footsteps, coming up the stairs now. Quiet, soft, almost soundless.

My senses were going crazy, I sweated, my hair stuck to my face. My vision narrowed, my eyes focused on the door.

Footsteps.

One shell.

One.

A tap on the door.

Someone was there, listening.

The doorknob rattled.

I forced the gun up and aimed at the door. My hands shook, the gun wobbled.

Too heavy.

"Who's there?"

No answer.

One shell.

The doorknob turned, I watched, unable to look away. Light flashed from every direction, electricity raced through my body and I heard the voices, screaming this time.

Put the gun down, daughter! We only kill for food!

He crashed through the door with his foot, taking the door almost off its hinges.

Mark.

He kicked the door again. It fell toward me, splintered pieces of wood, jagged, angry-looking.

He stepped into the room.

My hands shook.

He headed toward me, a knife in his hand, half hidden.

He held out his other hand. "Give me the gun, Raven."

One shell.

I stood frozen, watching Jack sneak up behind Mark, aiming his gun at Mark's head but he couldn't shoot, I was standing directly in front of Mark. Jack motioned for me to step aside. Mark caught my movement and spun around. Jack pulled the trigger at the same instant Mark lunged at him, slashing Jack's throat.

Mark fell first, blood oozing from his back. Jack dropped his gun and fell to the floor, half-draped over Mark's body. My heart almost stopped, I saw Jack's blood, so much blood, saw him gasping for breath. He forced his head up, his eyes glazing over, grappling for his gun. Mark rolled away, kicked the gun away from him, dragged himself in slow motion toward his knife, reached it, adjusted it to slash up, turned back to me.

Daughter! No! Never kill a man! It's wrong! It's wrong!

I cocked the hammer back, aimed straight at Mark's head and pulled the trigger.

Raven Talks Back

In the Quiet of the Morning

I stood in front of our bedroom window and watched the fog rolling down the mountains again this morning, remembering once again the horror that had engulfed our little town. The fog is dense, as always, but it no longer seems murky and threatening, as it did when the murders occurred. I still, once in a while, feel soft sounds coming from the fog, reassuring me that my ancestors are still there, and still watch over me.

But some things have changed. Now when I turn, early in the mornings, I see Jack sleeping, the scar on his neck visible even in the half-light. He'll always have that scar, but it's softened over time and it makes him even more endearing to me because I know what he went through to get it. To me, and to the people in our town, it's a visible symbol of courage.

He had a tough time for a while, not so much from the wound, and not even because I killed Mark before he could get him, but inside, because he felt he'd failed the town people by not recognizing who the killer was a lot sooner. They think of him as a hero though, and he has forgiven himself, although to me, he didn't have to.

The angle at which I see the fog roll down the mountainside now has changed a bit. A couple of months after Jack got out of the hospital, he was sitting in my kitchen having coffee one morning when he looked out back, where the new construction company was putting the finishing touches on my greenhouse, and remarked, "You know, Raven, with the view you have here, this would make a beautiful dining room."

One thing led to another over the next year. Before I would have believed it possible, Jack and I and the kids had moved into the new house we built on the empty lot next door. I only have to walk a couple hundred feet to manage our bed and breakfast, which was constantly full last summer, when we opened for the first time.

    The restaurant by itself has kept me busy enough the rest of the year. It doesn't hurt a bit that we're close enough to the highway to have a huge weathered-wood billboard with an Indianhead painted on it to attract the attention of anyone who might be driving through town. The ones who aren't just driving through come all year round for breakfast and lunch, unless the snow is too high to travel even a few blocks. I've always loved to cook and apparently I'm pretty good at it.

    A lot of security changes have been made here because of the pipeline and containers. We no longer have to worry about idiot kids with big ideas and stolen electronic I.D.'s trying to break into the terminal. When Charlie came home that night and told me what he'd almost done I wanted to have him arrested myself. Jack talked me out of it and we all put that episode into the past, along with my marriage to Red.

    Hopscotch is back in prison in Minnesota. I don't know if he'll be back, only time will tell. DeeDee McCoy is serving her sentence for obstruction of justice and her apartment house is up for sale. Red is serving a forty-year sentence with no parole in California. He won't be back.

    Charlie wants to go on to medical school in Washington after he graduates from college, which has surprised us all. He'll do his residency there and who knows where he'll wind up. We'd like for it to be here so there will be a replacement for Doc, but so many kids go to college in the lower forty-eight and never return, so we'll see.

    Alice is in high school now. Somehow she appears to be turning into a surprisingly responsible young woman, although she still hasn't a clue what she wants to major in when she leaves for college.

    Tim had a rough time for a while after the shooting, although we didn't let him see any of the carnage when we carried him out under a blanket. He still heard enough to set him back, but he's been fine for a long time now.

    He doesn't let anyone call him Timmy any longer. He wants to go into law enforcement like Jack. The two of them couldn't be any closer if Jack had been his real father; he follows Jack everywhere. As for his non-talking episode, he hasn't stopped talking since he started up again. We're encouraging him to get a law degree before he goes into the enforcement side. Jack likes to say that anyone who talks as much as Tim does should definitely get a law degree.

Kimberley has been a tremendous help with the bed and breakfast, if for no other reason than she's wonderful local color. She keeps the guests entertained with stories about her movie escapades although no one ever believes them. She's happy just to be here.

Today, Valdez is the same as always. Flowers bloom in the summertime, otters play down by the city dock, silver fish jump out of the water, owls and American eagles glide high over the countryside and up into the mountains. Once again, love and laughter runs beneath the surface of our daily lives and I can only pray that it stays that way, but you know what they say.

"If you want to hear God laugh, make plans..."

Acknowledgements

Thank you so much to all of the talented and generous people who have contributed so much to the authenticity of certain events in this book: Wally Lind, retired Senior Crime Scene Analyst, Brent E. Turvey, MS, Forensic Solutions, LLC, Cynthia Lea Clark, Psy.D., Forensic Psychopathologist, Anthony Mancaruso, retired NYPD and Dade County, FL detective, Ranae Johnson, Founder of the Rapid Eye Technology Institute, Ivan R. Futrell, Fingerprint Technology Consultant and Instructor, Robert W. Anderson, retired Alaska engineer, Ruth Black, Alaska Native, Athabascan tribe, Ginny Kubacki, Dorien Gray, Sloane Taylor, Melissa Bradley and Erica Dananay, who have all been so valuable in their editing and critiques, author Ken Lewis, who helped me fine-tune this manuscript, and Kathy Mierzwa of the South Holland, IL Police Department, who once said to me, her words so chilling while we were discussing another murder case:

"They're out there, Beth. They're out there."

About the author

Beth Anderson is a multi-published, award winning author in several genres including romance and mainstream crime fiction. A full time author, she lives in a Chicago, Illinois suburb. She has appeared on Chicago's WGN Morning Show, The ABC Evening News, as well as numerous other radio and cable television shows. She has guest lectured at Purdue University and at many different libraries and writer's conferences. She loves music, particularly jazz. Her website and blog are at:

http://www.bethanderson-hotclue.com